Electric
ICE

D. K. McCutchen

Leapfrog Press
New York and London

Electric Ice
9 8 7 6 5 4 3 2 1

First published in the United States by Leapfrog Press, 2024

Leapfrog Press Inc.
www.leapfrogpress.com

Coyote image on page 6 by Lydia Holloway © 2011
Map image on page 26 by Timothy Paulson © 2013

Cover and text design: Jim Shannon and Prepress Plus, India

ISBN: 978-1-948585-941 (Paperback)

The Forest Stewardship Council® is an international non-governmental
organisation that promotes environmentally appropriate, socially beneficial,
and economically viable management of the world's forests. To learn more visit
www.fsc.org

Electric
ICE

A Companion Novel to *JELLYFISH DREAMING*

In a thundercloud, millions of pieces of ice bump together from updrafts of up to 100 mph. Small ice crystals charge positive and waft to the top of the cloud; bigger ice pellets charge negative and fall to the bottom. The separation creates mega-volts of electrical tension — lightning.

— ELECTRIC ICE, NASA

LEGEND

In which Jellyfish Jack tells Joon the story of his 200-year journey before they met; of riding a Great Wave, a Ghost Bison, and being ridden by a trickster god cross-country to where 20 percent of the world's fresh water freezes while he sleeps. Buried under tons of snow, Jack climbs out through a chimney and joins a friend to ice sail, sail-skate, and hang-glide into a lighting battle.

PROLOGUE

ELECTRIC ICE

ICE HEARTS
ICE MAP
ICE SAILING
ICE SURFING
ICE SKATING
ICE FLIGHT
ICE SLEDGING
ICE THAW
ICE EULOGY
NEW BEGINNINGS

ICE-LESS EPILOGUE

Jack & Joon – In the Desert

PROLOGUE
JACK & JOON – IN THE DESERT

"How did you get here? And where were you going?" Joon asks one day as we ski across the desert sand on our quest to find answers to ... pretty much everything. We're looking for other towns that used to be connected to our University and the harbor town beside the Great Garbage Ocean. We're hoping to retrieve "half the known body of scientific literature," as our friend Charlie called it, to convince his partner Leo to come with us. But we aren't finding any living towns. This desert reminds me, just a little, of the time before I met Joon.

I've skated on ice in the past. Sand-skiing is so much slower. I think about what to tell Joon about flying over ice. Or should I begin the story further back, on that other ocean?

As we snuggle into our blankets that night under the desert stars, leaving our friends by our dune-grass fire, I start to tell my sleepless, pregnant Joon about the 200-year journey that brought me to her – and I begin to remember. But the further back I go, the more the memory feels like something that happened to someone else ... a story. A myth.

"Let me tell you," I say. "Without story, we are nothing." And the story becomes the memory.

• • •

INVISIBLE GODS

"The coyote is a living, breathing allegory of Want."
— *Mark Twain*

— THE NIHON KOKU ARCHIPELAGO

We knew the wave was coming. Across the water they knew it too, but chose not to know. California would fall into the sea. Perhaps a door would open – for us? The way across the ocean would be as lethal as navigating that distant border that had been closed and mined for decades. Even so, we'd ride the great wave an inevitable earthquake would send to destroy our home. Only that way could we reach the promised land, crumbling or not.

The Elders met with the Jellyfish Masters. The Masters were seafarers; they knew the monster coming better than anyone. The Elders would stay behind. They had a long view. Planning the voyage spanned decades. Many who'd felt the East was better for survival had left long ago. It was whispered that plague and pogroms had claimed them all. For years our scientists orchestrated family groups for their names, their status, and their genetic material. It was said that no child truly knew their own parents, though we all had family affiliations.

When the time was near, a quiet desperation of land families formally offered their children as fosters to the Masters for the ocean crossing. They took only the strongest. But we were all strong, healthy, well tutored. We knew what was at stake. We thought we knew.

We didn't have a clue.

• • •

— THE PACIFIC OCEAN

Waves towered over the small boats racing up them. Ours climbed a wave like a tall building about to collapse. We looked back as our boat of wood, reeds, and plastic managed to rise to the crest just as the wave began to curl. Behind us, in the shadow of the wave, was a cluster of unlucky boats about to be folded under tons of filthy seawater. Ahead of us, other boats raced toward even more waves. The alien landscape was a rolling, cresting animal trying to shrug us off its back.

Our boat tilted up wildly, and the men and women at the front leaned forward, shouting. Somehow we pierced the curl and were over. The wave crashed over the boats behind us, friends, neighbors, relatives. Not a single plank rose from the froth. Ahead, the next wave hadn't yet peaked. We might make it past that one too. That time I was the only one to look back.

•••

— THE OREGON COAST

The land was burning. It lit the dark sky ahead in disturbing electric greens, lightning blues, and bruised yellow-browns. We tried to steer north of the worst of it. The faster boats in the advanced line hit mines, joining the burning sky. Three boats alone were left after our terrible crossing. Damaged and soggy, they were barely able to navigate. These slower boats, pulped and bloated, tried desperately to navigate the path of wreckage left by the mined boats, flotsam that paved the way toward land. Surprisingly, all three made it to a long, dirty beach. Masters and proteges tumbled onto the shore, desperate for the feeling of stable land that eluded shaking sea legs. Almost all of us fell to our knees. Some kissed the blackened sand. A smoky sky rained ash on us as we kneeled.

Rustling in the long dune grasses alerted the Masters to danger and they staggered back to the boats for the few munitions that survived the crossing. It was a massacre.

When the monsters had feasted on the elite flesh of the crews that had worked so hard for so long to find this promised shore, only I was left alive, hidden when a Master had upturned a boat over me. When I heard the thump of a second wave of creatures arriving in a muffled thundering of hooves on packed sand, I gave up hope. But in the sudden silence that followed, I couldn't help my curiosity. Burrowing out from under the hull, I saw a herd of bison – known from books we'd left behind. The animals stood silently, staring at me like a group of hairy hillocks inspecting a small beetle emerging from the sand.

One beast, taller than any animal I'd ever seen, stood in front of the herd. Coated in a deep mat of chestnut curls, black horns jutted from its skull. It huffed like an engine of old. With nothing left of fear in me, I shuffled to the giant and reached out to touch its astounding fur. The bison stared with liquid eyes that were also long past fear. It swung its great head just as I gripped the curly mat on its shoulder, clinging like a burr with fingers and toes. The animal stilled while I climbed it like a wall, up through the tangled mane until I straddled its shoulders. The creature shook its hide in a full body roll, allowing me to dig in even deeper, sliding my thin limbs under coarse knots. Then the great beast trudged across the sand, followed by the herd. They trotted before breaking into a full stampede, taking us past the beach, over crumbling hills, crevasses and rugged mountains, past the Always-Burning, until we were on flat plains and out from under the dense smoke. Stars glared down at us from a wheeling splatter of pinprick lights. As the bison ran, they encountered the ghosts of many others, until a thousand, thousand animals thundered across the plains, wheeling northeast, creating a massive, thundering herd of all who had gone before.

•••

— VALLEY OF THE BUTTERFLIES (Nimiipuu: The People)

I came to the *Nimiipuu* reservation riding on the back of a great red bison, so entangled in the deep coarse curls across its shoulders that, even though I'd been half-conscious for days, I was unable to fall to my death. We'd been joined by a confusion of pronghorn antelope, by the ghosts of the bison-that-were, by elk, mule deer, grizzly bears, and wolves. When the huge bison I clung to gained the border of the Valley of Butterflies, he fell to his knees in front of the Elders from the *Nimiipuu* Fish and Wildlife Committee who, working together, untangled me from his back. Then they thanked him for his life and his meat. The herd was no longer with us. I often wonder if any of it was real.

The Elders of the Tribal Executive Committee, NPTEC, and the Fish and Wildlife Committee, CRITFC, along with the Natural Resources Subcommittee, argued about what to do with me.

I learned later that, because the People, the *Nimiipuu*, were a sovereign nation, they had managed their resources thoughtfully, so they were doing better than most in a time of flood, fire, and famine, when the coast was crumbling into the sea and tornadoes and lighting storms were taking out everything else. But water is always the limiting factor, and the Clearwater River had not run clear in some time. The river was barely running at all, and the tribe's salmon and trout hatchery would be in trouble soon. The Elders suspected a clan of Disaster Preppers somewhere along the North Fork of the Clearwater River, north of the Bitterroot Mountains, were diverting water above the long-broken Dworshak Dam Falls and their fish hatchery near Ahsahka. Names I only learned after they decided to let me stay.

The People didn't need a mythic bison-riding kid complicating the narrative. The only reason they nursed me back to health, when I felt near death from dehydration, was because of how I arrived – and because I brought food. Two thousand pounds of meat on the hoof.

• • •

— COYOTE (It'se-Ye-Ye) IN THE HAPPY VALLEY OF DEATH

"You know he couldn't have gotten here from the ocean in just a few days, even by buffalo," one of the younger Elders grumped. "Lewis and Clark took six weeks, and they were going downriver, in the opposite direction!"

"Coyote," another Elder said, frowning at the younger as she took me aside to tell me what she called a creation story while the others discussed my case.

"Coyote was a randy fellow, and he adored his wife, Mole Woman. When she died, the immortal *It'se-Ye-Ye* grieved. He spent years searching for the Valley of Death, which had always eluded him. Of course, that tenacious *Canidae* found it at last, and snuck down the mountainside. There he found all his old friends partying it up. It was *wonderful*! He got drunk every night with his friends, until the Happy Valley Committee came to remind him that a living being couldn't just stay in the Valley indefinitely. Coyote finally remembered why he was there and announced he would leave only if his wife came back with him. The wily Elder Committee agreed on the condition that Coyote couldn't sleep with his wife until they were beyond the mountains surrounding Death's borders. Of course, Coyote agreed but, like I said, Coyote was a randy fellow. He didn't make it through the first night on the mountain before seducing his lovely wife. His wife kissed him goodbye and returned happily back down the mountain to their relatives and friends before the sun was up. Since then, poor Coyote – *It'se-Ye-Ye* – has spent several lifetimes trying to find that Happy Valley again so he can party with his friends."

I tried to tell the Elders the Greek story of Orpheus and Eurydice, from a book I'd read before the crossing, but the Greek Hell depressed us all so much that we agreed to stick with Coyote's version of the Happy Valley, where all of our ancestors, friends, and families were waiting to party with us in the afterlife.

I did hope the Elders weren't trying to make a case for me to go there soonish, though.

●●●

— STOLEN WATER

Dust pattered down on our shelters like rain. I'd stayed with The People long enough I'd almost forgotten how I got there, and I never understood why I sometimes felt compelled to travel east. I tried to forget where I'd come from entirely, the crossing and landing so traumatic I preferred not to remember. But my survival training pre-crossing, when I was still on the archipelago, was in my muscle memory, and it made me useful in the Water Wars with the Disaster Preppers. DisPeps, I called them, because it reminded me of dyspepsia, stomach ache, though my team used worse names. Our strategy was to sneak in and dismantle any dams and diversions on the river. No people were targeted, just anything that blocked or changed the flow of water. DisPeps to the west had long ago broken the Dworshak Dam, creating the Dworshak Falls, so The People did the same to the DisPeps to the east when they stole water, though my team didn't use explosives.

The People's fish hatchery had originally been created because the steelhead trout and salmon couldn't make it past the Dworshak Dam-that-was upriver to spawn. The dam was too high even for a fish ladder. The dam existed no longer, only the Dworshak Falls remained, yet fish were becoming rare. So the hatchery continued to breed salmon and steelhead below Dworshak Falls and keep the sprat warm for faster growth. They released many into the river, keeping the rest for food. Somehow, they kept the hatchery going, despite less water reaching the falls every year. Some thought The People should move the whole hatchery west to where the Snake River joined the Clearwater. But the more time passed, the less possible that became. The *Nimiipuu*'s main mode of transport were their pretty Appaloosa horses. Moving heavy tanks was daunting via horseback. Besides, the People's hydro-electrics were still generated by the dwindling Dworshak Falls.

• • •

— IT'SE-YE-YE'S WATER WAR

Coyote was all about sharing. He went to the Frog People, who'd built a dam to keep all the water for themselves, and asked for a drink. Even for Coyote, the Frog People wouldn't just give anything away. They asked for something in return. Coyote thought a bit, then turned away and pulled out one of his own rib bones. He gave it to the Frogs, pretending it was a beautiful shell. The Frogs couldn't take their eyes off the giant shell and agreed that Coyote could drink as long as he liked.

Coyote stuck his whole head underwater next to the dam and started to drink. The water level dropped. An anxious Frog finally tapped Coyote on the back, asking him if he hadn't had enough water yet. Coyote lifted his head and said, "Almost!" But the Frogs didn't want him drinking up the whole lake. So he offered to take his rib bone underwater with him while he finished his drink, to make sure the lovely shell patina stayed beautiful forever. The Frogs eagerly agreed and handed Coyote back his rib.

Coyote put his head and front paws underwater, holding the rib. He jammed one end of the rib under the dam, dug it in and pried. The dam lifted and shattered, all the water running back into its riverbed.

The Frogs wailed and cried, blaming Coyote for their lost water. Coyote just shrugged and said that the water was for all the people. The Frogs wouldn't stop yelling, so Coyote plugged his ears with mud. He continued downriver, taking his rib bone, which made the Frogs peep even louder.

(Adapted from "Frog People" in
Giving Birth to Thunder,
Barry Holstun Lopez)

• • •

— THE PEOPLE'S WATER WAR

Frogs are long gone from the world, but the DisPeps, those gassy Frogs, still stole The People's water. My team always followed Coyote's lead and brought the longest, strongest pry bars we could carry on our mission to free the water. Sometimes DisPeps left a couple guards on the bigger diversions and dams. So I'd call on the ghost of the bison who once carried me to trample across the lake with his herd. Their feet did no damage, and my team had to supply sound effects by clacking our pry bars together, but whether they saw the herd or not, the DisPeps tended to run away when they heard the sound of trampling hooves and the yipping of hunters.

My team had little time to act before the guards returned with reinforcements. We attacked the spillways of packed dirt and the rock and tree branch dams with our pry bars. Sometimes I dived into the water to widen any weakened areas or drains. It didn't take much to destroy a dam once its integrity was compromised, because the heavy, waiting water did the rest.

The trick was to get out of the way before the water took us with it as it sought to fill its riverbed again. We leaped away, yelling thanks to Water Woman when we felt the dam start to break up. Then we ran like hell, often to the popping sounds of DisPeps' guns going off in the distance as they raced to protect their dam too late. DisPeps didn't sound like the frogs I remembered. And our plans didn't always go well.

• • •

Once there were armed reinforcements waiting for us, hiding among scraggly trees near the dam. The DisPeps couldn't have known the night we'd planned to attack, so they'd probably waited a long time. I spotted them from where my team planned to scramble down a rocky cliff to where the water was dammed in a crevasse below. Usually we snuck upstream. My team would have died that night if we had.

I never wanted to hurt anyone. But it was so easy to see where a rockslide could start, build momentum, and rain down on the DisPeps who kept diverting The People's water – who kept shooting at us! Just the month before we'd lost a team member, a friend, who was either shot or tripped into the foaming water when it released from the dam. We never found his body. He hadn't been the first. My team had become increasingly angry and ready to fight. So when I shushed them and pointed to the trees below, it was so easy to kick a pebble off the cliff. Show them possible vengeance. Each team member went quietly to the biggest rocks near the edge, wedging their pry bars. I was the one who gave the signal, but we all heard the cries of anguish from below when the boulders bounced and cracked and brought the rocky scree in an avalanche down upon the armed people below. I never led the team to destroy dams again.

The Elders were not happy with my refusal to protect the water. I tried to be useful in other ways. I looked after the few children, told stories. But my stories were not The People's stories exactly, and that made the Elders even more unhappy. I did try. I knew that stories also taught culture. But it was so hard to keep my own ideas and culture separate.

• • •

— JACK TELLS HIS OWN VERSION OF THE PEOPLE'S CREATION MYTH

"I'm not from around here," I told the kids. "But in my home we had similar stories, like a volcanic fumarole that became a Yokai and killed every animal that came close with its horrible breath. So this is my telling of the 'Heart of the Monster,' which led to the creation of the *Nimiipuu*."

"There were monsters before there were people. South of the Dworshak Falls is a wide valley surrounded by buttes stacking up into mountains broken by canyons that collect snow to add to the river. In that valley lies the cone-shaped, volcanic heart of a monster that once sucked up all the water, animals, and birds into its great maw, poisoning the air with its foul breath. It ate everything.

"Only *It'se-Ye-Ye* wasn't eaten. If Coyote came near the monster's mouth, it would snap shut, big round eyes squinching in panic. Even the monster knew not to mess with Coyote. Who knew what damage the Trickster could do to its insides if swallowed? But Coyote was missing friends who were being eaten, their bones littering the valley floor. This had to stop.

"Coyote and Fox snuck up on the sleeping monster one night. For once, it was full, and its giant mouth closed. Coyote leaped up to the great nasal cavity and Fox passed him a big ball of pine pitch and a flint before scrambling back to the hills. Coyote put a hand over his face to spare himself the worst nose mucus and the horrible fumes snorting forth. Then he slid on his back down the monster's nose-chute until he dropped down into a great cavern, his best boots splashing into brine at the bottom. It was dark, so Coyote lit the pitch Fox had given him. For a torch he used a bone sticking out of the brine that kept whacking into his knees. When he could see, a wall of animals were staring down at him from where they'd clambered high above the brine. There was White Bear and Hog Man, Bighorn, Red Tail, Wolverine Friend, and others. They greeted him with hoots and screeches, careful not to let go of their perches.

"Friends!" Coyote shouted. "Help me stomp the heart of the monster and we can escape together!" The animals growled and groaned and hooted in agreement. Coyote saw the ceiling thumping to a beat, so he sliced through it using Steelhead's serrated jawbone, which had been nudging at his ankles in the brine, wanting to help. All the animals clawed their way up to join him on the other side. They leaped and jumped and pounded on the giant's heart. The smoke from Coyote's torch began pouring from the monster's eyes and ears and the monster groaned as he woke. His insides churned, his heart kicked into a terrible uneven rhythm from the animals jumping on it. His distressed groan blew the lighter creatures right out of his mouth in a foul puff, with Bighorn charging after. White Bear escaped through his ear cavity. Prairie Rattle-snake wiggled out his nose. Visiting Hog Man was so angry that, counting on his tough hide, he tunneled out through the monster's guts, followed by his many piglets. Water Woman escaped through the monster's eyes as tears that ran quickly down to their bed to become the Clearwater River.

"When the animals had left, Coyote took the bone he'd used as a torch and struck the monster's heart a mighty blow. It rang like a drum. The bone had been the leg bone of Horse Woman, and her angry magic was strong enough to help Coyote stop the heart completely with a final thrumming stomp. "Horse Woman's bone and Steelhead's jaw helped Coyote dismantle the monster from the inside. Knowing how monsters grow from monsters, they chopped it into small pieces, flinging each far over the mountains. When Coyote squeezed out the last of the heart's blood, it splattered across the valley.

"Where the droplets landed, *Nimiipuu*, The People, sprouted. They still hunted but were thoughtful about how many animals they took, careful about protecting water and fish, and thankful for what Coyote had gifted them. They were wise, but small enough to understand that balance was important and resources precious. Coyote gave them Steelhead's jaw to look after, and Horse Woman's leg bone as a companion, so they would remember these things.

"To this day, Horse Woman and Steelhead Trout wear, as marks of bravery, pretty spots from the ash that fell from Coyote's torch."

I was kicked out of the community for changing the story.

(Adapted from COYOTE & Monster,
Nez Perce creation myth)

• • •

— CULTURAL DYSPHORIA

I suddenly didn't belong. Even my team avoided me when I wouldn't join them in what turned into full war with the remaining DisPeps. The voices of those we'd rained rocks down on haunted me at night. I was again an outsider, shunned at gatherings, sometimes punched for no reason that I could understand. No one would hunt with me, help me gather wood for heat, or let me help them.

I decided to go out into the nearest flatlands and try to talk to the gods. I told the *Nimiipuu* Elders that if their gods wouldn't talk to me, I would leave for good. They agreed – a bit too quickly. The sweet Elder who'd told me that Coyote was still searching for the Happy Valley of Death took me aside and gave me a big bag of dried fish. She also offered me a smaller bag she said could help me talk to the gods. She warned me about the Trickster and said with some sadness that I should bring my gear with me too: my flint and steel, my warm clothes and boots, my knife and pry bar. She clearly didn't expect me to return, no matter who I talked to out on the plains.

I felt like I should understand, but I didn't. Weren't the *Nimiipuu* my people? The Elder took my hands and commented on how young they looked, despite how long I'd been with them. How long had it been? A decade? A century? Her own face had aged into fine wrinkles that smiled for her. She told me my face had not aged at all. Is this why The People wanted me to leave? I sobbed while she hugged me tightly. I wanted to tell her I was not a monster, but then I thought of the DisPeps' agonized cries and wasn't sure anymore.

"This is the very last peyote from the far south, from the Mother Mountains. It will bring you truth," the Elder said, tucking the smaller bag into my hand.

• • •

— COYOTE GIVES JACK HIS IMMORTALITY

I walked out into the Eastern Plain, searching for a small plateau or hillock with enough height to hold me between the ground and sky. I sat and ate a little of the dried fish the Elder gave me, tying the bag tightly to my belt when I finished. I drank water. After wrapping my bison hide around me, I opened the smaller bag.

Inside was a dried leathery thing that looked – and tasted – like a tiny hoof. It was vile. I spent some time vomiting. When I looked up, the bison who's skin I wore was staring down at me, huffing like an engine of old. It shook its great head in a rolling motion, like shaking off water, then turned and walked away. I knew why. I'd used but not truly honored the bison who'd carried me to safety. The bison god had forsaken me. I wailed up at the wheeling stars in the dome of sky overhead. After a while I just stared out over the dark plains. Remembering.

Hours or days of wrenching introspection brought me to the realization that I'd never known who I was, and never would. The people who'd made me were long dead, their reasons with them. I was made of secrets no one was left behind to tell.

That's when the Trickster *It'se-Ye-Ye* appeared, walking toward me across the plains in a stutter, one minute far away, the next too close. Coyote sat in front of me, grinning. His mouth widened until I could see right down his throat. Coyote swallowed me up in one gulp.

Coyote ran across the plains while I watched passively through his eyes. The sage and limestone formations whipped past, faster than the trains of old.

"Take it," Coyote said.

I was confused; this was the first phrase the god had spoken. The words appeared in my mind like red streaks. "Take what?"

"My life," Coyote said. "It's your turn."

"I don't want it!" I cried out.

Coyote laughed and laughed.

• • •

— COYOTE IN JACK'S HEAD

The *Nimiipuu*'s *It'se-Ye-Ye* rode me like a wild *Kitsune* from Japanese folklore. They had much in common, those two trickster gods, including their *Canidae* faces. But he also made me feel that I wasn't alone. I talked to the god riding me as if we were friends. I asked for advice as if he were real. If Coyote really had given me his immortal life, it was clearly not a good thing. Why would he? What was the trick?

The Elder had claimed Coyote was finished with his work in the world and just wanted to go home to his Happy Valley. But where did that leave me? Forever watching my companions go on without me? Why *me*? But still, I talked to the god in my head, Coyote, my invisible friend. I was so alone without him. I did hope there would be no more of the creatures from my past, no Yokai. They were long ago and far away, in a land beneath the sea. This Coyote, a last gift from the *Nimiipuu* in my new land, was absolutely enough. Forever.

Despite the trickster god that lurked in my mind, I felt the faint stirrings of the old compulsion I'd brought with me, calling me eastward. I gathered my belongings and started to walk. And even though Coyote told me he would dwindle in the east, he didn't seem to mind.

• • •

Buffalo Man might have left me for good, but Horse Woman did not. When I reached the edge of the hills, I smelled smoke. Moving carefully through the sparse trees I found an encampment of DisPeps. Not water stealers, those, but definitely horse thieves. By the pretty spots on her rump, the gorgeous Appaloosa mare staked near their fire clearly belonged to the *Nimiipuu*. They would never have sold their precious ponies to the DisPeps. I waited until after dark before walking into their camp and untying the rope that staked her. I whispered Sahaptian words taught to me by the *Nimiipuu* before swinging onto her back. She calmly stepped over and around the guards that slept by the fire. I saw the glint of eyes under the lashes of one very young guard and grinned right at him, showing all my teeth. His eyes squinched shut and no one followed me. By morning we were miles to the east, climbing through the Bitterroot range.

I named the mare Yétiin, Crane, because it amused me to call her Yeti for short. She was anything but – dainty and quiet, so well trained I couldn't imagine how the DisPeps got hold of her. A simple nudge from my knee, or even a flip of her mane to one side, and she'd turn on my request. There was no need for a rope, which I coiled and placed in my bag on top of the dried fish. I gave Yeti time to graze as we traveled. There was no rush to get anywhere other than away. I considered tying her the first night, afraid she'd wander off, but we found a little clearing in the rocks with grass and water, and it seemed unlikely she'd stray. And she never did. The only time in our long association that I ever saw her angry was when a rare prairie rattler shook its tail at me. Then I got the full Horse Woman treatment while she stomped it into the dust with her sharp front hooves. Poor rattler.

Together we walked more than a year. Possibly much more. Time lost all meaning. Yeti was ridden by me; I was ridden by Coyote. We hunted and grazed as we went, walking far more than the 1,700 miles east from Idaho to the Mississippi River since we meandered through mountains and plains, avoiding dead cities and the rarer lights of live towns. We crossed so many broken highways, heading toward the great River. We wandered wherever the waterways and need for grazing took us. We aimed in a general way for the meeting place between the Mississippi River (2,350 miles long), the Illinois River (273 miles long), and the filthy Des Plaines River (133 miles long) that ran from the Great Lakes. Those names and distances I knew, because by then we'd acquired a map from an abandoned gas station. Pollution was also marked on the map. The landscape was so empty of people. Along the way, we never saw another living soul. *But is that even true?*

• • •

Coyote reminded me that water drew all types of life. So we kept moving slowly, usually just north of eastward, following water, fishing, hunting, grazing. I still didn't know why we headed east. Perhaps someone had once told me I must go east to find a safer salt sea, and that somehow justified my restlessness? I didn't really want to know, though at night I liked to watch the constellation Orion also running east, away from the scorpion that chased him.

"I will diminish in the east," Coyote said. Not for the first time.

"Should we stop?" I asked, as if I had a choice.

"No. It is my time," my invisible friend said (*the Trickster god riding me*). "I'm ready to go home."

I wished I could go home too. But Yeti left us first. We missed her terribly. I realized that somehow she got old during our travels. So much more than a year must have passed. We stayed with her until the very end, as she would have for us, if she could. As she did for me when I slept.

Coyote and I continued alone for a very long time, trudging up rivers and creeks, heading eventually toward the great bodies of water on our tattered map. Mostly eastward.

Snow started falling.

JACK & JOON – Lightning Memories

"But that's so sad," Joon cries, hugging her round tummy for comfort. Joon's lithe boy-body is lost in the glowing brown orbs of her belly and breasts. I no longer have to remind myself to use her new (to me) female pronouns. Joon has always known who she is. And she's bringing new life into this sterile world. It scares me to death. I could lose anything in this world except for Joon.

"Why did Yeti die?" Joon wails. "And was it really Coyote that gave his immortality? 'Cause it sounds like the Nimiipuu already suspected, Jae. I mean Jack. You were Jack then and Jae now – which do you want to be called? Did your original family mess with your ... what is the word Charlie used? DNA?"

I put on my thoughtful face. "The further back I go, the less it feels like I'm telling something I remember, and more like I'm just repeating a story heard long ago. As if it's my own creation myth, you know? The true memories are just brief, fragmented, flashes of light."

"Ooooh!" Joon teases. "So you're a tiny god, shooting lightning from your head?"

I ping Joon's tummy with my thumb and forefinger. Joon curls around it protectively.

"We all have to start somewhere. My story starts a few hundred years ago, so not too surprising I forget a few details, neh?"

24

"*Tell something more recent then,*" Joon says, cuddling down into her blankets in the chilly desert evening. "*We've got all night!*"

"*The thing is ....*" I hesitate. "*The thing is!*"

"*It's okay, love. I don't judge. You know that by now.*"

"*Well. Just don't expect consistency either.*" I sigh. "*There are things I forget – or leave out.*"

"*Do tell,*" Joon purrs.

• • •

In a small house near a broken city by a lake, there remained a spark of warmth. Soon it would be among the last seeds of life in a city solid and still under 10 feet, then 30 feet, of snow and ice. The boy inside was hungry, but there was no food, and after a while no heat. He dragged a blanket with him and curled in a cupboard by a chimney, shutting the door to keep his body warmth close. He was comforted by his invisible friend, who encouraged him to will himself small and still smaller as it got cold and still colder. He felt sleepy, so he slept. For a very long time he slept. The boy was me, floating alone in an empty sea of dreams.

And the world changed again.

Electric
ICE

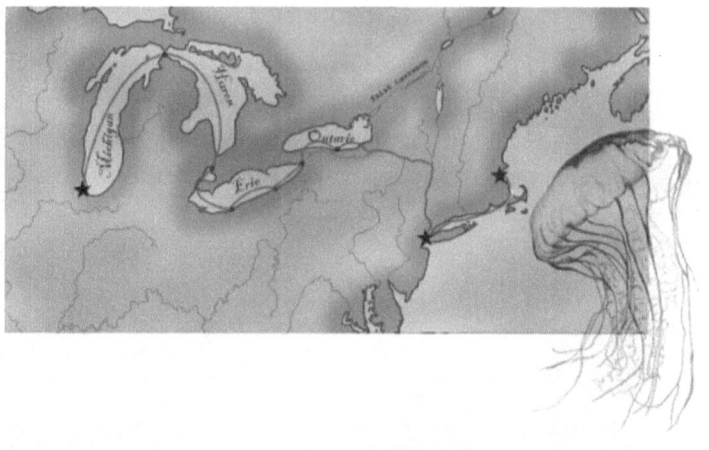

"The Great Lakes contain 21 percent of the world's surface fresh water .... It takes 400 to 500 years for a complete water change. A drop of water that enters Lake Superior can take 191 years to reach Lake Huron."
— *NOAA Office for Coastal Management*

ICE HEARTS

Some say the world will end in fire,
Some say in ice.
From what I've tasted of desire
I hold with those who favor fire.
But if it had to perish twice,
I think I know enough of hate
To say that for destruction ice
Is also great
And would suffice.
— *Robert Frost, "Fire & Ice"*

I wake in the dark. So cold. I try to stretch but my knees will barely unbend, as if it's been a while. My fingertips brush against a box of rough wood. A coffin? Have I been buried? In sudden panic I kick out and a wall *thunks* open on stiff hinges. It's still dark, but I remember now. The chimney cupboard. I crawled in for warmth. But the cold is absolute and frigid; every surface, including my body, is like ice.

Being born again stinks.

It's like this every time – disorienting. I've no idea how long I've been asleep, can only just access memories scattered like windblown trash. I take a moment to catalog.

It was cold. Snowing … a lot. There were two old people – kind – who fed me. But then they left me alone. A tear freezes on my cheek. I doubt I can afford the wasted water. If I don't get out of here I may sleep again for good. *Would that be so bad?* I feel around, fingers slipping through ragged tatters and thick dust. My clothes are shreds. I must've been here a very long time.

This is how I survive: when resources are scarce, I hunker down, grow small, sleep. When it's time, I start over. Eat. Grow. This has been my life for so long. Yes? Is that what I remember? Is this who I am? If I'm in danger, I sleep. *How long?* It hardly seems outside conditions have improved enough to wake me.

It's dark. Silent. So very cold.

A surge of angry disappointment shakes my hands. I want out, but there's not a fragment of light beyond the dark doorway. Why did I wake at all? The world could have ended and I wouldn't have to know. But sleep beckons like death. I'm awake now and I want to live.

The walls are smooth at first, then my fingers slide along rough brick. There's a faint smell of old char in a breeze so slight it's barely there; an absence of stillness. What if I *have* slept through the end of the world? Maybe dust and darkness are all that's left. I duck carefully inside what must be a fireplace, following the feeble draft. A pale light glimmers above. It brings a snapshot of memory: this was a cozy yellow place once, stiflingly warm from the heat of a wood fire. But now the yellow room is flat black, the darkness deafening. I tilt my face up toward the cold light beckoning from above.

It's no easy thing to shinny up a chimney half naked and frozen. Fortunately, the chimney is large and I'm small (*a skinny teen, the old people who fed me believed*). Brick crumbles in my hands and my fingers sink into rotten grout. At the top, bricks and ice collapse outward when I scramble free, falling onto a roof of white. After the dark it's too bright, but the air is sweet and cold. I stand shakily, afraid of falling into brightness. I cover my eyes, breathe the bitter air, and wait. I can wait for centuries – I think. But that only means waking to the grief of each new beginning. Everything dies and changes around me. Only I reset and start over.

Shapes slowly define in the white-on-white, swooping lines and lovely spires of ... just white. Perhaps I died this time and crawled up the flue from hell to heaven? In the cracks of light between my fingers, I start to make out a world of ice.

My feet are numb and my eyes are playing games. The world-that-was, the broken city in the jumbled snapshots of my memory, has become a long slope of snow punctured by twisted towers and horizontal stalactites of wind-carved ice. The city is completely gone. I've lived too long and earth has frozen over. I'd shed more tears if I could.

There's movement far down the slope. My eyes track the motion before my brain fully comprehends. It's a boat! A sail flits across a vast expanse of ice, a lovely human-made thing skittering far below – dark against the field of white. There are people in this bizarre landscape. The world is not dead yet.

I'm so relieved I stumble forward. My numb feet slip and I'm suddenly sliding out of control, careening down a slope toward the flats, sure I'm lubricating the slide with blood. There's nothing to slow me down. I hit a bump and go airborne, yelling rustily as I crash from slope to flats, skittering across smoother, darker ice, slowly losing momentum and gliding to a stop, gasping. The cold burns. I struggle to a crouch over my poor abused feet, shivering violently. Be still. Breathe. Assess. The despair that accompanies each awakening is dulled by shock and the need to focus if I'm to survive this next round.

A voice speaks into the bitter air. I give thanks to the imaginary deity I talk to in my head. I'm not alone yet. Thank you gods-that-aren't.

"You must be burned raw," someone says. A rough cloth lands on me where I crouch. I whimper but hug it tight to my abraded flanks. The cold steals my breath away.

"Where in the ice have you been hiding?"

In a cupboard, I want to say, but don't. Stuttering memories suggest it's best to say little. Strange as each new start is for me, people find me even stranger. Best to say nothing. Wait. Watch. Fit in. Do what I must to survive. I have no other beliefs left.

I focus watering eyes on a mummy of colorful rags standing over me. The feet and legs are thick bundles of wrapped cloth and plastic. The torso is a similar wrapped post. The speaker's face is hidden under a woven hood and behind a thick shard of plastic serving as wind glasses; a thin slit carved through the middle filters the light. Exposed lips are heavily greased against the cold. The light voice sounds female, though mine does too. And I am not female.

Oh, I would do a lot for that outfit and that grease. But she looks stronger than me, and seems kindly disposed, so I wait, shivering. The soles of my feet are numb pads.

"Come. Let's get you to the family." A clubbed hand hugs my arm and I lurch upward. The bundled woman half-carries me to a boat as ragged as she, a mishmash of boards and rusty metal topped with a colorful patch-work sail snapping in the wind. The sailboat fights to take off like one of the skittish ponies (*my Yeti!*) that disappeared from the west before I made it this far. *Ah!* I remember that I was traveling east, into the sun. I shake my head in frustration. My skull is a hollow gourd filled with scraps whirling unconnected. My memories have no cross-referencing.

"You're light as a child." The woman sounds pleased. She dumps me onto a wide plank making up the body of the boat. There are two parallel runners under the plank and a shorter runner under the bow. (I'm not a child, and I've sailed, but this is one weird boat.)

"Hold on!" She laughs, and I hold on to nothing since there's nothing to grasp. She leaps aboard, hauling the boom and planting her feet in one graceful motion as the sail catches wind and yanks us forward. The sail covers the glaring sun, and I can finally see.

We're sailing on a world of ice. The city on the lake that I last knew is gone, as buried as I was, swallowed in a frozen sea of white and speed and laughing woman bundled in multi-colored strips of cloth and plastic. The wind catches her laughter and plays with it, plucking it from her mouth and curling around the mast. Her joy helps me relax into this strange place that will be home for the next little while. Clear sky. Hot sun. Cold air. Brutal light. Ice.

• • •

Survival means focusing on clothing, food, shelter. Water is that necessary ingredient without which nothing else matters. The water in this frightening landscape is solid. I wonder what brought me out of my dusty cupboard. How long did I sleep? I don't remember my dreams anymore, between lives. The waking world is surreal enough. But there are people here, so I'll live a bit longer.

We fly over ice to the noisy scraping of the boat's runners. The wind shifts, the sail luffs, and suddenly we're among mounds of white-on-white, almost invisible irregularities in the vastness of the lake ice. My Captain heaves to, one foot dragging, and we scrape to a halt. It's suddenly quiet except for the crack of the sail before she reefs it.

The woman strides as if on skis – feet never leaving contact with the ice – over to a central mound.

"*Anaaanak!*" she calls. "Look what I found!"

There's only silence. I look around. We're in a village of white tombstones. Scuff marks between the mounds indicate other human occupants, but I see no firepits or obvious signs of food (*I'm so hungry*) or rubbish. The wind is calm and respectful between the mounds. I'm grateful for any relief from the fingers of cold creeping under my cover. I shift it downward so I can stand on the corner to save my feet from the ice.

I hear shuffling and a hand emerges and grips the edge of one of the ice doorways. An ancient woman steps out, dark against the white mound. Except for wrapped feet, she's as naked as I am under my covering. A deep criss-crossing of wrinkles clothes her like a full body tattoo. She gestures us inside.

We stoop to enter, but it's roomy enough inside to stand. The heat is solid as a wall. My body gives a great, involuntary shiver and relaxes for the first time since I woke. I hug the warmth, rocking in relief. The dome overhead is black above a banked fire. Everything is dim and dark and richly colored in browns and the rusty red of old iron. The wrinkled woman sits close to the fire but the younger woman seems uncomfortable in the heat and stays standing by the curved wall. She pushes back her hood and I see her face. She's young, with heavy blue-black hair, glossy ochre skin, and an oval, sweating face. Her eyes are rich almond-brown. Her face looks like home to me. She's so familiar I want to cry. She looks like me. But when I touch my cheekbones they jut out sharply. I envy her healthy roundness.

The old lady cackles. "You found a female!"

My head snaps up and I frown, trying to project *not a girl* at her, but she doesn't notice. I clutch my covering close. I'll keep my secrets a bit longer. Not her business anyway.

"Where you from?" she says slowly, as if I won't understand. Sometimes I can figure out migrations of people by how words and accents mix, though each new set of slang can throw me. I have Japanese, English, Sahaptian, and Wisconsin mixed into to my own patois. Because she asks, I realize I don't remember exactly where I started out. I do know I've been traveling east for a very long time, facing into the sun.

"From the west?" I say tentatively.

"Clearly." She stares. I look down first. "Where exactly?"

"Under the ice," I say. "In the city below." *Not a lie.*

"People living there?" she hisses.

"I'm the last," I say with conviction.

She looks pleased. She turns to the younger woman, suffering in the heat. "Akiak, give her Chu's things. He don't need 'em. Take her for a feed. Take her to Akycha. *Hmm.* Tell him ... she'll be the Akna." The girl flinches. I don't know these words, all "*ahs*" and hard consonants. The names all sound alike. *Akiak, Akycha, Akna.* The old woman was *Ak*-something too. Maybe the old gal never got past 'A' in the alphabet?

The old woman leers at the girl's downturned face. "Bring her back later, to meet the family."

The girl nods and we leave the warm hut, stepping back into air so cold my lungs burn. We duck into another round lump, this one dim and cold. Dry lakeweed is piled beside an empty firepit. Spears and nets are tidily stacked against the walls alongside a pile of tattered cloth and plastic. I wonder where the owner is. We ransack his stuff. The girl hands me strips of material to wind around my numb feet, calves, and under my covering, which I cinch with a wide strip of old cloth.

The girl works on my hands, showing me how to wind cloth so fingers can be exposed at need. I get my own little plastic pot of grease. She caps it with another rag after applying it liberally to the exposed skin of my face. I tuck the pot into the wrap at my waist, making sure it's knotted

33

securely. I even get a hood woven from strips of plastic tarp and ancient woolens. I feel so much less vulnerable once I'm properly wrapped against the cold.

The boat skitters impatiently when we climb aboard and surges over the ice as soon as the sail is raised. The cold is less of a crisis now, the air still so dry my nose hairs tickle. The girl sets our course westward, leaving her own hood off, long black hair snapping in the wind. It's good to be among real people again. In counterpoint, an urge to turn eastward pulses in my head like a phrase of music too often repeated. I ignore it for now. It makes me tired. We fly over ice to the harsh scrape of runners instead of the rhythmic slap and knock of waves. And the speed! I've never sailed so fast. The girl's expression is joyous as she leans into the wind.

Shapes in the distance resolve into a series of dimples in the ice as we approach. We scrape to a stop near a giant hole with a man crouched inside. He greets the girl as *"Akiak."* So that wasn't the old woman just clearing her throat. The girl responds, *"Lluq."* There's no warmth in the man's face when he looks at me until she says, "This is our new person ... the *Akna.*" Then his expression shifts from dour to ... delighted? He stares at me until the stick he's holding dips sharply toward a smaller hole through the ice at his feet. Akiak hefts a spear from a nearby pile and stabs deeply into the hole, and together they haul out a squirming monster. It's as long as I am, with a pale-yellow belly – a snake, an eel ... a fish?

"Laker." The man grunts and slashes it open with one swipe. He reaches inside the body and pulls out fistfuls of warm yellow-orange eggs. Roe. He gestures me over and fills my cupped hands. "Eat."

I'm trembling with sudden, overwhelming hunger. This is food I understand. The things I've had to eat in past lives .... Compared with bugs, vermin, and rotting things in walls, this is *my* food. The food I'd have dreamed of – if my dreams haven't failed me. Fresh, slippery, raw fish eggs bursting with energy like tiny suns. And the size of them! I suck them down, moaning. The man fills my hands again. I look up for more once my second helping is gone. Lluq is popping the last of the roe into this own mouth and looks guilty when he sees me empty handed and eager for more.

Akiak laughs and pins the fish with the spear, ripping off the skin and slicing through muscled sides to make instant sashimi. So good. My body vibrates with well-being. This is what I woke for. We eat the fish down to skeleton and skin. Lluq scrapes the guts into a scaled bait bucket. My stomach bulges. We've just eaten a 20-pound monster down to its bones and I want nothing more than the old woman's fire and a normal sleep. I climb on the boat and nestle into my patchwork covering, already half-asleep when Akiak leaps aboard and lets loose the boom in one smooth motion. We scrape out across the ice, back toward the frozen city.

• • •

The city is more beautiful in death than it ever was in life. As we race toward the southern shore, towers and bridges of ice become a warped fairy tale of frosted shapes, wild curves and violent stalagmites of ice protruding sideways in wind-twisted tentacles. Only the tallest structures jut above the rolling hills of frozen snow, and all are distorted and strange. I'd wondered why the lake is so clear of snow, but the wind at my back makes it obvious. The city is buried *because* of the lake.

"Akiak?" I call loudly over the wind and scraping runners. "Where are we going?" I'm half afraid she expects me to go back under the buried city. She jerks her head toward shore. "To the sun god!" I think she yells. I wonder if she also has an imaginary god she talks to in her head? I like the idea. Maybe everyone needs one in order to cope?

We rattle over uneven drift near shore, slowing as she eases off the sheet. We jump off and I help drag the boat into an ice cave that leads into a deeply buried building. Narrow tunnels dug through the outside crust let in light and air. The wind follows, whistling noisily, like someone blowing into a multitude of bottles. We walk past rows of sailing hulls in various stages of completion, through a tunnel of dense-packed snow, and into a quieter, dimmer space further in. There's a fire inside, and a boy, bent over some kind of parchment or skin.

"Akycha," the girl says.

I'm wondering again what's up with all the harsh "*Ak*" names when he turns around – and he's breathtaking. It's suddenly quite clear who the sun god is.

• • •

Akycha and Akiak are siblings, they tell me, named by the old witch with a penchant for spitting out names like hairballs. They were swapped for a season's worth of dried fish by traders moving through a decade earlier. *Akiak* means "brave" in Inuit, since she protected her brother when they were small. *Akycha* means "sun god," they tell me again, grimacing at each other. Akycha shares his sister's (and my) blue-black hair, dark eyes, and ochre skin tone. He's more muscled and moves with extraordinary grace. Akycha invented the ice-sailing craft. His workshop is dug in near the city so he can scavenge for materials. He also makes fishing spears and nets – whatever's needed. He'll be village leader when the old woman dies.

Akiak says this with some bitterness.

"My sister should be leader." The boy sighs. "I just want to make boats."

36

"Yes. I'd be better. But my job is to make *babies* for the family." Akiak slants her eyes at me. "That'll be your job too."

"Not me!" I laugh, stomach clenching. "I don't do offspring."

The siblings stare as if I've uttered a heresy.

"Why not?" Akiak's voice is tense.

"It's against my religion," I say lightly.

Akiak stands abruptly and leaves the room. We hear her dragging the boat back onto the ice. I start to follow but Akycha stops me. "Stay for now," he says. "She's upset."

"Why should my personal beliefs bother her?" I say bitterly, as if wars hadn't started over these kinds of things.

"She hopes you'll take responsibility off her. We have few females ...."

"Not. A. Female," I say, a little late.

"What?" The sun god stares. "Does the Grandmother know?"

"Apparently not. She sent me off to be fed by a hopeful-looking fisherman," I laugh. Argh! Never laugh at hospitality. I could kick myself.

"You lied?"

"She didn't ask! Not even my name! She just decided I was *Akna*. She seems to like '*Ak*' names," I add, lamely.

"Oh my. That's ...." The boy named after the sun sits on the ground. He's grinning.

"Meaning?"

"Goddess of Fertility."

I thump down next to him. "*Feh*. Why would anyone bring children into this world?"

"Then how would people continue?" he asks naively, this innocent, smart-as-hell boat builder who thinks life is simple.

"All evidence to the contrary," I mutter.

"She'll still want you to breed," he says. "You aren't related. You really male?"

"Never said that." I stand abruptly. "So. Where do I sleep?"

When he starts to ask the obvious, I cut him off. "Call me Jack, okay? And you're Keycha and sis is Aki, or I'll get everyone mixed and call you all '*Ack*.'"

"Huh. Jack and Akna sound similar."

"Not a fertility goddess," I say firmly.

He sighs. "If we call you Jack, the Grandmother will know."

"Better than old witchy woman dishing me out to the local fishermen, yeah?"

I really hope I don't hear him mutter "that might not stop her" as he leads the way to his sleeping area.

• • •

Over the following days, Keycha shows off his boat designs. There's little he hasn't thought through, creating working art from scratch and stories, testing and re-testing until his inventions fly across the ice. I like the way he lives in this harsh landscape: fishing, scavenging, building on the ice. I try to ignore that thing that's been tugging at me since I awoke: an itch, a vague memory of an obsession telling me to move on. I find myself staring eastward when the sun rises, sniffing the air. But it's good here with Keycha. Maybe this time I can stay.

(*Maniacal laughter from my imaginary trickster god.*)

I get Keycha interested in trying to build an auger. He has no trouble at all with the principal of a screw for digging fishing holes in the ice, but what to make it from? Currently the fishermen chip out fishing holes with old rebar they scavenge from the city under the ice. It's hard work.

Keycha has worked out a method for ice fishing using nets. The fishermen dig two holes in the ice, 20 or 30 feet apart, then send a float with a light line through, pushing it downstream with whatever spears or wire they have (a tedious business), until it finds the second hole and bobs up. Then the nets are attached to the line and pulled through the ice to make a curtain between both holes. It's time consuming to set up, and most of the fishermen prefer to spear fish through watched holes or leave trips on unwatched holes. The real trick is to dig over the current. If the water moving under the ice is narrow, the fish are concentrated in that narrow current. But if the fishermen dig in an area with no moving water underneath, it's wasted effort. The witchy woman is their water dowser and, as her hearing fades, she's been training Aki to take her place.

Aki never misses finding the current, Keycha tells me. He makes it sound like she has an almost religious affinity for moving water. Ice is Aki's god, and flowing water is something even more elevated.

• • •

Keycha lets me explore his workshop and we share heady ideas while he tells me about this new world in which I've found myself. Then he decides we need to search for more metal under the iced city. He wants to try making my auger. "It'll be a chance for you to see how we mine the ice-city," he says. But I stall, deeply reluctant to return to the dark.

As reassurance, Keycha shows me a precious piece of flint and steel he uses to light rebar torches wrapped in fish-oil-soaked rags. He also has a working crank flashlight.

"Another city find?" I ask.

He nods. "We sometimes find more than we can use, but you have to dig deep for unbroken things." We're huddled around his culvert stove eating dried fish when Keycha asks me one of those questions I try to avoid.

"Why don't you want to go back under the ice?"

"It was dark," I say reluctantly. "It was cold." I shiver involuntarily in the heat blasting from the lakeweed and fish-bone fire. I'm a fool. I want to tell him everything about my not-so-recent origins. But I can't stand the thought of that expressive face turning rigid with suspicion and dislike.

"How do you decide where to look?" I ask instead.

Keycha looks sheepish. "It's just luck, though the grandmother does like to make a big deal out of it when we get it right. Kind of like her water dowsing. We're supposed to throw the black stones to point the way."

I can't figure out just how religious Keycha is. Or what religion it might be. He criticizes a lot of the Aanak's traditions and rules – at least the ones I'm hearing about. He seems to question everything, testing truths. I remember someone once telling me, "Belief is a kind of blindness." And though I have my own (*mean little*) imaginary mini god for company, I often watch for cues to see how people's beliefs will drive their actions. It helps me stay alive.

"Black stones?"

Keycha pulls out a bag of uneven shiny black stones. They're all stuck together.

"The Aanak found them in the belly of a fish – supposedly. I don't know how they work, but they stick to most metals."

"*Ooh*! Magnets! Ever tried making a compass with one?"

Keycha looks at me oddly. "I've seen ... a compass."

I sense a way to stall our expedition.

"If you float one of these in a bowl of water, it ought to align between north and south."

"You want to float a rock."

"*Ah*, just let me shave a bit off one side ...." Keycha snatches the stone back. I look up, surprised.

"These are sacred stones," he says. He isn't kidding. "You may not *shave* them."

40

"Okay, okay. Do you have a little piece of steel or iron?"

We spend a happy half hour magnetizing a needle-sized sliver of metal against the black stones and then trying to find something light to float it on in a bowl of melted snow. It actually works. We spend the rest of the hour arguing about what north means. To my surprise, Keycha knows about navigation, especially by the stars. He's even more surprised that I do.

"I learned from my other family. Before we were sold. To the Lake people it's more important which way the wind comes from, though to be honest, it usually blows out of the north or northwest anyway. But how would people living under the ice know about stars?"

"Other people came from under the city?" That was a dumb thing to ask. As if anyone could survive under the ice without other people. As if anyone but me could have.

Keycha hesitates before answering. "They have. Not for a long time. It was not a happy meeting – so I'm told."

"Well, I'm glad you took me in."

Keycha smiles his brilliant sun-god smile. "Me too, Jack. Imagine, floating stones to find the north star!"

"You have to have the right stones." I beam back. I like Keycha. He's so quick. "I think you can just bash a bit of metal with a hammer if you haven't got magnets, but it might be weaker."

"Bash them?" And we're off again. Soon it's – thankfully – too late for our expedition.

The fire burns down, more to ash than coals, and Keycha invites me, not for the first time, to share his blankets. I've been sleeping chilly, something I can do, but I hate it. I don't sleep well and wake cramped. The patchwork covering Aki gifted me protects from the bitterest cold, but crawling into the pile of oddly soft covers Keycha sleeps in looks as close to heaven as I'll find in this world. I like him. Maybe I can trust him. Well. Trust is relative, of course.

I watch Keycha organize the sleep corner. I'm still not sure how close I'm allowed to get physically. Every culture I've encountered when traveling seems to have its own personal space requirements. As formal as Keycha can be speaking, he doesn't sweat physical contact. If anything, he sticks a bit closer than I'm comfortable with, often leaning on me to talk, or taking my hand to show me something. It's so natural to him I'm getting used to it, though I'm not sure how this will extend into the sleeping arrangements. But what really matters now are those piled blankets calling my name. No, not blankets after all. Skins! I finger them in surprise, trying to tell what they came from. They aren't thin or scaled like Keycha's fish-skin trunk, but thicker and soft, though I see no sign of fur.

"Snakehead eel," Keycha says slowly, as if I won't know the words.

"I thought eels lived in saltwater." I can't help yawning suddenly. When my eyes stop watering, Keycha's staring.

"Salt?" he says.

"Yes?" Have I said something wrong? Given something away?

"You know about … the salt sea?"

"Yes?" Why would this be important to him? I'm still trying to remember why it is to me.

"We have a lot to talk about, my friend." Keycha yawns too. "Tomorrow."

And it turns out that Keycha's people don't have a heckuva lot of taboos about physical contact at all. Keycha climbs into the tidy pile of skins, spoons up to my back, pulls the heap on top of us, and falls instantly asleep, one arm draped around my middle, his long hair tickling the nape of my neck. The sun god snores.

I can't sleep after that. I lie in the dark, wondering why it's always the sea that's important. Wondering why a stranger's sleeping body feels so warm and comfortable.

Wondering what this alien feeling of well-being is, and whether something as simple as a friend's touch can be called happiness.

• • •

The snow tunnel behind Keycha's workshop narrows and twists until we eventually lose the light. Keycha has to ask me to walk faster. I grab the back of his wrap and he laughs.

"How old're you?" he teases. That's a question I never answer.

(*That's an answer that frightens everyone.*)

Keycha stops and pulls my hand from his clothing.

"You're worse than the fishermen," he complains, digging the crank flashlight from his pack. His voice echoes.

We've just left the tunnel for what sounds like a bigger space. The whizz of the crank announces our presence to the dark. I imagine tons of shifting weight overhead. We must be right under the frozen city. Even after the population crash preceding the snows, this must be the grave of thousands – including two who were kind to me once. *Don't think.*

I can't do this. If I take one more step into the dark I'll panic. I'll abandon Keycha and he'll see me for the self-serving coward I am ....

Keycha turns on the light.

How can it be beautiful, knowing what it is? But the lit cavern is so otherworldly it takes my breath away. Light fractures away into the distance along a broken maze of ice shards. The cavern is held up by a massive skeleton of iced steel under a high roof of frost. Shining columns angle away in all directions. We're below the broken city looking upward at the end of the world. We walk silently into a catastrophe frozen in time, a catacomb of broken things.

"People lived *here*?" I ask, voice tamped small.

Keycha looks at me sideways. "Who knows?"

I sigh. "I'll tell you later. Promise."

Keycha grins and takes my hand. I'm relieved by his trust. I watch his profile as we walk. He's warm-toned and lithe in contrast to the backdrop of glittering blue and angular white shadows. I imagine his internal thoughts as richly organic, like dark loam.

"What're we looking for?" I ask after we've climbed over and under iced beams and debris for a while. I've relaxed a little, though I cling to Keycha's warm hand.

"Who knows?" Keycha answers. "We're on a treasure hunt."

Keycha's idea of treasure includes piles of twisted rebar. He exclaims over one piece of frozen metal then rejects it to choose a flatter piece of iron that he chips from the ice and pads with a tattered plastic tarp before tying it to his back ("for boat runners," he explains). We contemplate a pile of old cans concreted into a single lump.

"A pity." He sighs. "I remember getting food from these once. But people got sick, so we avoid them now. I remember, when I was small, something so delicious. It was yellow and soft in sweet thick liquid."

I'm remembering peaches when there's a *snap* and the light goes out. We're pitched into absolute blackness. The crank light failed. The hair rises on my arms until I feel Keycha's hand squeezing mine. I really can't stand the dark.

"Easy," he says and starts to hum.

It's surprising enough that I listen. Someone humming is not a frightened person. Keycha removes his hand and I flinch, but the humming keeps us connected. I hear him scrabbling through his bag. But without his touch to ground me the darkness becomes heavy. I lose my breath, crushed under the silent weight of it. Invisible tons of ice overhead press the dark down until my knees buckle. I slump into a ball, small as I can make myself. My body is ready to do its thing: heart rate slowing, breathing shallow. Conditions are poor. It's time for the sleep that's not quite sleep. It's dangerous to do here, but danger and hardship are the triggers, after all. What happens when one's survival strategy works against one?

I tell myself to stand, to say something. But I'm frozen in a small space. Only Keycha's humming keeps me connected. There's the scritch of a torch being lit. The under-city appears again, no longer a blue-white glitter but yellow with flickering, red-filled shadows. It smolders. I manage one deep, shaking breath, then lose it again in the smoke.

"Jack?" Keycha's voice calls out, but I've become small and distant. I can barely feel the world around me. I'm invisible. "JACK!"

• • •

My skin burns. I've never, in a long imperfect memory, been interrupted during regression. Now I'm stuck halfway and it hurts. I'm sitting in what seems to be a giant kettle by the fire in Keycha's room, boiling. Am I being made into soup? I think I ask him that before I pass out again. But this time it's just the little sleep.

• • •

I rise to the surface of awake. I'm skin-to-skin against Keycha's naked chest, under piled blankets. It's distressing (*but so lovely and warm*). I keep apologizing. Keycha tells me to shut up and go back to sleep. There's a sense of time passing, so I can't have been in the deep sleep. I keep talking, just to be sure. I hear myself, and the rumble of Keycha's responses, but I'm enough in the dream world to know I'm talking nonsense, a conversation that only starts to make sense at the end, as I fully wake.

"No, I'm not gonna cook and eat you. Yes, I figured out you're not exactly a boy or a girl. Sorry. Couldn't be helped.

No, I'll never take you under the ice again – why the *frack* didn't you tell me it could get that bad? Yes, I get that you never lived there, not the way you react to dark. So. You awake enough to hear what I'm saying?"

"Yes."

"Really?" Keycha rolls on his side to face me. My head slips off his shoulder and we stare at each other. "Welcome back."

"*Ah.*" I've never wanted so badly to explain myself. "What happened?"

"Dunno? I dragged you back – and warmed you up. Sorry."

I sigh.

"What are you?" Keycha asks softly.

I don't know how to answer. I'm a boy and a girl. I'm neither. I'm nothing.

"I've heard of folk like you," he says hesitantly.

"Really?" I say bitterly. "Where can I find them?"

"It was just stories," Keycha apologizes. He reaches to pet my hair. I hold my breath, afraid he'll stop. "My first family were traders. They told of a tall woman ... like you. She traveled with the family for a time. She knew things ... helped when folks were ill. She told tales about the world."

He had my attention. "You never saw her?"

"No. But every story ended with her traveling into the sun toward a great salt sea that never freezes."

"I was heading east," I say breathlessly. (*But why?*) "When the ice caught me."

"Will you keep going?" Keycha whispers. It sounds like it matters to him. I want it to matter. We stare at each other in the firelight until his warm hand slips down to rest on my cheek. My eyes flutter and I fall asleep, dreaming of chasing the sun.

• • •

On the full moon Aki returns to tell us it's time to meet the family. She watches the two of us closely. I don't want to go, but I feel responsible for Aki too. She found me. Fed me. And I've let her down just by being who I am. I'm all too familiar with that feeling. Keycha hugs Aki and her expression lightens a little. I smile, thinking of the warmth of his hugs.

We've spent our time together talking about anything and (*almost*) everything. We've been making things. Keycha worked on new boat designs and I explored different versions of my auger. I don't want to leave. Ever. How often does one meet a friend like this? So few times in so very many years.

I'm not eager to meet the family. I just want to stay here building useful things with Keycha. I imagine checking in with the group now and then to get food or present our latest toys for their use. But Aki needs us to go with her now.

Keycha and I sail out on his newest boat into a night that's almost day, spotlighted by the moon. The new boat is made of wind. We heave to near the mound village minutes before Aki, ruddy from cold, our laughter gusting away behind us.

Aki pulls up beside us, her eyes wet, also from cold – I hope. But it's sobering. The laughing girl is quiet and distant now. The three of us walk toward an orange bonfire competing with the silver moonlight. People in familiar mummy-wraps are silhouetted around the fire. The old woman is, thankfully, dressed against the cold. I doubt Aki has mentioned my disinterest in breeding to the grandmother. And there's still the secret I haven't told Keycha. *A fresh tingle of worry; once he knows, will this warmth be taken away?*

"I am *Aanak*!" The old woman calls out as we approach. "Grandmother of all! Who comes and how will you aid this family?"

"I'm *Akiak* the brave!" Aki responds. "I bring … glory … to the family."

The Aanak is silent, as if this is unexpected.

"I'm *Akycha*!" Keycha calls quickly as we move closer. "Maker of fast boats. Inventor!"

The Aanak frowns with every wrinkle of her leathery skin. In the firelight, hoods thrown back, I can see the faces of the waiting people. All have the same ochre skin, black hair, and eyes with heavy epicanthic folds that give me a feeling of home. There are faces carved with experience, with wind, darkened by sun and cold; shy, resigned, grinning, attentive faces. Hopeful faces. Grim faces. For a dizzy moment I imagine them all as adult possibilities of myself – if I'd ever made it to adulthood. They lived the lifetimes I missed while sleeping …. And this is Keycha's family, all that's left of the fertile earth, standing in warm contrast to the silver and white of the night ice.

I breathe deeply in the bitter air. *Aki and Keycha took a stance. It's my turn. What's to lose – other than endless lifetimes chasing a distant sun? I want a place here, with these people. There's a warmer sun hidden in this ice.*

"He-ey!" I say conversationally since we're face-to-face now and I don't want to yell. "I'm Jack. Teller of … unfinished tales?" Keycha stifles a laugh. Aki is stone-faced.

"*Akna*?" the old woman asks.

"Jack," I reply firmly.

"Female?" she says, hopefully.

"Not at all," I say.

"Shit," the old woman says, breaking the mood. Everyone starts talking at once.

ICE MAP

"The ceremony of innocence is drowned;
The best lack all conviction, while the worst
Are full of passionate intensity."
— *William Butler Yeats, "The Second Coming"*

Aki is furious. She'd heard me say I had no intention of bearing children, but she didn't know I couldn't. Or that's what she's assuming now, I guess. Keycha understands that's not quite the whole picture, but he keeps his mouth shut, thankfully. A friend who can really keep a secret when it matters is worth his weight in ... what? Crank lights? More. Worth his weight. Full stop.

"You bitch!" Aki is just stunningly mad. "I even gave you my brother. You've had ages to get to know him. You were *flirting* with him on the way over here!" I look at Keycha in surprise as he tries to hush Aki, but there's no stopping her. "And now you say you can't when I thought you just needed ... *frack*! What are you, a freak or something? What have you two been *doing* all this time?"

Keycha looks at me and I hold up my latest auger reflexively, to show her. I've been clutching it ever since we escaped back to Keycha's cave. Aki made it very clear we would be having a "talk" there. We left the Aanak speaking to the disappointed adults.

"We've been making things?"

"Ice forbid, another freaking *boy*."

Now Keycha is angry. "You left Jack with me thinking we'd get on with making babies after what he said about not wanting to? Who's the freak here, Aki? You're as bad as *her*. You *would* be the kind of leader *she* wants. You just want to manipulate everyone." Keycha turns abruptly and stomps into his sleep room. I grab Aki's arm to stop her following.

"Give him some space," I say.

"Don't you tell me what to do!" she spits at me.

"Same to you," I say as calmly as I can but with some heat.

Aki yanks her arm away and stalks toward the boat-house. It's deep dark now. The moon has gone down and the stars are swallowed in scudding clouds. I can't imagine how she'll sail in this. I follow her, still holding the auger. Keycha left a torch to burn itself out near the boats, but it's truly black outside. I don't want to see her disappear into that.

"Don't go out there," I say a little too sharply. "Come back in. We'll talk."

"Just die," Aki says, dragging her boat toward the dark outside.

"I can't," I say without thinking.

Aki turns toward me. She's standing in the entrance with her back to the dark, frowning, her mouth open to speak. There's a single loud crack behind her, and a night-mare creature, long, pale, and toothy, erupts through the ice and launches at her silently, the only sounds skittering shards of ice and my own choked cry of warning.

● ● ●

My auger might never have drilled a good hole in the ice, but the sharp blades work for decapitating a sea monster. They snap and break but last long enough for me to hack desperately at the neck of the thing that attacks Aki, chopping repeatedly at a pale, scaled neck below a triangular head. The jaws hyper-extend to sink curved fangs deep into her leg. Its long body whips and writhes across the floor, making it hard to aim. The blades slice open those white scales to an unexpectedly deep red. Sign of an air-breather. An impossibility. It all happens so fast. By the time Keycha comes running, Aki is sobbing in my arms while I pick helplessly at a long, curved tooth embedded in her shin. My hands are shaking and slippery with blood. The creature is still flopping and twitching a few feet away, the head mostly severed from its body, several broken blades stuck in its skull. I'm afraid that my last reflexive blow to the head is what drove the tooth so deeply into her leg.

Keycha reaches us just as the body starts to jerk backward toward the entrance, its long snaky length juddering as if it's being yanked. Aki cries out, but I'm so sure it's dead I just stare in disbelief. Is there something even bigger and meaner out there, pulling it back through that new hole in the ice? Keycha stomps on the head just as the body is yanked again, and it parts from the neck. The length of the creature disappears into the dark. Only the mangled head is left behind under his foot. He kicks it away and pushes us toward the living quarters.

"Quickly. Get her further in. I'll block the entrance."

"Don't go over there! It came out of the ice right there!"

He hesitates, then follows us, dragging a boat across the passage to his kitchen.

"Go on. We'll block it from the inside too."

"Water," Aki says, still wide-eyed with shock and pain. "Why am I hearing running water! What have you done?" She's speaking to Keycha, who for some reason looks shamefaced. He keeps going though, upending his fish-skin trunk to block the passage, something we tend to do nightly to keep in the heat.

"Fracking hell. Calm down, Aki, he's not responsible for that horrible thing. Sit. I want to get that tooth out of you."

Aki barely flinches while I work the tooth loose. It's big. The sharp, conical tooth of an aquatic reptile. But the reptiles, like alligators – right after frogs and amphibians – were among the first to go extinct several long sleeps ago. I remember the first affected were the creatures that lived and fed in and around water, including sea mammals and birds. Aki keeps muttering about running water being impossible. Keycha takes the bloody tooth and hands me a rag and something that smells like alcohol for Aki's wound. It's deep.

"Not a coward after all," he says to me. "Sometimes it's good to be afraid of the dark." He puts a hand on my shoulder. "Thank you for helping her." He rubs at his eyes and sags down beside me. Aki's wound tended, for now, I end up with a sibling slumped against me on both sides, staring into the dying fire.

"What was that?" I finally whisper, after what feels like a long time.

"Snakehead eel," Aki answers, surprisingly. I thought she'd gone to sleep. "A really, really big one. Usually they can't get through the ice. The adults are too big for the holes we make for fishing, though they'll steal fish, and your hand if you reach into the water to hook your catch. How it could have broken through .... It doesn't make sense. And there shouldn't be running water under here anyway ...."

"Jack?" Keycha's voice on my other side is slow and logy. "Where did you test your auger?"

Uh-oh. "*Um*, outside the door?" I say tentatively. "But I never cut very far into the ice. They were just shallow

52

tests ...." Mostly because the test augers wouldn't cut without me leaning hard enough to bend them.

"Close together?"

Maybe ....

"Still. Shouldn't be running water under here ...." Aki's voice, insistent in the dim firelight.

"Shouldn't be snakeheads either," Keycha says. "Didn't used to be."

"It looks like a reptile tooth," I add, forgetting what I should and shouldn't know. "*Uh*, but they died out a long time back. And ... they breathed air. Or ... so I was told." I picture a fish with an alligator head, but it doesn't fit. This thing looked more like a super-sized pike or a barracuda with a fat eel body – though I never did see the whole length of it.

"The Grandmother saw a huge one once, frozen in ice," Aki says. "Old ice. Maybe the ice is giving them back."

"Maybe we're heading for a thaw," I say to a stunned silence. That's something to think about. What else could the ice be hiding?

• • •

Next afternoon the Aanak sends a scowling fisherman to get us, and Keycha sends him back with the giant eel's head and a message that we have other problems. He doesn't mention that I'd thinned the ice near what is now the old entrance (*good man*), but even Aki doesn't seem too concerned about that, lucky for me, since she'd almost had a chunk taken out of her because of my mistake. Right now, she's obsessed with the water running so close under the ice – and by the idea of thaw.

Moving water is visible through the new skin of black ice forming over the snakehead's hole, which has cracked and widened enough that it could pose a danger to the boats. Keycha's solution to the unsafe area was to dig out a new entrance on the other side of his boathouse first thing in the morning. I helped. More than once we stopped digging to see Aki kneeling too close to the black-ice window at the old entrance, just watching the bubbles moving past in the current. Keycha growls each time and stomps over to pull her farther back, asking if she wants to be eaten again. But the giant eels either don't hunt during the day or they had enough to eat with the body of their companion. Keycha tells me we'll need to block the damaged entrance soon, but he's loath to do it while Aki is so focused on understanding the moving water. At dusk, we drag a boat hull back across the tunnel to the kitchen before we retreat into its warmth.

During the evenings, Aki acts intensely happy, despite her wounded leg, which must be aching. It isn't the kind of joy she showed on my first day, that laughing freedom while she sailed the ice. But she radiates edgy excitement. She asks constant questions she clearly doesn't expect us to answer. Are we heading into the time of Thaw? Where might we expect to see open running water? How long will it take? And if the fishing channels open up, how will the boats cross them? That sobers her momentarily, and Keycha starts mumbling something about needing longer runners.

Without thinking I say, "But eventually the whole lake will melt, so longer runners won't help."

"The lake?" Aki laughs. "Don't be silly. The lake is *ice*."

"Ice is frozen water," I say reasonably.

Aki stares at me. "Are you trying to be funny? You aren't. Listen. There has always been, and always will be, ICE. It's true that ICE is what will bring us running water in the Great Thaw. But ICE gives us our lives and our fish, our homes and our deaths. ICE is Everchanging, Everlasting." Her voice has gone all singsong. *Ooh*, I know those symptoms. This is Aki crossing over to some flavor of religion and blind belief. And just when we're starting to get along.

"This whole lake used to be water," I say sharply, no longer caring what I'm supposed to know and what I'm not. And she was so cute just after the fish bit her. I was hoping she'd allow me a place in her family at last and drop the damn business about making babies.

"Don't be stupid!" Aki says, and laughs right in my face. *Gah!*

"Aki," I say patiently – condescendingly really. I can't help it. "What happens when we take a chunk of ice and put it over the fire? We get drinking WATER. What happens when the ice that makes up the surface of this lake melts? We get to swim in water – with the snakeheads." That's mean, I know. Aki rubs at her bandaged shin.

"*Psha*, that will never happen," she says. "Why would the ice melt?"

"A water lake?" Keycha frowns. "But my boats would sink. I'd have to replace the metal runners with, ah … hmm."

"Wood," I say abruptly. "Wood floats. Fish skin or snakehead hides on a light frame. Plastic, bone, wood. Maybe even tarps. But the snakeheads –"

"Maybe if I used snakehead hide they'd leave it alone?"

"They ate their dead friend quick enough."

"True." And Keycha's mind is off to solve the problem of a light, tough, floating boat.

"You two are thick as – as thick things!" Aki yells at him, clearly not wanting to insult ice.

"Aki, it isn't likely to happen right away."

"See!" she says. "So you admit it." But she looks disappointed.

"Honestly, haven't you ever wanted to see open, running water? To be able to go outside freely, with bare skin if you choose, because the wind is warm? To see green things growing …," my voice breaks a little.

Aki's eyes swim with sudden tears. "My whole life," she says.

• • •

Aki has a secret too. Keycha knows, because he gave it to her. Aki has a book. Keycha taught her to read. Even the Aanak can't read. But Keycha learned before he came to the lake. The Aanak's own secret is an old, folded, waterproof map of the lake and of other lakes to the east. Keycha's first family handed the map over with their children and it's treasured. Aki and Keycha have seen the map, but the Aanak told them that it is for no other eyes. The lake is their life. She wants no one imagining life on other shores.

Keycha tells us he used to wonder how his family could have given up that map, which he remembers as the keystone, the focal point, of their zealous belief in an unfrozen salt sea to the east, and the motivator of their wanderings. They were on a lifelong pilgrimage to the sea when they came to the lake. Keycha still thinks about this sometimes. They believed there was something important to the east. Something they must have valued more than they valued him and his sister. Sometimes Keycha wonders how they could have given him and Aki up. But he needed to put that from his mind, so he also put the map out of his thoughts, for a time, and what its existence might mean. He decided that it is enough to simply live. To create. He's satisfied that his creations improve the lives of his current family.

This is who Keycha is, and what he values. But Keycha has gotten close to no one other than Aki – though now he has a new friend he can share these thoughts with, I hope.

Aki's book is a child's reader, with simple words and pictures. The Grandmother has never seen it, and never will. Keycha gave the book to Aki, taught her to read it, then put that from his mind also. The book isn't reality. Its pictures are of green things and running rivers. It shows men and women, boys and girls, so many people, on boats and on land. It shows a city not yet under snow, and so many strange animals and trees. It also shows something that looks like the lake but is too blue, with rolling ripples and frothy edges. No one is wearing the winding grave cloths to keep warm, so it can't be a real lake. Aki hopes the people aren't too cold. The book has pictures of busy crowds in the sun, sometimes lying on something that does not seem to be ice. There are pictures of fish, but no pictures of ice. There's no word for ice in this book. Aki doesn't know how to spell the name of her god.

The book has become Aki's internalized proof that the Aanak's tales of the Great Thaw are true, but somehow, maybe because there's no ice in the pictures, she has decided that ICE is something outside of all the happy images, surrounding them, invisibly framing them, orchestrating even the Thaw. Ever-present. As it is and ever shall be.

At least Aki's god is tangible in the real world, unlike the imaginary god I talk to in my head (*less lately, since I'm with people. Is he finally diminishing? – Huh. Where did that thought come from?*). Aki's god fits the category of something greater than herself. We live on the ice, drink the ice; the ice gives us fish to eat, fish-skin, bones and weed for our fires and our beer. The ice both invites and keeps the ever-present wind at bay. A world without ice is unimaginable to Aki's – except that she does imagine it when she reads her book, looks at the pictures, and envisions a warm, rippling salt sea that her parents eternally travel toward but never quite reach. These things make up the dichotomy that is Aki's personal world view.

The Grandmother Aanak's personal beliefs are significantly darker. But it takes a while for us to discover just how grim they are.

• • •

Keycha, Aki, and I discuss these things far into the night. Aki flips through her secret book, its once heavy pages dog-eared and worn. Normally she keeps it under her wraps, close to her heart. Keycha admits to being angry at his parents for abandoning them (*to which Aki reacts with surprise*). And me? What do I share? Useless information. That the lake is water, that extinct reptiles breathed air, that my own god is an imaginary voice in my head who likes to play tricks on me. That my personal religion is simply to survive. I say too much, even so.

"It's time," Keycha says. "Jack has promised to tell us more about where he comes from."

"From the ice," Aki says sleepily. "I saw him. He came right up out of the ice." Then she seems to hear herself. "Oh! The ICE?"

Before she can get some dumb idea in her head that the ICE sent me to save her from that toothy fish, I say even more. Dumb, dumb. But no one else has been interested in so long, and they don't seem the witch-hunting types. Blame exhaustion, and the odd weedy-smelling beer from Keycha's mismatched still. We're bonding, I suppose, hardly knowing what that means.

"I climbed out of the ice, but I got myself in there too," I say. "Nothing supernatural about it." I pause, considering. How much to say? Though it scares me, I almost think I could tell Keycha about my multiple lives, but Aki is too aggressive, too volatile to trust. I start with what I've already told Keycha, the short version.

"I was traveling," I say tentatively. "Like your other family. I need to get to the salt sea." As I say it, a yearning awakens in my stomach.

"You were naked," Aki snorts. "That's a tough way to travel if you believe survival is everything."

I remind myself that when it isn't about matters of religion, Aki is pretty darn sharp.

"Yes, about that," Keycha adds.

"Some people under the ice took me in," I say in a rush. It's all true, just not all the truth. "But I fell asleep. When I woke, it was dark and I was naked. So I climbed up toward some light and you saw me sliding down the ice onto the lake. You saved me." I smile warmly at Aki. That should let her off the hook about paying me back for saving her from the eel. Knowing her, she'd hate to owe me.

"Jack doesn't like the dark," Keycha adds. "It makes him pass out. They probably thought you were dead. I did, for a while."

Keycha is pretty sharp too.

"How many people were under there?" Aki asks abruptly. "How were they living? What were they eating? Could you have just imagined them? I thought you told the Grandmother you were the last?"

"They were old," I say. "An old man and an old woman. They were kind. They fed me. I don't believe they're still living." I feel sad. How could I ever tell Aki that this was before the snows fell, before her lake had so deeply iced over. That the old couple took a homeless kid off the long winter streets and fed me the most amazing meal of eggs, from chickens they'd farmed and fed in the poor dirt between slabs of the broken city's pavement ... things Aki couldn't even imagine. That when I woke up they'd been dead so long my clothes had turned to dust. That it would always be this way for me. That I would lose everyone I loved, that all I had was moving on.

Keycha's warm hand is on my shoulder. Aki quietly refills my cup with weedy alcohol. They silently accept my small tragedy. This is now, warmth, food, friendship. This is enough.

"I'm older than I look," I sniffle. Leaving it at that.

"You act younger than you are," Keycha snorts and gives me time to pull myself together by telling Aki the story of my terror under the city, which makes her laugh. Somehow, instead of being rejected for my fear, it becomes the thing that helps them accept me. I can be afraid of the dark, or I can be a hero fighting a toothy fish. I'm fallible. I'm only human.

In the morning we wake slowly by the cold firepit, woozy from the alcohol, the taste of swamp weed in our mouths. Aware that there's something between the three of us now. We know each other a little better.

Keycha gives us a purpose for getting up: "Today we race!"

Aki's bleary face brightens. "The new boat design?"

Keycha smirks. "Only one is ready. But you can have my old boat."

"Nuh-uh!" She punches his arm. "I get the new one. Jack, you sail with me this time. I'll need the extra ballast." And she grins at me. "Let's whup this lazy boatbuilder!"

• • •

We're flying. Keycha's sail is slightly ahead on our right. We creep up to steal his wind, but he grins over at us and kicks something. A second sail snaps open, billowing out in the westerly wind. He stalls a moment just before the huge sail fills and jerks ahead, the scraping of runners abusing our ears. The lines snap and rattle. Aki swears and looks for any sign of a second sail on this new boat we're chasing him in, Keycha's prototype. He's been bragging that it's his most innovative design yet, but we still can't catch him. Instead of the single board Aki usually sails, this is a catamaran, with an old tarp slung between two hulls. I don't trust it with my full weight. One side lifts as Aki pulls closer to the wind. I lean out, terrified. But the confidence on her face, the sheer beauty of her love for this speed and freedom, infects me too and I face forward, watching Keycha's sails pull away, imagining long-gone birds in flight.

We pull up, cursing and laughing, near Keycha, who's heaved to near a group of fishermen, far out on the western ice. We stop and one of the men grabs Aki's arm. I try to swat him away, realizing belatedly that Keycha's arguing loudly with the others. Aki looks panicked. I try asking nicely for the large fisherman to let go of her arm.

"Aki!" Keycha yells suddenly. "Go to Grandmother. Now!"

I kick out hard and catch the fisherman right on the elbow and he lets Aki go. She never set the brake, so I roll off, using my weight to swing the boat around. I give it a shove, and she's off, letting the wind push her southeast, back down the lake, a fleeing bird. The fisherman rubs his elbow, staring at me, face deadpan. I start wishing rather badly that I was on that boat with her, but Keycha has it covered.

"Snakehead!" he yells, and gods help us, but all those big stolid men turn around to look – and me with them. Then Keycha flies past me and I catch onto his stern and drag for a minute, barely keeping my feet, but it's enough to get us out of range, and he flings the sail wide, slowing to let me climb aboard. Then he hauls her in and we're off, flying after Aki.

"What th' hell?" I pant.

"Just a minute," he says, "gotta control this sail ..." and to my sorrow I see him cut away that second, lovely sail – it was flapping uncontrollably and catching against his mainsail when he tacked – and it flies free across the ice, belling out and rolling in the wind like a giant patchwork sea creature, lines trailing like tentacles. I wonder if the fishermen will catch it.

"*What* a waste," Keycha says regretfully. "Only good for downwind. I need to find a way to reef it faster."

We're silent for a few moments, and I wonder what kind of situations might require more speed in Keycha's future. Aki is far ahead of us now and angled southeast toward the village and the Aanak.

"What did they want?" I finally ask, shouting over the scraping of the runners.

"Aki," Keycha answers shortly.

• • •

We arrive at the mound village, only minutes behind Aki. Her boat is already tied down, sail heaped messily where she's just let it drop. Aki is standing in front of the Grand-mother's ice-hut. The Aanak is naked again and leaning out of her doorway. Aki's hood is back and her hair is flying around her face. She is screaming at the old woman. We tie down our boat. Keycha carefully reefs the sail, and we start toward Aki just as the old woman steps out and slaps her hard across the face. Aki sits down suddenly on the ice, hand to her cheek. I break into a run, but other adults, who are closer, emerge from their huts and surround Aki and the old witch. I feel a flight-or-fight surge of adrenaline, and Keycha must have too because he barrels right through the crowd, shoving them aside. I slip through behind him.

The old woman has Aki by the hair. There are large people all around us waiting to do her bidding.

"You will do your duty, girl," the old woman says, her voice disturbingly calm. "If you won't choose, I'll do it for you."

"Keycha!" Aki sobs out, asking for help, and at the same time, Keycha bellows, "JACK!"

"I'll be the next leader and I have a say in this. Let it be Jack," Keycha says in the sudden quiet.

Aki and I stare at him in horror. There's an icy lump in my throat. What's he doing?

"*Hmph*." The old woman drops Aki's hair. "Not the worst idea. For now. New blood." She looks me up and down. "Can you do your part for the survival of this family, boy?"

"I'm not a –" I start to say, but Keycha claps his hand down hard on my shoulder and yanks me roughly around to face him. He looks directly into my eyes.

"Help us," he says.

• • •

This is when Jack panics. It isn't pretty, but it's one of those things I do best.

"No!" I yell in Keycha's face, this once-in-many-life-times-friend who I thought understood me. I jerk away and turn to run but he has me by my hood and I hang up, gagging. Then Keycha, my smart, gentle, almost-brother, drags me by the scruff of my neck across the ice to the empty hut. He dumps me roughly inside and bellows in a loud, deep voice I hardly recognize.

"Stay. Or you will die. Understand?"

"Yes," I choke out, bitterly. I turn my face away.

"I don't think you do."

"I get it!" I shriek at him. "I do what you and that old bitch want, or I die. I go against everything I believe in – everything Aki wants – or we both die. I get it. So *frack off*, you traitor!"

Keycha's face is impassive. He drops the door flap, leaving me in darkness. I spend a moment feeling horribly betrayed and sorry for myself, then take a deep breath and tell myself to just get over it. So I put my trust in the wrong person; it's not like that's never happened before (*but why him?!*). I take a few more deep breaths and scoot to the door to peer out.

Aki is being marched into the Grandmother's hut. Keycha follows them in. Bastard. The adults are still gathered around the door, faceless in their wraps. Maybe those wrappings of cloth are really empty shells, colorful mummies torturing the living. I hear a mutter from one of them, shaking its head. A larger adult pats it on the back, but the mutterer knocks the clubbed hand away and stomps off. So there's dissension in the ranks. Good.

I must have made a noise because Big Mummy comes over and parks his leggings in front of my doorway, right in my line of sight. *Hmph.* Not like they can make me do what I don't wanna. Clearly, it's time to leave. But I think about Aki's face, and Keycha's warning. I think about what little I know of the Grandmother, other than she needs to be in control. I think about my days and nights with Keycha. I try to decide what's in my best interest right now.

I hear Keycha's "help us" in my head and mull over his tone. Help the family? Or help Aki and Keycha? Could that be it? Because I'm not stupid either, I decide that if there's any possibility that Keycha might actually know what he's doing then, whatever his plan might be, it probably offers a better chance of survival than being out there on the ice by myself with no supplies. So I do that other thing I do best, when I'm not panicking or running away, and I wait.

In the meantime, I build a fire with the weed and fish bones the previous owner thoughtfully left stacked by the firepit. I wonder, in passing, where he went.

• • •

Keycha comes back well after dark. I'm waiting for him. After the hut warmed I let the fire die down to a dim glow. When Keycha ducks in the doorway, I leap on him in a full-body tackle.

Keycha's flat on his face with my entire weight across his back. I hear a muffled "Wait?"

"You gonna help us or psycho-granny?"

"You?"

"Thought so." I let him up. I'm feeling smug, but Keycha looks exhausted. More, he looks terribly sad.

"What?" I say.

"What," he says back.

"Wha's the plan?"

Keycha unfolds a lovely map of faded blue and green and gives it to me. The print at the top reads: "Great Lakes Waterways." It's creased and old, but the plasticized paper has kept it intact. I should have clothes so sturdy.

"So we run?"

"That or you and Aki give up your personal wishes for the good of the family." Keycha sounds so tired.

"That's not an option for me," I say quietly and he nods.

"Thought so." We're quiet for a while, looking at the map.

"Keycha, it's not just selfishness." I start. "Well, but I am selfish. It's how I've survived this long. But you don't want to replicate these genes. You don't want another me in this world. You don't know the half of it ...."

"So tell me then! What's so bad you have to abandon me and my family?" Keycha sounds bitter.

"Wait. But. You'll come with me! You can't want to stay here. They aren't your family!"

"I'll be the last young person here," he says. "After you and Aki leave. How can I leave them with no hope?"

He shifts restlessly, pushing the map aside.

"See, that's just it." I want to shake him. "That's what my personal beliefs do for me. I can leave people if it's in my best interest." *If my survival depends on it.*

"Like my parents left me."

"I'm not your parents and I don't *want* to leave you! Come with us!" I'm pleading now, surprising myself with my own intensity. "How can you care about those faceless mummies? They'll leave *you* when the ice melts!"

"You don't know them."

"I know you."

"Then you should understand what I'm making here. My creations help the people around me, even if I don't … love them. Being useful to others is part of *my* personal belief. It's what I need to do."

I need *you*, I want to say, but I can't. I can't *need* anyone enough to pull them away from a primal belief that's as strong as my need to keep moving on. I can hear the surge of the sea in my head again. I feel a yearning toward the east I'd almost let myself forget during my time here with Keycha. How could I have ever thought this would be a place to rest? It's time to move on.

Oh, how we lie to ourselves, again and again. Blinded by our own beliefs and blinkers. What would happen if I could just reach out to him honestly? What if I ask him who *he* loves?

"Keycha …." I touch his cheek. He closes his eyes and presses his face against my hand – just as Aki is shoved into the hut, and the moment is lost.

• • •

Aki is hyper-alert and wild-eyed. But she figures out Keycha's plan as soon as she sees what we're holding. She scans the room and drops to her knees by the map.

"I haven't seen this in years."

"The Aanak had it hidden in the old city. I didn't realize there was another way in. Do you remember footprints, Jack? Before you passed out? She has a hiding place in there. Lots of stuff." He sounds like there is more to say.

"What kind of stuff?"

"You don't want to know. But it was enough to tell me you two will have to do what she says," he raises his hand as Aki protests, "or she's crazy enough to have you iced. Do you understand me?" Keycha cups Aki's chin with one hand. "Will you really leave the family just to live the way you want?"

Aki stares at him belligerently. "Why don't we ice *her*?"

Keycha's face pales. His hand must have gripped Aki too tightly because she jerks her chin away. "You gonna kill everybody who disagrees with you, Aki? That how you wanna live your life?"

"I'm more the run-away type myself," I say quietly, trying to ease the tension. "And what do you mean by 'iced,' exactly?"

Aki turns away and busies herself with the fire.

• • •

There are stories, Keycha tells me, as we warm ourselves around the fire, gnawing on dried fish. Stories of folks choosing to go to the ice before their time. The family was bigger once, but lack of new children, and loss of elders, reduced its ranks, especially recently. Family lore told of a time when elders were abandoned on the ice in times of famine, something that seems terribly wasteful now, when family members are so few. The Aanak always told the family proudly that under her leadership there was no need to consider wasting the collective knowledge held by the old people, and no lack of fish and weed to keep everyone healthy and alive – whether they could actively hunt or not. And it was mostly true. There were times when the current flowed too deep, and fishing was hard. Winters when it was almost impossible to cut a hole in the ice before the wind clogged it with snow and it froze over again. But the Aanak had always insisted they store dried and frozen fish for such times, and it had always been enough. And yet the family continued to shrink. Middle-aged adult males, in particular, seemed prone to depression, and sometimes wandered off, leaving behind any tools or clothing that might help them survive on their own. Chu, whose hut we're using, disappeared not long before I arrived.

"Could he have been grabbed by a really big snakehead eel?" I ask sleepily, not terribly interested in the despair of aging males.

"No," Aki says sharply. "Chu was a seasoned hunter. And we'd have found his fishing gear on the ice. You can see it's all over there, carefully stacked." And indeed Chu's belongings seemed well organized.

"Any word about Lluq?" Keycha asks, quietly.

"No," Aki says shortly.

"The fisherman who fed me the day you found me?" Now I'm interested. When I think back, Aki had taken a long time to return to the boat after we ate that Laker. Lluq certainly hadn't been depressed when I saw him. Had I heard raised voices while I was napping? It feels very long ago.

"Lluq is gone. His belongings have been given to the family." Aki doesn't want to talk about this.

"What about Chu's things?" I ask.

"Those were given to you."

"Oh!" I look around the hut. I seem to own quite a lot of fishing gear. I get up and start digging through a tidy pile of cloth, looking for pieces long enough for my leggings. The siblings watch me silently. Perhaps I'm not acting in the best of taste, considering our conversation, but I'm alive, and I'll need extra coverings for the cold if we're to leave this place.

"Did you like Lluq?" I ask Aki, on a sudden whim.

She shrugs uncomfortably. "I didn't like or dislike him. He was family. He could be pushy sometimes."

"Pushy?"

"I finally asked the Aanak to tell him he wasn't on my list of possibles. He was getting – arrogant. It made me angry. But then he found out Jack, the new *Akna*, was a boy ...." A tear rolls down her cheek.

"Oh, Aki." Keycha is by her side in a moment, hugging her close.

"Am I missing something?" I say.

"Lluq gave up. He no longer had any hope of passing on his skills and knowledge to a child. That hope was what made his life worth living, it seems," Keycha says quietly.

"And that's Aki's fault?"

"No more than yours," Keycha says without looking at me. I'm not really sure how to take that, but it makes me a little mad. When I'm mad, I tend to lash out.

"Are you saying it's my responsibility to fulfill the needs of every aging fisherman who feels the urge to procreate? It's my *fault* that this – stranger – who I barely knew, gave up and walked out onto the ice? You really believe I ought to go against everything I know is right and correct for me – my body! – for someone else's needs?"

"I'm saying that we're all as responsible for our inaction as we are for our actions." Keycha is mad now too. Aki is looking at us both with concern. "I'm also responsible as the next leader. I should have been more aware of Lluq's – and of Chu's – sadness."

"And handed over your sister, and your friend, to stave it off? How about the next one, and the next? Are we puppets to satisfy others? We have our own needs and sadness, damn you!"

"I didn't say that!"

"You mean you *aren't* a boy?" Aki's sharp comment cuts across our rising squabble.

That shuts us up.

"I never said I was," I say sulkily. "That was you."

"Ooh, I will kill you myself," Aki snarls, pushing Keycha away to get at me. He automatically blocks her.

I'm angrier than I've been in … as long as I can remember, and that's saying something.

"You want to see?" I ask, a certain viciousness creeping into my tone. "Do you want to see what I am?" I stare at Aki, who stares back. Keycha keeps his face averted, still blocking Aki from reaching me.

"Is it so awful?" I say to the back of his head, "that you have to look away?"

Keycha turns toward me, but his eyes are on the ground.

"I see." That hurts. A lot.

"I am neither male nor female," I speak directly to Aki while unwinding my wraps. The fire is warm; there's no danger of freezing, unless you count my heart, which feels like a block of lake ice. "I was born a hermaphrodite. Intersex was the polite term, once upon a time, or third sex. For me, it's effectively no sex, since I won't curse another generation with my genes." Nor it seems, would I be offered the chance. I'd no idea Keycha found me so repulsive he'd need to look away. "Odd as it may seem, it is *not* my dual gender that makes me feel that way." Let him chew on that. "Am I ugly?"

"No." Aki breathes, looking me over with frank interest. I'm completely naked now, and probably appear more like an immature male than a female. I have no real breasts and my penis is small, partly hiding the female half of my anatomy. My shoulders are broad and my hips only slightly curved, my waist narrow. When I look down I do not find my body ugly. It's smooth and muscled and golden brown, and has served me well, too well, over the years. The scars I accumulate over time never reappear after a long sleep. Once I even regrew a toe. But I never develop either. I never manage to stay awake long enough to grow to adulthood. I wonder if Aki's ever seen a naked body before. But then remember the old woman's habit.

"Prettier than the Aanak?" I ask, posing and hamming it up, though I can hear the shake in my voice. I've never – ever – shown anyone purposefully before.

Aki bursts out laughing. Keycha finally looks up, surprised. He even manages a grin as I twirl and prance, hunching my back and pulling grumpy Aanak faces. I rub my hands together greedily over the banked fire.

"Much better," they chime together, giggling. (*Thank goodness, neither is looking at me in disgust ....*)

"You knew about this?" Aki asks Keycha.

"Yes."

"Then why ...?"

"Aki," I say patiently. "You and I do share one belief. That we should have control over our own bodies – over whether or not we love, or have children. Isn't that so?"

"Yes." Aki has the grace to hang her head.

"So by all means, save yourself, but don't use me as your scapegoat."

"What's a *scrapegroat*?" Aki says, never having seen a goat in her life.

"But that's what I'm saying!" Keycha interrupts. "That we're each responsible for what we do – but also for what we don't do. You believe you should look out for yourself first, yes? That's your survival belief. But if Aki believes that sacrificing you will save her, how is that wrong – within your *own* belief system? And in fact, by not telling who you are, and what you're capable of, your inaction has an effect on Aki too – and Lluq. I'm not *saying* it's wrong. Just inevitable. I don't know if any of us could have saved Lluq. And I would not have sacrificed either of you. But ... I should have talked to him.

"The best we can do is help each other. Think a bit about what each action or inaction might result in, and take the best course we can, no?"

This is the longest single speech I've ever heard from Keycha.

"Here's the best response I can manage," I say, knowing they won't necessarily understand. "I look after myself first, my family next, my community after that – if I can. But what you call family, I call community. I didn't know Lluq. I was grateful for the fish roe, but I didn't owe him my life."

"Are Aki and I your family?" Keycha's voice sounds tragic.

"Almost," I whisper. "I would help you if I could."

"Is there never a time when you might put family before yourself?"

I can't answer him. But my expression must say it all. "How can I know?" I finally say. But it's too little, too late.

"That's unfair," Aki says and takes my hand. We're in agreement, for once, though I know she would battle a dozen giant eels for her brother, and perhaps I would too, though I would never purposefully put myself in their way (*"And there's an equal possibility that you would run,"* my mental mini god reminds me). But Keycha, with the weight of leadership and responsibility for the family on his head, cannot see past the words, or at least the intent, to keep true to my own body and beliefs. Is he done with me now?

"Keycha. Aki." For no good reason I suddenly want to share the secret no other living being knows. A part of myself that has been hidden much longer than the ice has covered the lake – and as far back as I can remember. The curse I won't pass on to another. It's a secret that frightens me, and by telling, makes me vulnerable. Perhaps I can trust them to help me understand it. I want to give up this boulder I've been pushing uphill far too long. I want so badly to let it go.

"What would you say ... what if I told you ... that ... I'm older than I look? That I'm older than the ice on this lake? That I've never completely grown up? When food resources are low, or weather conditions bad, I go to sleep, regress, and start over again. But conditions are always bad ... so I never ...."

I'm out of breath, my chest constricts with panic at what I'm doing, but I manage to pant out, "I've seen your Thaw come – and go again. I've ... seen it all. And ... everything ... except the salt sea ... is covered in ... ice."

I see sparks in front of my eyes and the room dims. I'm about to pass out. Not now! There's no threat! I'm just afraid! That's all it is! That's all!

• • •

Keycha has a gift for not letting me regress. He grabs me as I collapse and supports my head down low, telling me to breathe deep.

"Is it a fit?" I hear Aki's voice from far away.

"Get a blanket," Keycha barks, and then I'm warm, and being held by friends.

This life is good. So I'm allowing myself to live it a bit longer. You hear that, imaginary god in my head? I choose to stay.

And yet staying means leaving, in the end. As I doze in their warmth, I can hear Keycha and Aki speaking quietly. Talking about what we will take away with us, and where we will go. It's been decided. Keycha has already said he'll stay behind, but with Aki's help maybe I can still persuade him to come with us. We have to try.

"Does she have the seizures, do you think? Like Auntie from last season?"

"He," Keycha corrects absently. I perk up. It's complicated, but Keycha remembers the pronoun I prefer ... for now.

"Maybe so. But where *did* he come from then? The people under the ice were not like him. Aanak described them as pale and half blind. And they've been gone since we were small."

"Aanak says from disease."

Aki shudders.

"If this is illness, I think it's just his own body's." Keycha's voice is dry. "He's healthy as a snakehead otherwise."

"Who will you miss more?" Aki says bitterly.

"Oh, Aki. I don't want either of you to go. So badly. I don't want to be left here alone."

I reach up and pull Keycha's head down onto my shoulder. Aki lies down with us so we're all bundled together. We breathe each other's breath, creating commonality. And finally, we sleep. My last thought, as I drift off, is that the reason I haven't talked to my imaginary god much lately is because I'm doing it all out loud for once.

• • •

I wake when I hear noises outside, but I don't get up right away. It's too lovely and warm, and the day promises only cold and conflict. Sunlight filters in through the smoke hole in the roof and I see Keycha watching me – watching him. Neither of us speaks. Once we move, unhappy events will follow.

Finally, I groan and stretch, jostling Aki awake. "It's time, I guess. We should collect what we need before we leave the hut."

We untangle silently. I start rewrapping my cloths, softest on the inside, toughest out, plastic strips of tarp throughout, to hold it all together. As I wrap, I add knives and fishhooks, a bone needle, and a long line of dried fish gut around my middle, careful to keep all sharp objects several layers away from my skin. A few knives I leave near the surface, where I can slide them out quickly. I tie a fish

74

bladder around my neck that holds flint and steel, others at my waist for powdered lakeweed. All of us rewrap our feet, find hoods, tie our clubbed mittens so our fingers can escape at need. We add every bit of extra cloth we can. There's no food left here. We'll have to find that elsewhere. When we're done, Keycha pushes back my hood and takes my face in his mitts. He stares into my eyes and then leans his forehead gently against mine and we breathe each other's breath, softly, lingering. He does the same with Aki, then hugs us both close. Aki makes a hiccupy sob.

"Perhaps ...," he starts, just as the Aanak's voice calls loudly from right outside.

"Who emerges, and how will you aid this family?"

We go out into the daylight, Keycha in the lead. The Aanak takes one look at him and snarls.

"Do you want this child twisted?"

"There will be no child," Keycha says firmly. The entire family has gathered to listen. In the light I see them clearly. They're fewer than expected. Less than two dozen colorfully wrapped adults crowd around the Aanak. I see faces turned to the sun, rather than just hidden mummy shapes. Each adult has a face carved by their own experiences, standing out in warm, living contrast to the blinding white and shades of blue surrounding us.

"Aanak. These people are leaving with my blessing, because they feel they cannot be part of the family anymore. We have no right to keep them. I may go with them, depending on how you answer me now." Keycha's voice is deep and booming. Everyone hears him, all the wonderful faces turn to him, suddenly tense, attentive. Aki and I also tense. I was right; Keycha hasn't completely made up his mind. We might still have a chance.

"Are you responsible for the deaths of Lluq and Chu?" Keycha takes us all by surprise, and the Aanak flinches. "Whose bodies are frozen in the ice under the city? The bodies where you hid the map?" Keycha holds up the map, and begins to unroll it ….

The Aanak shrieks, "Stop! That is a sacred item! It must not be seen!"

"I will show it."

"No!" The old woman is furious, but also scared. "I'll tell you what you want, but you won't be happy knowing."

"The truth," Keycha says. I hardly know him. He's suddenly become not just adult but the one they all look to. He's stepped into his role, and by the expressions of the listening family members, they are accepting him. Subtly, the Aanak has lost stature. My confidence in taking him with us fades as he speaks.

"Chu and Lluq," the old woman spits, "were useless to the family. They left their responsibilities and went onto the ice to selfishly wait for the Thaw on their own. I forbade them from taking belongings useful to the family, since they no longer were. No doubt they're one with the ice, now." She cannot hide her contempt. The family turns away from her and waits for Keycha to speak. I see the Aanak eyeing our extra wraps.

"You could have stopped them."

"I could not."

"You hid their bodies under the city."

"I did not."

"Who then!" Keycha suddenly roars at her. I know he's angry because he feels that she, and he, could have done more for the lost men.

The Aanak flinches. She looks small, tentative. But she tries to regain that presence that has let her guide the family until now.

"Boy," she says to Keycha, who has never looked more like a man, "I brought you into this family. I saved you and your sister. You would have died under the city with your parents if I had not."

76

"Died?" Keycha stares at the map in his hand. Aki grabs his arm. "I *knew* they would never have given you this. They never would have given you *us*. You killed them too?"

"We traded a season's worth of fish for your ungrateful lives." The Aanak is still going for control. "As you know. As you all know!" She appeals to the crowd. "It was a hard season, with little food, because of our sacrifice!" She turns back to Keycha. "Your parents died in the under-city. They didn't know any better than to eat the pale-peoples' food. I took you in. The rest of that 'family' was afraid of you. They believed you carried the ice-people's disease. They sold you for safe, dried fish. They moved on and, yes, I hid their precious map."

"The frozen bodies?"

"Your parents," Aanak says, her voice a little softer. "I poured running water over their bodies and gave them to the ice."

"You weren't afraid of disease. You knew the food was contaminated."

"They abandoned you. I did not."

"You knew Chu and Lluq were sad, that if you didn't help them, they would go to the ice."

"It was their decision. They were no longer useful to the family."

"You make bad decisions that hurt the family," Keycha says coldly. He's trembling beside me.

"I saved you!" The old woman shrieks.

"We might not have needed saving if you had only warned them …."

"What I did was for the good of our family. Can you say the same? Will you let our only breeding female leave and doom us all?"

"It is her choice," Keycha says grimly. "I no longer trust you to do right by her."

"Then take over leadership," the old woman says slyly, "and *you* can make the right choices."

For a moment, Keycha's whole body relaxes. He looks like a hopeful boy again. "Yes, perhaps that's the answer ...."

But the old woman goes too far. "You can even take her first. If we get one damaged child, if it's too twisted, we give it to the ice. She's young; she can bear many."

And it's over. I know how this will play out; the Grandmother will control Keycha the way she controlled Chu and Lluq, playing with his mind and body's urges, and perhaps losing control the same way, with Keycha escaping into the death that is the open ice without protection. We need to get to our boats. We need the food stocked over at Keycha's cave. Then the three of us need to leave.

I underestimate Keycha and his methodical mind. He tests things before making decisions. He strides toward the Aanak as if he's going to hit her. Immediately, several large fishermen step in his way.

"I see," Keycha says thoughtfully, "that my leadership would be limited." He looks back at me and Aki. "Let's assess the truth of our present leader. I suggest we all go to the under-city. The Aanak will show us the entrance she uses, and we can all discover the truth of her words. Perhaps there are other secrets she's not telling us." No one moves, so I push Aki and we walk slowly toward our boat, wondering if they'll stop us. Instead, one of the smaller fishermen holds our bow while we raise Aki's sail. We thank her, a craggy older woman with skin like a wrinkled walnut, and climb aboard. I look over my shoulder where Keycha's still facing off with the Aanak. But other family members are starting to raise their sails. It's turning into a family outing.

Aki and I invite our helper aboard, though it's crowded. It isn't politic to look like we're running away. Yet.

"I've watched you grow from a child to a fine young woman," the walnut woman says in a quiet voice. Somehow she's gotten hold of Keycha's map and has it partly unfolded in her lap. That makes me a little nervous, but she just traces her wrapped hand along the huge lake, our lake, that dominates the image, then along toward a series of other lakes folding around each other toward the east. They're huge lakes no one would know existed if they'd never left the icy delineation of this one.

"If you need to explore other lakes, find other people, I support you," she says quietly. "Perhaps, one day, you'll come back and tell us stories of what you've seen?"

"Perhaps," Aki responds quietly, "if I can." She gestures for the woman to hang on. Like lemmings building up momentum, the family is finally moving.

• • •

We're a ragtag flotilla of odd sailing vessels, some standing singles no larger than a board and sail, some bigger, but overcrowded with extra adults ducking under low booms. Some vessels are merely mats of plastic, half-drums, and scavenged wood. There are a few pre-ice sailing hulls, heavy and unwieldy over their added runners. I wonder if these represent all of Keycha's experimental designs over the years.

We stop near the mounded city, just out of sight of Keycha's boathouse cave, which is just around a curve of the buried shore.

At the lake edge, the great mounded hump of the buried city effectively hides the mouth of the Aanak's tunnel. The tunnel isn't natural but the Aanak didn't dig it out either. It's too smooth and sculpted. Keycha approaches me as everyone drops sail and anchors their boats to a few metal stakes quickly pounded into the ice.

"You and Aki stay and watch the boats," he says, gesturing in the direction of his boathouse. I know what he's implying but I'm not done with him yet.

"We'll wait for you," I say firmly. After a moment he nods.

"I'm going in," Aki says. "I want to see my parents." Keycha throws his hands in the air and stalks off toward the tunnel. But the Aanak wants us to know she's still in control.

"*Both* the girls will come with us," the old witch says loud enough for everyone to hear. "Isn't that right, *J-akna*?" I wonder if she'd been listening at our door last night. What did she hear?

"*Jack*," Keycha says, just as loudly, "cannot come. *He* cannot be in the dark without distress."

"We have torches," one of the men offers helpfully. The old woman sniggers.

I pull Keycha aside. "I'm good to go. I'm curious. But there're too many people. If there's anything that can tell us what she's been up to, it'll get trampled."

"The Aanak goes first," Keycha announces. "Then Jack, Aki, and me. The rest of you follow a little behind. Be careful where you step. Be watchful. Notice the things around you."

Keycha has effectively pinned us in the middle, which doesn't make me happy either. But at least we'll be able to see whatever there is to see. The Aanak agrees a little too quickly.

"It's like a murder mystery," I whisper to Aki, who stares at me blankly. "Scene of the crime?" She shakes her head. *Oh well.*

Torches lit; we walk into the snowy tunnel. Daylight is behind us, throwing odd shadows ahead. The Aanak becomes a long-legged spider scuttling up front. I tell myself she believes she's doing her best for the family. It's a hard sell.

The tunnel is lower and narrower than is comfortable, but we move along quickly. I hope it will widen out soon. We pass a series of shallow rooms cut into the ice beside the tunnel. They're piled high with cans like the ones Keycha and I saw when we were exploring. These were stacked neatly, once. But the cans are very old and some have exploded and refrozen, so the stacks are distorted and lumpy. Most have marks dented into their sides. Each stack has a different mark, though the sizes of the cans differ. This was a lot of food once. Enough to feed a family for years. Clue number one.

The tunnel suddenly widens out into a circular space with shallow shelf-like areas cut into the sides. These are interspersed by more tunnels, like spokes branching outward from the hub of a wheel. On the far side, I see a glitter through a dark archway. Air streams in from that direction, setting our torches flickering. We've come in from a different opening on the lake, but I'd lay bets the ice-covered girders from that fallen bridge – or whatever it once was – where Keycha and I explored are through that arch. The broken-bridge cavern itself spans the shore of the lake at least as far as Keycha's boathouse. I wonder where the other tunnels lead.

The Aanak gestures toward a shallow ledge in the hub. In the flickering torchlight we can see the room is a round, domed crypt. Keycha sidles up and puts something in my hand. It's a crank flashlight.

"Hide it," he hisses. I drop it in one of my waist pouches. What a guy.

The torches flicker, shadows jumping. The family shuffles in behind us, and Keycha asks some of them to wait. I'm glad. We aren't under the city proper yet, I don't think, but I can still feel the weight of ice overhead. The Aanak leads us to a shelf with several long shapes lumped up out of the ice. They could easily be bodies.

"Your parents, who I laid out with respect after they died, dedicating them to the ice." Her voice is oddly triumphant.

Aki holds her torch closely over one of the forms. A great dollop of layered hoarfrost suddenly slides off as it melts.

"What are you doing!" the old woman screeches.

Keycha loops an arm around the Aanak's shoulders to hold her back. "Keep going, but be careful," he says to Aki.

"That's solid ice under the frost," the old woman snarls. "The ICE won't let you commit this sacrilege."

"Wanting to see our parents' faces is hardly a sin," Keycha says calmly. "Is it?"

The old woman tries to twist away, but he holds her firmly. A few more adults shuffle in to watch. We're surrounded by mummies in a snow crypt. I feel like laughing – but not.

Aki jams a torch into the ice shelf, at what's presumably the head of the frozen dead. We watch ice shed away from the forms. She grabs another torch from one of the watchers and swings it up and down over both bodies. The roof of the alcove quickly becomes black with soot.

"Careful," I say. "You don't want anything inside to burn."

"Let them burn," the old woman says bitterly. "I should have."

The torches flicker and melt slides away. The alcove roof is melting as well, dripping onto the torches with periodic hisses. The hiss and drip is punctuated by shuffling feet and heavy breathing as even more family members crowd around. The presence of so many bodies warms the air, and I imagine the whole round room softening – rotting. I push my hood back and gasp. Keycha looks at me with concern, but I nod at him. I'm good. I can do this.

Aki's melted off the crust over the ice, and with each pass of the torch, she polishes the water off with her wrapped hand.

"You'll get your hand wet," one of the adults says reasonably, his voice breaking the firelit silence. "Then it will freeze."

Aki ignores him. I tear off a long strip from around my arm, careful to tuck the ends back in, and give it to her wadded up. She takes it without comment. Her face hovers over the ice mummy's face now, and she's polishing like mad. Suddenly she sits up and waves Keycha over. I peer over his shoulder. I can see something in there, light and dark, through the window she's creating in the ice.

"Keep going," Keycha rasps.

I have to get more air. I sidle over to the breezy archway where I saw something glitter and peer through. Torchlight leaks out and I make out footprints leaving and returning. They can't be as old as the stacked cans, can they? But no, there's hoarfrost on most things under the iced girders. Surely that would have covered any traces of the small, pale people I imagine carefully stacking their winter stores – before their own scavenged food poisoned them. Did they ever break out onto the ice? Keycha said they were almost blind, so perhaps not during daylight. I take a few steps out into the wider space and immediately feel the dark weight overhead. This place is hard to be in. I'm amazed anyone could survive under the sheer terror of it. But I recognize some of what I see, and that helps. There's a wide track (*from a body being dragged?*) under the crossed girders we climbed over before I fainted. I smile a little, imagining Keycha having to manhandle me home. I'm tempted to flash the light over there but don't want the Aanak to notice. That trail should lead directly back to Keycha's kitchen. Better than a trail of crumbs.

I turn back into the torchlit cave.

Aki is the center of everyone's attention.

I push through the crowd to the shelf of ice. Aki and Keycha are staring down at the window Aki's creating. The Aanak watches from a little farther away. Most of the adults have crowded in now. Waiting for clue number two, if only they knew it. But the Aanak doesn't look particularly worried.

Keycha waves me over.

"What do you see?" His voice is grim.

I peer through the ice window. Through the distortion, I can make out a sunken face, eyes shut, lips writhed back in death.

"That is a face that died in pain," Keycha rasps out, a little too loudly. I don't contradict him, though I'm not convinced. Death often seems to have this effect. But I'm uncertain whether that rictus would still happen however a body died. I start to say something, then realize he's testing the Aanak again. He wants to see if she'll react.

Keycha steps toward the Aanak. This time the crowd makes way. Aki remains crouched over the ice window, examining the face of the parent who didn't abandon her after all. I can't imagine what she's thinking. I've no memory of having parents. I wonder if I'm losing memories again. Maybe there's only just so much room in any one head for remembering.

"*You* poisoned them." Keycha's squarely in front of the Aanak now. I can't see her expression, but neither can she see me or Aki. I try to pull Aki away from her window into the past. The past is dead. We need to live. She ignores me.

"No!" The Aanak's voice is sharp. "They poisoned themselves. They almost poisoned you!"

"You could have told them about the contamination. You knew what it did to the ice-people."

Suddenly I have it. I know.

"How did Keycha's parents know where the ice-people stored their food?" I call out. "How is it you were there in time to save the children?"

"I … I gave them dried fish to suck … before they found this place. Children wouldn't want anything else …."

I remember Keycha describing long-ago treats from cans, something yellow and sweet in heavy syrup.

"You're lying," he says flatly. "Why were my parents here alone? Why were the other family members so afraid they left us behind? Why were you in the middle of all of this?"

"I followed them."

"You sent them."

"I saved you!"

"You told the others it was disease."

"What if I did?" the old woman spits. "We needed children. We still do. The good of the family …."

We've ignored what the heat from all those people and torches has been doing to the ceiling over our heads. Ice sheets have been softening and sliding unnoticed down the walls. But suddenly a great swath of slush collapses down into the middle of the room and onto the people crowding in. I'm not as scared as I should be, because I've no intention of fighting back up that narrow tunnel to the lake. "*Run!*" I shout, grabbing Aki's arm and hoping Keycha will follow. I yank her through the archway leading under the dead city, just as the low ceiling of the crypt collapses behind us.

• • •

Aki's torch is still burning. I drag her over to the steel girders and we hunker down underneath, right on top of the trail to Keycha's. I want to be sure nothing else is falling from above before we move on. We peer back toward the cave. There's not a smidgen of torchlight behind us. I can't make out the opening we've just run through. The silence is deafening. I haul out the crank light and start winding, the sound alien and wrong in this space. Aki watches apprehensively. I aim the light back the way we've come. The archway is completely blocked. We run back. I put my hand to the fresh fall and Aki calls out for Keycha, but there's no answer. We dig at the packed ice in the doorway, but the slush is already refreezing between blocks of ice, wedged tight and hard as metal. My chest tightens in panic. I hear the silent city overhead, listening to our faint cries. I have to get out of this place. Now.

"We can go to Keycha's from here." I hear the breathlessness in my voice. "Then we'll go around the outside. Make sure everyone got out."

"It'll be too late!" Aki cries.

"It'll be worse if we stay. Can you find your way out alone?" I'm gasping now, my fears of the dark returning as the crank light loses its charge and starts to fade.

Aki takes the light from my hand and cranks it carefully back to full power, the sound whirring into the offended silence. How long did our old crank light last?

She peers at me. "Let's go. I'm sure they got out."

I tell myself Aki needs my help to get out. But in the end we simply follow the drag marks Keycha made saving me. Saving me twice by making this path. I try not to think about him trapped in the crypt.

We hurry over debris, tripping and stumbling. Once we're moving, the glittering cavern holds no wonder and no ghosts. It's just an obstacle, worry about Keycha's safety overwhelming even my fear of the dark. Faster than I would have thought possible, we burst out of the long tunnel into Keycha's cold living space and run smack into him, coming in the other way.

"Oh, thank any gods left," I breathe, while Aki buries her face in his chest. "We thought we'd lost you. Did everyone get out?"

Keycha pulls me into a three-way hug. "I saw you run into the cavern. Then the roof collapsed. I wasn't sure ...."

"I didn't pass out!" I say proudly, wondering why Keycha's cave-like home doesn't affect me the same way as the cavern, or the snowy crypt we've just escaped.

Keycha smiles at me. "Everyone got out except ... the Aanak was not with us. I need to go through and see if I can find her."

"You won't get through this way," I say. "It's solid."

"I have to try," he says simply.

"Just leave her," Aki says. She's still stuck into his shoulder.

"If I do, the family will have no leader, and I can't go with you," Keycha says. Is he teasing?

Aki leans back, grinning.

"Then we better find the old bat!" I say, smiling so hard my face hurts. Keycha's leaving with us!

"The old what?" Aki asks.

"Small flying mammal," I say happily. "Liked caves. Been extinct for two hundred years."

"Off to the bat cave!" Keycha says. I choke with laughter.

"But if they stink ...," Aki is saying, just as the Aanak staggers in from the cavern tunnel, her face clammy pale and her iron-gray hair full of hoarfrost.

• • •

Despite her tough talk, it's Aki who leads the old woman to a seat by the dead fire. Aki who lays weed and fishbone in the culvert stove and lights it with the flint from around her neck. Keycha stands apart, as if he can't bear to go near the old woman. Even I am confused by her. She seems fragile and in need. She reminds me of someone. The kindly woman who fed me before the snows? But I don't like the Aanak. I don't trust her. And how in the world did she get through the caverns in the dark?

"I live, as you see," the old woman finally grates out. "No thanks to you," she aims at Keycha.

"That's not fair," Aki says hotly, but the Aanak stops her with a wave of the bent claws she's released from her mitten wraps.

"Enough, girl. No more of this. I live. You live. The dead no longer concern us. We all have things we must do to continue on. *J'akna* understands this, I think."

"That is not my name, and I owe you nothing," I say casually, no respect in my tone. I might agree with her about the dead, but who is she to tell me what I '*must* do' to continue on?

"You would not have survived the ice without our help," the old woman snarls.

"You'd be surprised what I can survive," I say.

"Prove it! Walk out there! Follow Chu and Lluq. Useless girl. You need us as much as we need you."

I don't answer, and she snorts. There's truth in what she says. I've no wish to sleep under, or on, the ice again. There's always the possibility the bitter cold of exposed lake ice would finally kill me, if the snakeheads didn't eat me while I slept. I need people to survive. More importantly, there are people here I care about.

"I'm not a girl," I say instead.

"You'd better decide otherwise, or our future leader ..." she says sarcastically, "will fall prey to his body's urges and either make twisted babies with his own sister, or fall into depression and let the ice take him."

"You witch," I breathe, but Keycha has had enough.

"Leave my house," he says furiously. "Go! *Now*. You kill our parents, you trap us here, but you will not decide my moral life. The 'good of the family' should not include actions hurtful to others. To family members! Go back to the village. If I choose to I will follow – eventually. But if you do not leave now, I'll kill you myself."

"Come on." I yank her roughly to her feet. "I'll walk you out."

"Don't touch me!" she spits, clawing at my wrappings. I'm surprised. She's strong. "*Freak*. This is your fault. The only reason I let you live today is for the family. I followed you through the under-city. I could have brought the ice down on you at any time. But for the family, and to save Aki, I did not. But I see now that you will bear freaks too. Freaks I will send out onto the ice!"

My face is burning, but I manage to say, "We're in agreement then." The witch slaps at me again and Aki moves forward, whether to protect me or help the Aanak, I don't know. Keycha puts her aside and holds out his hand to his family's leader. His voice is cold with fury, but his words are polite.

"Grandmother. You may take my boat, since yours is still some way off."

"Yes," the Aanak says. "Keycha will take me home."

"You will take yourself. You may use my boat."

"Insolent boy." I hear her hissing as they walk away, her clawed hand gripping his arm. "You'll do as I say if you want to be leader."

"I never wanted it ...." Their voices fade.

• • •

When Keycha returns to the kitchen, we have the weed fire smoldering and Aki and I are packing food for three into cloth and fish skin bags. We've decided to leave at first light.

"We should get my boat back over here before dark," Aki says and, thinking of the snakeheads, I'm agreeing just as Keycha comes in.

"She's gone?"

"She should be by now. I didn't wait."

"Pity you gave her your boat," I say, then remember. "You warned her about the east entrance?" Keycha's eyes widen and we all race back to the boathouse.

• • •

The evening winds have died down. There's only the sound of water lapping. The three of us stand at the east entrance to the boathouse. In the late afternoon light, with the sun behind us, we can see far out over the ice. It's empty and bare, the ice-field just starting to shade purple and gold, completely void of life. At our feet, almost to the doorway, a fractured plate of black ice wobbles and dips. The thin ice had been lightly frosted with hoarfrost so that it was no longer a clear window into the water but, recently submerged and broken, it's become a dark collection of opaque shards bumping together. The gap is so much larger than it should be. Normally one would think a boat with long runners might glide right over the weakened area, the runners bridging it to reach stronger ice. At some point, while we were digging the new entryway, arguing with the Aanak, and melting Keycha and Aki's parents from their snowy crypt, the dark ice must have absorbed enough sun to grow and soften the thicker ice around it, before being covered in a light frost again as the sun dipped, rendering it invisible.

There's no sign of the Aanak, of Keycha's boat, of any living thing. The water splashes at our feet, the edges immediately refreezing into small, descending ridges.

Keycha grabs a spear from one of the remaining boats and lowers the butt into the water. He runs it around the circumference of the hole, as far as he can reach. The water is deep here, deeper than I would have guessed. His spear does not touch bottom, and starts to become slippery with ice. I notice the wrapping on his hands getting wet. That's dangerous in the dropping temperatures.

"Stop, Keycha." I grab at his arm, but the spear has already slipped from his hands, and we watch as it bobs once and then slips under the thicker ice, disappearing.

Aki and I have to pull Keycha away from the edge of the rotten ice. The sun is dropping and the shadows lengthening out across the lake. The cityscape takes on a new life in shadows that suddenly become long buildings again, stretching away over the lake, a black and white moving picture of an invisible city. There's no longer the sound of waves lapping, but it continues in my mind. The cold is seeping in and we have to lead Keycha firmly back into the warmth of his kitchen. I upend the old fish-skin trunk across the tunnel, from habit. Aki sits Keycha near the fire and starts unwrapping his hands, laying the wet cloth beside the fire. He's sliced through several layers of cloth holding the sharp end of the spear. He stares at his hands as if he expects to see wounds gushing blood.

"I didn't tell her," he finally grates out.

"You were arguing. You had other things on your mind," I say. Who knew the rotten ice could have grown so big? *(Maybe the ice wanted her, an evil voice whispers in my head.)*

"She raised us." He looks up, his eyes red-rimmed.

"She was also a cold killer," I say grimly. I'm worried. With his belief that we are also responsible for our inaction, Keycha could go on a bad guilt trip with this.

Aki surprises me. "She was old. She lived a full and useful life in aid of the family. We need to remember her properly, good and bad. Then, tomorrow, we will tell the family and put her to rest."

Keycha nods, still staring at his hands, but he seems less brittle. This is what grieving traditions are for, I think. Aki will take the lead in this. Keycha's shoulders slump and he allows Aki to nudge him against the wall. He leans there, hands between his knees, head tilted back, watching us prepare food and the ceremonial weed beer to properly mourn the death, and celebrate the life, of the Aanak. Normally we'd wait for the family, Aki whispers to me privately, but it's clear Keycha needs this now.

We talk far into the night. Aki tells stories from the Aanak's teachings. The story of the Wish-Fish whose granted wishes always result in the fish getting away and the fisherman going hungry. The story of the Fisherman-Who-Forgot-His-Hood and had to wear his catch home on his head, where his wife spent the night removing frozen fish guts from his hair. This made even Keycha snort with laughter. The story of the Lady-of-the-Ice, which makes us quiet and thoughtful, contemplating the eerie messages the dead have for the living. Wondering what the Aanak would say to us now, from her boat under the ice. Nothing good, I feel. But I keep that to myself.

Eventually, Keycha speaks. He talks about the care the Aanak gave him as a child. The support for his creations, her fierce pride when his first boat fell apart and she told him to stop sniffling and try again.

"But she let my parents die," he says. "And I let her die. And they have all gone to the ice now." And Keycha finally weeps.

After a while, staring into the fire, Aki says, "I knew a different Aanak. A slothful Aanak who would lie naked around her fire, burning it throughout the daylight, and order me to bring her weed beer, even when there were no ceremonies. A warmer Aanak who would tell me stories while she drank, and talk to me about what it meant to be a woman in the family. I believe Aanak herself was resentful of having to put the family before her own wishes." Aki falls silent for a moment. "She was harder and more distant with you, Keycha. Because she expected more from you. I hated her and I loved her," Aki says, but she sheds no tears.

"The Aanak I knew," I say, "in the short time I've been with you, was hard and fierce. Ready to sacrifice anything and anyone for what she felt was best for her family. And I think," I choose my words carefully, "that you two were the ones she thought of first when she said the word 'family.' I believe, now that she's freed by the ice from her narrow understanding of the world, that she would want you both to do what you think is best for yourselves." In the end, messages from the dead are always interpreted by the living, so teaches the Lady-of-the-Ice.

Aki nods. Keycha sighs. We drink weed beer and keep watch over the fire so it doesn't die until the first daylight seeps in from the outside world.

• • •

We retrieve the new experimental catamaran and bring it around to the new west entrance of the boathouse. Aki throws the ashes from our fire over the black ice at the east entrance (*ashes to ashes, ice to ice*). We discuss building a berm so others will avoid the area, but leave it for later. Instead Keycha places two crossed spears in front of the entrance. Aki and I load up the catamaran with supplies, since Keycha's best boat is under the ice, taking the Aanak on her final journey.

I notice Aki emptying the larder, which means she hasn't figured it out yet. But I'm not the one to tell her. We even take three of the biggest snakehead hides from the bed and discuss ways to make a shelter from them, using spears, perhaps, to create a tent. Keycha says nothing while he watches Aki bundle the skins aboard with his best hunting spears.

"It'll be crowded with three on this thing," she says cheerfully, and still Keycha remains silent.

Aki and I sail together on the loaded boat, but Keycha takes another, a tiny single-sailer, nothing but a board on runners with a sail. I admire how he handles it; he stands, leaning on the mast, his arms tilting the boom to catch the wind. He tacks so gracefully. Keycha was made for iceboats. Someday there will be stories told about him.

We tell the family about the Aanak. They take it with remarkable calm. They're used to loss. But, to a person, they turn their hopeful faces like flowers toward Keycha's sun. Then I know I'm right. He won't be coming with us.

Aki doesn't react well when she figures it out. I sit by the ceremonial fire with the family while she and Keycha have it out in the Aanak's hut. But arguing changes nothing. Keycha will stay. He'll be the next leader. Already, before Aki understood, one of the younger adult men asked if Keycha would teach him to build boats too. So I'm no longer needed. I imagine Keycha turning them all into a family of boatbuilders, plying the lakes during the thaw. I'm sad I won't see this happen. But I hear the lap and crash of waves again in my head, the salt sea calling me eastward. For me, this has always been the sound of goodbye.

"Then we'll stay too," Aki says as the siblings emerge from the hut, coming to find me.

Keycha and I both say "No!" at the same time. Keycha's speaking to Aki but looking at me, his voice bitter and terrible. He hasn't figured out yet that he's actually doing what he wants, in the end, though he believes he's doing what he must.

"The Aanak was right. If you stay, I'll ask of you what she did. For the good of the family. Spare me that at least ...." Aki looks at his red-rimmed eyes and nods.

We wait no longer. It's late in the morning, but we're packed and ready. Aki tries to take the snakehead skins back off the boat, but Keycha stops her.

"I have what I need," he says, waving toward the Aanak's hut.

94

"But you'll keep building boats," I say firmly. Keycha's mouth turns down. His eyes are tragic. "You will, Keycha, and you'll get everyone else helping you. What could be better for the family? When the Thaw comes, who'll be best prepared to float on water? To hunt snakehead eels? To explore the rest of the lakes?" *To come find us*, I want to say.

"Send your boats east, Keycha," I whisper in his ear, hugging him close. I want to tell him I'll never forget him, but the words hang up in my throat. Who knows what this rotten brain of mine will do, melting a little with each life I live, like ice in the sun? I want to tell him I love him, but if I do I'll never be able to leave. Keycha tilts my face up and leans his forehead against mine. I want to break this great sadness weighing down my chest with a little wickedness, so I press my lips to his.

"Oh!" Keycha says, touching his lips, eyes startled. Maybe I've started a new tradition.

Then we're aboard and sailing away. Keycha and the family are receding in the distance, the only patch of color in a world of snow. We tack laboriously north, leaving them all standing on the ice, watching us go. I always wondered if it's harder to be left behind than it is to leave, but my chest is heavy. Aki is quiet and seems depressed.

"Penguins," I say, trying to laugh while I wave vigorously back toward the watching figures, our touchstone, now looking like a photograph fading in the sun. One simply can't cry when thinking about penguins. There are a confused few minutes while I try to explain penguins to Aki. Then we lapse into the silence of runners scraping on ice, the rattle of lines, and the sound of sails snapping in the wind on each tack as we travel north, our ancient map telling us that we are (*probably*) sailing toward the top of Lake Michigan and a whole new land ahead.

ICE SAILING

"Talk of your cold, through the parka's fold
It stabbed like a driven nail.
If our eyes we'd close, then the lashes froze
'til sometimes we couldn't see ....

'It's the cursed cold, it's got right hold
'til I'm chilled clean through to the bone.
Yet tain't being dead, it's my awful dread
Of an icy grave that pains.
So I want you to swear that foul or fair,
You'll cremate my last remains.'"
— Robert W. Service, "The Cremation of Sam McGee"

We leave behind our only landmark when the family finally recedes from view. There's nothing on all sides but white and snow and ice and distance. The scrape of the boat runners, so loud when we plied our way between the triangle of Keycha's boathouse to the family huts, to the fishermen's holes, is diminished somehow, lesser in the vastness of the ice field. We've also lost the edge of the lake along with the mound of the under-city, and now have only ice stretching in every direction, seamlessly matching the bright white sky; limitless. It's so large, I wonder if it could be the reverse of what my mind is telling me. Perhaps we're in a white box, closed on all sides. For a time the vast emptiness becomes claustrophobic.

We scrape on and on through whiteness, until time means nothing. A niggling fear surfaces, one that may be partly to blame for wanting Keycha along so badly (*do I need a practical reason for needing him?*). We've no idea what's ahead, or whether there will be other people, those difficult beings that are so necessary for survival. We don't know if the ice will ever end. I have my perpetual goal of reaching the salt sea. But what in the world does Aki have to push her forward into this endless unknown?

The steady north wind helps us remember which way we're headed as we tack, weaving to catch the wind. Even so there are constant flashes of disorientation. Are we sailing north? South? I have to breathe deeply and let my skin feel the direction of the wind. The setting sun lets us know when the wind shifts a bit westerly, and finally Aki heaves to. There's no shelter, but better to set up something while it's still light. We're both exhausted.

"How do we know?" Aki asks miserably. She's been silent most of the day, as if she's also lost her sense of direction and purpose in this vastness. The immense lake makes me doubt we've moved at all. Or perhaps we've turned around – the family only just over the horizon? If ice covers the entire world, then the distance we travel is an ant's progress around a room, hardly moving forward, never finding an endpoint. The lack of landmarks is deeply disturbing.

We reef the sail and upend the boat sideways, keel to the northwest wind. The tarp is an amazingly effective windbreak. I've been cold all day, shocked that we've left, battered by the constant blow, unable to move around much to warm up. We put a snakehead skin down on the ice, then hang two, to complete a triangle from mast to stern, so we can feel partially closed-in for a while. Outside is just too big. Our makeshift shelter is open to the sky, which crowds with stars as the light fades. The even vaster dome of the sky, speckled with recognizable points of light against a soothing blanket of darkness, is a relief after the all-day glare.

"Maybe we should sail at night," I say, pointing to the stars. We've barely spoken all day.

"Too cold," Aki says. She's fumbling a bale of dried weed out from under a tarp lashed to the stern.

"Is that a good idea?" I say, but shut up when she doesn't respond. We need the light and warmth of a fire as much as the heat right now. It's been a hard day.

"When we get to the northern shore," I say sleepily, "you can listen for moving water and we can dig more weed."

"What if it's all like this, Jack?" Aki says. "What if this is all there is?"

"Do you want to go back?"

"Sometimes …. About every time we tack."

"Yeah."

Once the fire is burning, Aki scrapes up some ice to melt in an ancient metal container on a small folding tripod Keycha made for her. The container is so beaten up, I've doubts it started out life as a pot. She drops in dried fish and a dense fistful of weed she pulls from the bale. I miss salt.

I unroll the map, careful not to hold it too close to the fire.

"What does this mean, other than there are more lakes of ice?" Aki gestures at the map.

"Well, it will guide us to the salt sea," I say, surprised. I thought she'd understood what the map was.

"How?"

"We started here." I point to the bottom of the largest lake shown on the map. "And we're traveling north to the top where it links to the next lake. Water always runs to the sea. If we sail south down the next lake, then east across the next …."

"Does ice also run to the sea? We're sailing on ice," she reminds me, speaking as if to a backward child. "And how do you know where we started?"

It's a very good question.

"Because I went to sleep in a city called Chicago," I say quietly. "And when I woke up, the city was under ice, and you were there."

Aki looks at me skeptically. I shrug.

"See here." I show her the illegible print in the fold of the map. "That says 'Chicago.'" *Maybe.*

"If that's where we started today," Aki is clearly not convinced, "where are we now?"

I hesitate. I've no idea how far we've come since late morning. We've been tacking and weaving north – I hope – but how far?

"How far can you sail in a day?" I hedge.

Aki frowns. "I can sail from the family to the fishermen to the weed beds to Keycha's all around three to four times in a day if I want to." That doesn't help. Aki's world on the lake has been limited to the triangle of home, collecting food and fuel and harassing her brother – no wonder she wants to escape.

I find the map's legend and check the scale. But the lake is so large, and the map so relatively small, that measuring the triangle of Aki's previous life in kilometers is impossible. I take a blade of weed and hold it against the scale.

"If we measure straight from the under-city to the top of the lake, it should be about 500 kilometers, or maybe 300 miles?"

"That is a lot," Aki says thoughtfully. "But three is less than five, so let us go 300 miles."

I snort. "We're also tacking a lot, which is slower and adds more distance. If I knew the distance we can cover in a day I could figure it out." I'm frustrated. Knowing this information could have a big impact on how we ration our food, when we stop to fish, and on our morale. I bet Keycha could figure it out.

"How far can you walk in a day?" Aki asks.

"Uh, I think I heard once that a full-grown man can walk about three miles an hour?"

"How about a half-grown herm-af-rodite?" She stumbles over the word.

I stare at Aki, offended, until I see she's laughing.

"Why don't you walk north for a day," Aki says reasonably, "and I'll sail. Then we'll know the distance we can sail in a day?"

"Why don't you walk and I'll sail?"

Her voice becomes very serious. "I've sailed Keycha's boats from the time I could hold a line. When we're onboard, I'm in charge."

"Aye, aye, sir," I sigh. I can tell she means it. It's just as well. I don't particularly like having another being dependent on me. But I also can't imagine being able to achieve the kind of shared synthesis with Aki I felt working with Keycha. Still ….

"I don't have to walk all day," I say. "Just three miles."

"If we knew what a mile was, we wouldn't have this problem," Aki points out.

"Then I just have to walk for an hour, and we know what three miles is. More or less." Though the ice and wind might have a thing or two to say about my land speed.

We both try to figure out how to measure an hour.

"Keycha made a sundial once," Aki says.

"I don't know how to do that when we're moving," I snap. Damn. That would be handy.

"Okay," I say. "We just need a rough estimate, yeah? So we figure out how many hours of light we have in a day – this time of year – then divide the sky into those increments. When the sun is directly overhead, we'll call it midday, and I'll walk for the duration of one of those increments."

"Incra-wha?"

"Ah!" I draw a semi-circle in the hoarfrost. "Okay, there are 24 hours in a day."

"If you say so. Ha ha. *Nah*, I'm just messin' with ya."

"And it's light longer this time of year, yeah?"

"Absolutely."

I think that on the longest days there're only eight or nine hours of dark. But what season is this?

"Almost summer solstice." Aki surprises me.

"Thank goodness you know that. It makes this possible."

I add to my half-circle in the frost. I put the sun at the apex, a circle at the very top of the curve. Then I divide the curve with seventeen evenly spaced marks, eight on each side of the sun. "If there are 16 hours of light this time of year then, when the sun is directly overhead, I'll walk until the sun is this far to the west." I hold one arm straight above my head, toward an imaginary sun, and the other angled about one-eighth of the way toward the horizon, the angle of one mark, or hour, away from the overhead sun.

"This is *not* very precise," Aki says.

"Sorry for not being Keycha," I snap. "It's the best I can do."

Aki holds her arm straight out from her body, angling her hand sideways, fingers together, parallel to the horizon. "It's easier to put the bottom of your hand on the horizon and count the number of hand-widths to the sun. One finger-width from horizon to the sun is a quarter of an hour. The width of your whole hand is an hour."

I stare at her.

"What? Every sailor knows that much. That's time."

We test her measurement against mine. They mostly match.

• • •

We try several times. Again, I miss the lack of landmarks. Aki sails so much faster than I walk that, in the end, I just tell her to sail for the space of our one imperfect hand-width-hour, then stop and wait for me. It takes me three hours, as best I can tell, to catch up with her. Which means she's probably traveling due north about nine miles per hour when tacking. Clearly we could cover a *lot* more distance if we had a following wind.

"That means if we sail ten hours a day for three days, we're almost there!" Aki is very excited.

I'm flat-out beside our fire, exhausted, but at least I didn't get so cold today with all the walking.

"Aki, just how many miles do you think we traveled today?"

"Well, not much, but that's 'cause you're slow."

"And yesterday?" We'd left the family when the sun was high and been exhausted and chilled by the time we camped, after less than half a day. "We're probably averaging about twenty to thirty miles a day so far. I doubt we're more than forty miles from home." *From Keycha*, I carefully avoid saying. "If we continue at twenty miles a day, it could take us fifteen days to the top of the lake. Thirty miles a day would take ten days. Fifty miles a day is six days. We have food for five and a bit."

We're silent while Aki figures. "So six hours of sailing a day gets us to the top of your map in five more days? So we double our current sailing time."

"No. We'll have to stop and fish," I insist. Forget freezing our tails in this northerly wind for six hours a day. Ugh.

"Out here?" Aki shivers.

"Can't you hear the current?" I'm curious. Keycha said dowsing was Aki's gift; that she could always find the narrow currents through the ice where fish concentrated.

"I can't hear anything out here but ice," Aki says in a small voice. We look out at the expanse together. Ice is everywhere. Its sound is very big, even to me.

"Change of plan," I say. "Let's head east and hug the shore. That way we have landmarks, weed, maybe better fishing?"

Aki's expression is disdainful. "And this is why I'm in charge. Have you felt the difference when the boat hits drifting snow and hoarfrost, how the runners hesitate? You want to wade through even deeper drifts? We stay in the middle where the wind brushes the ice for us." She has a point. "I'll listen for running water," she adds with less confidence.

We head out the next day intending to sail at least six hours. We bundle up with every extra scrap of cloth and plastic we own. Aki looks like a fat multicolored dumpling and I spend a good half of our first hour trying to explain what those are. It makes us both hungry. I've insisted we need to stop and move our bodies periodically, so we don't freeze. Now that she has a goal, Aki just wants to push on. I don't mention that this is only our first goal – to reach the top of the lake. It's just the beginning of a much longer journey to the sea.

We're not even fifty miles from the under-city when we crash.

• • •

The man-sized pillars of ice appear without warning. Like everything else, they're white and mostly formless, so our ice-burned eyes don't distinguish them from the endless horizon of ice until we're on top of them. We're on the easternmost point of our tack when a gust of weirdly warm air curls around and pushes us from the south. We're whooping with the sudden tail wind, picking up speed for a bare few moments, when the boat jerks to a bone-crunching stop, upends in slow motion, and dumps us onto the ice before coming down on top of us.

It takes a long moment to catch my breath, and when I do it's with a gasping, shallow effort. My chest can't expand properly. I hear a groan nearby but can't breathe deeply enough to say Aki's name. I gasp like a fish until my breathing deepens. I can hear Aki rustling, the sail flapping.

"Jack?"

"Hah," I manage.

Aki crawls under what I hope isn't our mast, because I'm looking at splintered wood. She peers into my face.

"You alive?"

"Yup," I say, optimistically. Not moving though. Everything hurts.

"Good." And she drops her head down for a minute beside me.

"What did we hit?"

"Some damn thing."

"Yeah."

The cold starts to creep in from below, so we finally crawl out to see what's happened to our boat.

The boat's a mess. The fickle wind is playing around a small field of iced stumps, one of which we've hit and knocked over. The stumps are evenly spaced, creating a subtle, knobbed texture of white on white that's difficult to look away from now that I can actually see them. Any texture is compelling after the flat white of the last few days. Aki moves to control the upside-down sail, which is flapping but doesn't look torn. No such luck with the tarp that makes up the body of our catamaran. It's ripped in two. The thin forward strut that created one side of the square holding the tarp to our double keel is broken and jagged. We turn the boat over and she lists drunkenly, her two hulls no longer parallel. Aki hammers a stake into the ice for an anchor. I reef the sail. Thankfully, the mast itself seems okay. But we may be here awhile.

"What'd we hit?" she says angrily, turning to survey the odd landscape. Then, "Oh! I can hear water running underneath!"

She's turning back to the boat, presumably to get our fishing gear, when I put a mittened hand on her arm. She stops but doesn't turn around. I think she already knows there's something here she doesn't want to see. But then she turns toward me.

The ice pillar that we hit has toppled sideways, the base exposed like upended tree roots. Underneath I can see cloth wrappings around frozen leggings and feet.

• • •

We stare silently, then stare out over the knobbed field. There are dozens of them. More than all the family combined. I can see now that some are clumped together, but most are single pillars of ice, almost evenly spaced.

I hear an odd sound, like the Doppler whine of a distant engine approaching. It's rising from Aki: the sound of pure panic. I know it well, but feel no answering emotion bubbling up. There's no crisis or pain in this place. This is another kind of ice memorial, though far less threatening (to me), out here in the sun-washed open ice, than the heavy message of the under-city.

I brush at the top of a nearby pillar. I can almost make out the form of a bundled man sitting cross-legged. I imagine his eyes closed peacefully, asleep in the sun and snow under a wide sky, among fellow sleepers.

Aki's head thumps into my shoulder, hiding her face. She's shaking. "Who is it?" she whispers. "Is it Chu? Is it Lluq?"

"We'll never know," I say firmly. There will be no melting of these peaceful corpses. "These are not like your parents. These people chose to come here, to sit together and wait for the Thaw. There is no fear here," I add.

After a while Aki stops shaking and we turn to the boat. She doesn't look toward the frozen forms of what may be family members or strangers. They are wanderers who found each other, found this place, and chose to wait here together. This is a place, distinct from the rest of the lake. Like the place the Aanak chose to build the family huts, separated from the flat, relentless horizon only by a warmer south wind playing around the frozen sleepers, and deep within the ice, the faintest thrum of running water.

• • •

We do not fish near the sleepers. We work on our boat, wrapping the broken strut with precious fish-gut line, supporting the break with spears. Aki takes time to patch the tarp, sewing it with more fish gut so it will still work as a windbreak. It will never hold our weight again, but so far it's holding our gear. We'll have to be careful how we move, keeping our bodies directly over the separate hulls. It's going to be even less comfortable for long hours of sailing. The boat looks less like a boat now; it's more fragile and tentative. The two hulls don't seem as sturdily connected but move somewhat off-kilter, like a wobbly, badly glued chair. I imagine her falling apart while we're at full speed and shudder. I don't want to pitchpole onto my face again. My body aches and Aki is also moving slowly and painfully. We probably look a lot like the boat, suddenly fragile.

I'm about to climb aboard, leaving our usual running start to Aki, when she turns back toward the sleepers.

"I should stay with them." Her voice is heavy with exhaustion. "Maybe this is why we were brought here. To give ourselves to the ice."

My stomach clenches. I'm afraid again, though not for the first time. But then, suddenly, I'm angry.

"How dare you!" I hear myself saying, hardly knowing why I'm so mad. "How can you squander what the ice has given you? You wanted freedom, remember? And now you want to waste it? You don't know why these people are here. You have your own life to live."

"Freedom is hard," Aki says humbly.

"Life is hard," I say. "But there are always good moments ahead, if you give yourself time."

"Besides," I tell her later, once we've sailed far enough away to camp, making good time thanks to that fickle south wind. We're cuddled together between snakehead skins behind the ruin of our tarp. Our tiny weed fire is warming last night's frozen fish-weed stew. The stars are overhead, reminding us that there is texture that does not always mean death in the world. We've started creating our own constellations each night. Telling stories about the sky. Aki is very good at it; her gods are powerful and interactive, unlike mine, who is good only for complaining to.

"Did you ever think," I say, "what you icing yourself would do to *me*?"

"No," she says simply. "What?"

"You!" I growl, trying to tickle her through her wrapped clothing. It's pointless so I stop. "I would be very sad and lonely without you."

"Ah," Aki says, snuggling closer. "What about Keycha?"

"I'm very sad without him," I reply. "But you make it less lonely."

"Yes," she says.

• • •

We reach the top of Lake Michigan before the boat falls apart. The south wind stays with us, saving us several days of travel and giving us just a bit more needed warmth, taking the bitterness out of the air. By the time our nor'westerly returns, we're heading east and make good use of that wind behind our struggling sail. We reach what I hope is the intersection between the giant lakes that should lead us to Lake Huron. We can see the almost subliminal presence of the lakes' shores as rounded mounds in the distance, a relief after oppressive, unending flatness. There's more powdered snow blowing and accumulating on our ice road though, and the tugging quicksand of one of these drifts finally finishes off Keycha's experimental boat, our home, shelter, and transportation for the last ten days.

The boat slows, struggles, and then with a crack, one keel moves ahead while the other stays behind in the drift. Our mended stay pulls apart again. We stop, our square boat a sudden parallelogram. Aki drops the sail before it can pull us into any weirder shapes.

You can't call something a crisis when you've been expecting it. I have a sudden urge to just get out and walk. We've been sitting far too long. I slip from the boat. I want to explore. The landscape is like fairyland after the wide-open flats. The lumps and bumps and even the drifts are charming, and – is that color I see? A shadow on shades of white? Could I be seeing green ...?

Aki calls to me urgently from the boat, but I can barely take my eyes away from that compelling color. Snow-blasted for too long, nothing but white above and below, my eyes are hungry for it.

I'm up to my thighs in drift before I've taken five steps.

"Jack, you idiot!" Aki yells behind me.

I turn my head reluctantly. Aki is holding onto our mast, clearly distressed. I wade back to her.

"Aki, there's green over there!"

"The mast is splitting. *Fracking* help me!" It's true; the mast, normally a long tapering pole, is splitting into two half rounds.

I'm standing on the ice behind the rudder; Aki is still up on the boat. "You know," I say, "it looks like Keycha made the mast from two pieces." There are a series of latches up the back I've never paid attention to before.

Aki jumps down from the hull and stares at the back of the mast. Metal bands wrap periodically up its entire length, but I never realized they could be released from the back. I'm starting to understand what Keycha has done.

"Aki, take the boom completely off. I think it's meant to separate."

"Bloody Keycha," she says.

We take off the boom and unlatch the mast, which becomes two masts for two separate hulls. Suddenly we have a pair of windsailers on our hands. Just big enough for one person each.

"But there's only one sail," Aki says. "And one boom."

"I think the tarp was meant to be the second sail," I say, looking at the poor ripped tarp, the stitches pulling badly from the cockeyed hulls. "Could that broken front stay have been the other boom?"

"Too weak," Aki says, "and this boom is too heavy for a single-sailer."

We examine the boom more closely, then start unlatching the bands circling that as well. It's also a double.

We spend the rest of the day reassembling our catamaran into two single-sailers, one with a pathetically patched sail. Without the tarp forming the body of the catamaran, there's very little room for supplies. But Keycha seems to have thought of that as well. The hulls are slightly curved rather than flat, with space inside for skins and what's left of our weed bales if we tie them in for safety. There are flat boards across the hull's width for standing or sitting – somewhat uncomfortably. The gunnels have carved insets perfect for setting a spear into. But overall the effect is somewhat troubling.

"I think by making this into two boats it was never as strong as a single boat," Aki comments and I agree.

"They aren't as comfortable as his normal single-sailers either," I say. I lean down and take a good look at the hull on mine (I'm getting the patched sail of course). "Aki, I think he's curved these enough so that if we shed the runners the hull could float. Look, the runners aren't even one piece. The two on mine look like they're bolted in the middle. Wouldn't that make them weaker? Easier to remove, though, I suppose ...." I don't mention that the heavy double runners probably slowed us down quite a lot on the way here.

"He's being too clever." Aki rubs her face with her mittens. "It's such a mix-match, how can it be good at any one thing?"

"Like me," I say brightly. "It's a hermaphro-sailer."

"A hermailer."

"A boat-dite."

"A bite-sized boat."

We're so funny.

"Let's race!" I say, forgetting all about the green.

ICE SURFING

"There's a certain Slant of light,
Winter Afternoons –
… When it comes, the Landscape listens –
Shadows – hold their breath –"
— Emily Dickinson, "258"

We fly down Lake Huron in half the time it took us to beat upwind to the top of Lake Michigan. Our sails run before the wind like the ghosts of fleet greyhounds, heeling over so far that Aki's hair brushes the ice when her hood flies back (she's faster and always ahead). We stop more often to stretch and rest. Aki has regained her sense of water and we fish for Lakers, sucking down the yellow roe and stuffing ourselves until our stomachs groan. After a hard beginning, we have this traveling thing down. The clouds shift, and the sky, blank white on much of the trip north, is large and blue and sunny as we head south-ish again. We shed layers. Sometimes the surface of the ice is wet. Our newest worry, when we can be bothered worrying, is keeping dry. When the sun goes down, everything, including our outer wraps, freezes. Even so, our moods lift with each day in the sun. We're flying free. We cannot be stopped and life is good.

Later, toward the bottom of the lake, the sneaky southerly creeps in again, and we find ourselves tacking into the face of it. This time it slows us down and quite possibly saves us from crashing again.

• • •

One night among many, while we watch the stars above Lake Huron, Orion rises bright in the sky and I tell Aki the story of the hunter being hunted. Orion, son of the salt sea, was always my favorite constellation, though it was Orion who bragged about killing every animal on the planet, and the world-mother's rage that set the scorpion on him. Despite his sins, there he is, unchanging in the night sky, racing away from death by scorpion, keeping me company on my own long journey around the curved horizon. He's also the Heavenly Shepherd, symbolizing rebirth and the afterlife. The serpent-bearer waits for him in the east with the scorpion's antidote. *What will be waiting for me?*

Aki talks about feeling less oppressed, less watched over by her Inuk ice god, since this Lake Huron is not the Inuk god's lake (this lake, which sometimes reflects back Orion's stars from the ice; stars glimmering above, their echoes below). We found a little windswept bay free of drift that we explored, realizing quickly it was only a large divot in the otherwise unimaginably big expanse of the lake. The map tells us Huron is slightly smaller than Aki's lake, but we will always be ants on its surface. We're happier in the sun and following wind, but still minuscule against the horizonless backdrop.

Aki finds a current under the bay, and I chisel out a fishing hole with our pike (grieving for my auger, laying broken back in Keycha's boathouse). I dig down deep and manage to snag the pike in some weed, but Aki forbids me to reach in with my hands to pull it up. Remembering the snakeheads, I do the best I can with the pike and a spear, and we pull up fresh weed and catch fish for dinner. Later, also remembering the snakeheads, we move the boats a little away from our fishing hole in order to cook and star-watch.

Our two boat hulls, upended and angled together, make a larger camp. At night we often pull the sails over the top, after the fire dies down, for extra warmth. But tonight we watch the stars longer than usual, telling stories about old gods, stars and ice, until Aki becomes quiet, listening to something on the night air.

"What is it?" I ask. I can hear the ever-present wind, and farther away the slap of water deep at the bottom of the hole we'd carved in the ice. That's unusual, in a way. Normally the hole would have filled with slush immediately and frozen over by now. But lately, with the south wind, and the air losing its bitter edge, each exposure to the ice is less like an emergency, and the refreeze takes a little longer.

Aki's expression changes from interest to alarm, then, oddly, sadness.

"What're you hearing?" I ask again.

"The water running beneath the ice is telling stories too," Aki says, her voice taking on the rhythmic quality with which Aki tells her best stories. I slide under one of the warm snakehead skins and wait with anticipation. But with the next sentence, her rhythm breaks.

"The water of the lake is churning in the wind, rising to touch the clouds." This is different. Aki has never yet admitted that these lakes are anything – could ever be anything – but ice. "There are boats without runners, huge boats, with many, many people, riding on the water – in the water! Tossed about by ice turned to water thrown by wind …." Her eyes are closed, her head cocked, still listening. "The people are groaning with fear …," and she's silent for a long time. "They're under the water! Everywhere! The boats and the people! Their ghosts are crying in the water weeds!" Aki's eyes pop open and she stares at me. I pull her wrap around her more tightly. She's shivering.

"The ghosts are old?"

"So old," Aki breathes, some of the tension leaving her.

"Why would they still be there?" I muse, though I remember feeling something similar in the under-city.

"The Thaw is coming. The ice is turning to water." This idea clearly makes her afraid again. "But Jack, water is much more frightening than ice! The wind is stronger on water. Ice is powerful. The wind clears it for us, pushes us along its surface. But the wind on soft water is terrifying. I don't know if I want to go to the salt sea, Jack!"

"Can you *not* go? Knowing it exists?" But the idea of a sea even larger than the vast expanse of these lakes and the image of boats tossing helplessly in water stays with me too.

The sound of slapping water from our fishing hole changes into something else, catching my attention. Across the ice I hear a faint scraping. For a horrified minute, Aki and I stare at each other. I imagine the skeletons of old sailors struggling up from the weedy water. Aki's the one who thinks of the crank light. She winds it under her covering, so it won't be so loud, then we crawl warily out of our cage of boats and shine it across the ice. I have the digging pike in one hand and a spear in the other. But Aki bravely steps ahead with just the light.

Something is indeed struggling up out of our fishing hole. It's a face far more horrible than my imagined drowned sailors. Squeezing inch by inch up out of the ice, a gaping mouth emerges, edged with sharp teeth and followed by wide milky eyes and a bulging body. It's too small, and the eyes are too big, to be a snakehead eel, but there are similarities. I step forward, but Aki arm-blocks me. We wait to see what it will do. The light shining on its face stops it, so Aki aims the beam a little to the monster's left. We can still see it clearly. The creature oozes up out of the hole, its body a pulpy caterpillar mass. The head swivels toward the light spot where it hits the ice. It continues to wriggle forward, aiming for the glow.

Aki moves the light a little, and the creature follows, its body going on and on, some on the ice, a lot still rippling and shrugging up out of the hole. When its very fishy tail finally follows it out, it's as long as I am tall and bigger around than my thigh. The fish thing gulps, its body humps forward, and it snaps at the light. Aki shifts the beam farther away, and the fish follows, humping across the ice, gulping and snapping. It's horrifying. I want to hit it with the pike.

"Think it's any good to eat?" Aki often surprises me with her practicality.

"Let's find out," I say grimly and step forward. As soon as I move closer, the fish lunges at me. I leap back with a yelp. "Aki! Do something!"

Aki is laughing so hard the light in her hand shakes. The monster's head snaps toward the quivering glow on the ice again and I can see it kinking its fat neck slightly, like a snake about to strike. It lunges for the light and I swing at the creature. It doesn't die easily.

• • •

"Damn! Did you see that?" We're eating what turns out to be quite delicious Monster-I-Dunno-What, recapping my heroic dance of many thumpings and leapings. The fish lunged and I hit it, then scrambled away (yelping, I admit). Even when it was dead, it jerked about convincingly, making Aki howl with laughter because each time it jerked I jumped. I can tell this is going to go into Aki's collection of humorous tales.

"I don't know what you're laughing about," I say sulkily. "That thing was dangerous!"

"This *thing* is delicious," Aki says, still giggling. "Sure you wanted to plug up the hole? We might get more." While Aki had prepared the fish, I'd scraped and dug out ice to fill our fishing hole, pounding it in tight with the pike. Nothing is going to creep up out of that again while we're sleeping.

"We have enough monster to eat for days," I say righteously. "No point killing more than we need." This sends Aki off into giggles again. It's amazing to see her laugh.

For some reason, this is the night I choose to begin the story of Odysseus, or at least as much as I can remember. We stay up late after our second meal, bundling wasteful amounts of weed on the fire, watching the ever-entertaining sky as clouds move in and out of star fields, making the myths come alive in the night.

It must be the fish monster that inspires it, and I may confuse Sinbad and Odysseus just a bit, because I begin my story with the hero landing and building a fire on the sleeping fish island. That's enough to keep us up half the night, telling each other our tiny fire is going to wake the lake, which will then swim away with us to the salt sea.

As the days go on, Aki asks me more about the story and, each night as we camp, I reach back into my memory. I have to go backward quite a lot. I tell the story of Circe's island, and the Cyclops Polyphemus, but then have to go back even earlier to the Trojan War, and then back further to Helen and Paris. Then I remember it all started with the golden apple, and the three goddesses asking Paris who was most beautiful. His prize for choosing Aphrodite is the love of Helen, the face that launched (and sank) a thousand ships.

Aki is entranced. "Am I beautiful?" she asks me one night.

"Oh come on!" I stall, "you've just heard where that kind of question can lead!"

"It's just," she hesitates, "I've never thought about it before. It has always been more important to be good at sailing and fishing and finding running water."

"That is more important," I say.

"But now I want to know!" Aki says. "You say you've lived so long. If that's true then you've seen other women? Young women?"

I nod reluctantly. I don't want to talk about the world before the ice, except for in stories. My memories are so fragile and ephemeral out here. Right now, sailing on the lake with Aki is all there is. No starting point, no final destination. Even my time with Keycha is starting to feel a little like a story told long ago – though picturing his face still makes my heart ache and eyes sting. But I don't say that to his sister.

"Compared to them," Aki insists, "am I beautiful?"

"Beauty is relative," I say pompously. "It has more to do with how we feel about a person or a thing than anything else. What I find beautiful, you may not."

"Am I beautiful to *you*, idiot?"

"Aki," I sigh. "You are the most beautiful woman on the ice. The most beautiful woman I've ever, ever seen. Helen had a monster-fish face compared to you."

She looks satisfied and leans against me. Like Keycha, she doesn't sweat physical contact, and traveling in the cold means we cuddle every night under the snakehead skins, for warmth and needed companionship in the big empty. Keycha was beautiful too, I remember.

"You're not too bad either," she says, wriggling in more comfortably against my side. "Bit skinny, though."

• • •

A southerly shift in the wind finally slows our speedy down-wind flight as we're forced to tack into the everchanging gusts. It's Aki who spots and names Odysseus's clashing rocks ahead, Scylla and Charybdis, when they loom up suddenly out of the ice; tall, heavy, rust-red metal. Are they giant gates? We avoid crashing into those.

We check our imperfect distance estimate and discover that we may well be close to the bottom of Lake Huron already (give or take a day or two). The new wind brings unfamiliar scents as we tack slowly and uncertainly into it. There are smells I've almost forgotten, including the smell of weed above water and of mud. Is that the fresh chlorophyll smell of green and dirt? I'm also reminded of the unsettling tang of tidal rot. And do I actually smell engine oil? Metal? The scents on the warmer wind cause waves of unrest and anticipation in both of us.

It's the odor of cooking that brings us to a complete stop, bows together. My heart thumps with anticipation. Things are about to change again. I feel regret as well. Aki and I've found a rhythm during our journey down Huron. We've worked together well, not unlike the magical synthesis of collaborating with Keycha. Already we know what to expect from each other. But all that may end if there are people around.

We sidle up to the two huge metal doors rising into the sky. Odysseus's famous "rock and a hard place." This particular Scylla and Charybdis are each at least three inches thick, covered uniformly with umber rust. They loom high above our masts. The doors are partially open, ragged and threatening. If they were to slam shut, our boats, and we, would be nothing but an organic smear, atoms gone back to the beginning, our long evolution wasted. A path of ice, suspiciously free of drift, winds between them in a narrow channel, heading due south. We seem meant to sail between those metal doors. But they look dangerous.

"How did Odysseus pass through?" Aki asks, her voice muffled by the presence of yet another huge land sculpture (the lake being the more impressive of the two).

"He stuffed wool in his ears?" I whisper back.

"Wasn't that for the singing snakehead eels, luring sailors to their deaths?"

"I get those mixed up," I say.

And ice help me, I see Aki pulling tufts from her wrappings and rolling them into a ball, getting ready to stuff them into her ears.

I stop her. "We need to hear if other people are around."

Aki gets this but isn't as worried as I am. People mean family to her and, as irritating as they can be, family helps each other.

"Remember the Aanak's stories of the under-city people, before they died?" I warn urgently. "We don't know if these people will be friendly or not."

"The under-city folk were slow and half-blind," Aki says dismissively. Then, "Will these be blind too?"

"I sincerely doubt it," I say. But that only makes her more cheerful.

"Halloo!" Aki calls out suddenly, the sound ricocheting off the dense metal and bouncing away. The echo rumbles down the canal as if she's yelled into a bent tube.

"Are you an idiot?" I'm saying angrily, when we hear a distant thump. Thump. Thump.

The small hairs stand up on my neck, and even Aki is silent. We stand completely still and listen. There's only the sound of wind riffling our slack sails, and then again: three distinct thumps.

"You know, I think maybe we should find another way?" I'm spooked.

But Aki throws off her headgear and removes her bone glasses. The wind whips her hair as she squints down the canal, waiting.

"Here comes something," she says.

My eyes water when I take off my glasses. I see, blurrily, a small shape moving with great speed up the canal.

The thumping in the distance isn't getting louder, so it isn't coming from that same fast-moving source, which is almost on top of us in a matter of seconds.

Aki and I watch, dumbfounded, as a child swoops gracefully up the canal and slides to a dramatic stop in front of us. The stop sprays us with ice. He's wearing skates.

• • •

"Why didn't you sail in?" a sharp little voice asks us. Aki is staring at his skates and I don't know what to say. So I try, "Hello?"

"Are you friendly?" the small, aggressive person asks, a hint of anxiety in the voice.

"Very friendly," I say firmly. "We didn't come in because we weren't invited."

"Ah. Good." The child says thoughtfully. "What do you have for trade?"

I look at Aki. "We have … monster-fish steaks?" I say. "And …."

"And we have stories," Aki adds.

"Yes," the child says in a very mature way, nodding his head. I realize for the first time that he's not wearing wrapped rags, but has a real winter jumpsuit on, the kind I remember fishermen wearing long ago. On close inspection, it's patched and sewn, maybe to cut it down to his size, but it looks in good shape for skating and wouldn't bind as much as wraps.

"You like my clothes?" The kid is sharp. "I like your boat."

"I need my boat," I say. The boy looks disappointed. "May we come in?"

The boy turns and glides over to the intimidating metal doors. I can see, now, that Scylla and Charybdis are firmly iced in. No clashing possible. If they're some kind of river lock, would they be so tall, looming far above the surface

120

of the ice? The child takes a small mallet off his belt and hammers on the door. The deep thumps reverberate down the canal.

"You may enter," the child says, in a ritual singsong, "to trade and to pass through, at your own risk and none of ours." I'm not sure I like the sound of that. Let's hope the singing snakeheads are iced in too.

• • •

I should have known better. There's no way that giant Lake Huron, with Aki's even bigger lake behind it (*and other lakes beyond these, until they run off our map*), could have drained its massive contents through the relatively narrow gap between this particular Scylla and Charybdis. It's just another landmark in the vast ice, though I am glad we weren't going full speed when we met it. The huge lake dwarfs the metal rising into the sky in the same way the metal doors dwarf us, throwing off my perspective. We follow the skating child between them and find ourselves on a clear ice channel, protected from the wind but open to the sky above and ahead, lined on both sides by the rotting metal of what must be a giant barge. We've mistaken a single boat, split in two, for a river lock through to our next destination.

It's a big boat and well lived in. I saw pictures once of a civilization carved into a cliff face. But those dwellings had been as soft and rounded as the stone they tunneled through. Above us, lining the ice canal, are jagged, rusted layers of metal, twisted, holed and sharp. The smell of cooking and old diesel is stronger here, with an underlying tang of rotten iron. I can hear movement above and see a few shy faces peering down on us from the stacked layers of rusty shelves above. Down on the ice, where it meets the great curving walls, are piled masses of stacked and sorted debris. There are broken pieces of small boats, rusted sheet metal, glass bottles, rotting rubber tires, a more savory stack of dried snakehead skins, weed, bones. There's even a mound of empty shells, which surprises me. A pile of plastic doll parts sits next to intensely color-saturated piles of same-color plastic items: Buckets, pop-apart Easter eggs separated from their other halves, cartons, boxes, bags, chairs, and unrecognizable pieces of presumably once-useful things. Each pile is sorted by color rather than shape, with all the greens in one pile, pinks in another, then blues and faded yellows. The concentrated colors glow in the filtered light. They're beautiful. Above the piles someone has strung more colorful plastic trash and hung long cheerful lines of it around the grim metal walls. The occasional eyeless doll's head, strung among the rest, undoes some of the gaiety.

It's like some obsessive-compulsive kids' version of the apocalypse. Which fits.

We walk slowly, leading our suddenly windless sailboats like horses on tethers. We stare. More heads pop out of the recesses in the walls and bodies start climbing down to us, so we stop and wait. There's a broken stair welded in along one wall, but many of the figures just spider-walk down the rusted holes peppering the curved walls. I wonder about tetanus.

They can't be doing too badly here; there seem to be a lot of children. Most of the figures scampering about are very small. Aki watches them wide-eyed, and I wonder what she's thinking. Will she get all clucky and want to have children after all? That would be a waste of leaving home. Then I shake my head. I'm not Aki's keeper. But I don't like kids. It's too hard to look after oneself without needing to take care of some helpless being. And it would just be too terrible to worry about what lay ahead for them. No. Better to just keep moving east and think about one's own survival. That's hard enough.

These kids seem pretty competent, though. I watch one swing down on one of the decorated lines and wonder if they'll make it. The kid drops right in front of us, staggering, then straightens with a gap-tooth grin, teeth all brown and black. They look like they hurt, but the kid's expression is cheerful and excited.

"You like colors? You have a trade?" Clearly what's exciting this urchin is a chance to do business. So I assume they get other travelers through, though I can't imagine there are many.

Our skating friend glides up and pushes the smaller boy (if it is a boy) away.

"I found them. I trade first," the bigger boy says, and the growing crowd steps back deferentially. But then an adult steps up, frustrating our skater.

"But these travelers have all the things they need," the man says unctuously. "Your poor baubles wouldn't interest them. I have food and fire and a warm place for them to rest. This I can trade for … a mere …." A desperate expression crosses his face. "*Half* of what you brought!"

The crowd of children groans, as if wondering why they didn't think of that.

"No!" Aki says quickly. I'm more than happy to let her field this one.

"What we have is ours, needed for survival on the ice." Again the crowd looks terribly disappointed. More adult figures are joining the group now.

"Why are you here then?" A firm, authoritative voice rings out. A woman steps forward. Like everyone, she's clothed against the cold, but wears another uni-suit like our skater, and it fits voluptuous curves that would have put Aphrodite to shame – I can easily imagine her as the goddess who started the Trojan War and Odysseus's long journey. She seems only a little older than Aki (*who's looking at her with a slightly stunned expression*), but she has a powerful, mature presence. The crowd of children parts for her to pass, even while leaning in toward her, several pressing themselves against her sides. She absently pats a few heads, but the face she turns to us is challenging. I have a premonition that something bad will happen if we say the wrong thing.

"We were invited in," Aki says hastily, "to trade." Which reminds me how sharp she is. She's picked up the threat too.

"Good," the woman almost purrs. "I will trade for your boat."

"We have stories to trade," Aki says, "for passage through to the next lake. *With* our belongings."

The children gasp and the woman hesitates.

"We also have stories," the woman says, but it isn't a rejection.

And Aki shows that she has the soul of a true busker. She's magnificent.

"Ah, but I have stories about star gods racing across the heavens, of fish who walk upright like men, of snake-heads who sing ice sailors to their deaths. To show my good faith, I'll give you all a story for free so you can test my wares. This is the tale of the Lady in the Ice ...." And without waiting to see what the adults will say, Aki sits on the bow of her boat and starts to tell the children a story. They creep closer and sit at her feet, enthralled. A few adults join them, standing protectively at the edges of the group. I stay farther back, clutching the bowline of my precious boat, and find the curvaceous woman suddenly beside me.

"I know a different version of this story," she says dryly.

"That's surprising," I say. "Then you've traveled?"

"Yes." Her tone does not invite further questions. "And what do *you* offer in trade? You understand that we must make use of the resources that come to us."

I sigh. It's just another version of the same thing. "For the good of the family?" I ask.

"Of course." She looks offended by my tone.

"I have information," I say, my eyes on Aki speaking to the crowd. "I know more of the far past than anyone living, and how it can affect the future."

"The past may be useful," she says thoughtfully. "Give me something for free."

"Is that in your rules of trade?"

"No." She grins. "But it was worth a try."

"I'll tell you something useful from the present," I say. "But I want our belongings protected until we leave."

"You are always protected by the Trade," she says automatically. Then, quickly, before I can renegotiate, "It's a trade." We bump fists.

"You have a lot of children," I say, scanning the crowd. The few adults seem very protective, but there's something hopeless about their expressions as they watch the children's faces, alight with the magic of Aki's story.

"This I know," the woman says, eyes narrowed.

"There's a family who lives far out on the ice." I'm still watching the kids. One of them is swaying in his seat. Another seems to be twitching with excitement, his neck angling oddly. One little girl keeps falling asleep, her neighbor poking her when her head nods. "This family has no young women, and no children."

"You'd trade for children?" the woman hisses at me.

"No! Of course not. I'm just saying this family eats clean fish and weed. They live a hard life, but they're good to each other. They have boats and sun and wind. They live long and – they're healthy."

The woman says nothing.

"Why are there no older children here?" I ask.

"That is what you must tell me." The woman's voice is hard. "As part of this trade.

"Tell me!" she yells out suddenly, and Aki pauses her story. Everyone looks back at us.

"You should trade for Aki's story about the fall of the under-city people," I say, as calmly as I can. The woman is like a lioness beside me, ready to rend me with her teeth to protect her young. "And I'll tell you what I know, though it may take some time for you to understand." The nodding child tilts over and is caught by her neighbor. One of the adults steps forward and scoops her up, rocking the little body and murmuring. She carries the tiny figure away toward the iron stair, the whole group watching somberly. "I'm tired," I say sadly. "Will you share your fire with us in exchange for clean fish from up-lake?"

"It is a trade," the Lioness says dully, her eyes on the child. We bump fists.

• • •

Fortunately, the Lioness's lair is not up on the rusted shelves. Her home fire is in what must be a broken engine room. Odd shapes, tanks, and pipes are frozen into the ice, but she has a cozy corner curtained off with tatty plastic curtains and a padded bench for sleeping. The ice underfoot is scattered with weed and cloth strips. Her fire is in a cozy space open enough for many of the children to follow us in. The rest leave reluctantly with the other adults. There seem to be anywhere from three to five children herded by each one. The Aanak would have drooled with envy.

"It's amazing to be so protected from the wind," Aki says happily. She's already figured out that the children are happier if they can trade something small for her stories, no doubt allowing them to feel they got the best out of the deal. She's the proud possessor of quite a number of color-ful plastic trinkets now. She trades for a lanyard and starts stringing them around her neck. The children look very pleased, then demand the next story as payment.

"Food first!" the Lioness roars, and there is a moment of chaos while everyone fetches from their own small stores. After a flurry of trading, the children settle, some heating their food over the Lioness's fire after first leaving her small gifts of beads or glass.

I inspect the children's food while Aki fetches our fish and her kettle. It seems prudent not to use anything belonging to our host without first stipulating a trade. The children can trade trinkets, but I believe the woman wants more from us.

I smile at a small child crouched at the outer edge of the group and ask what she's eating. She looks around, as if trying to figure out what she should trade, then simply holds out her hands and grins. She doesn't speak.

She's eating a double handful of black mussels, prying each apart with the blade of a broken case knife.

"Ah," I say, trying to smell them, but she clutches her food protectively, then looks up expectantly. I remember the pile of shells out in the main "hall" of the boat. "Do you eat these a lot?" The child nods once, watching me.

"Would you like to know what I eat?" The little face brightens. "I eat a lot of dried fish and weed stew." I stick out my tongue as if it's yucky, then realize it probably isn't, to her. I slip a tiny piece of dried fish into her hand. "Don't tell anyone. This is just our trade, right?"

The fingers close tightly around the sliver, hiding it from sight. She's shaking slightly. I make my way back to the fire.

"Can she speak?" I ask, but the Lioness says nothing. "I need more information to be able to tell you what you want to know." This trading game is irritating, though I notice Aki is having no trouble with it.

"I need to know what they eat, and where they play," I say. "I need to know what kinds of symptoms, of odd things, happen to them. Do they grow abnormally? Do they lose speech? Do they stagger? Do any of these things happen over a long time? Or is it only just before they ...." The Lioness leans forward and claps her hand over my mouth.

"And what will you trade for this information?" She is angry.

"Answers, if I can. Though you may not want to hear them."

"What's going on?" Aki asks softly. The children, having eaten, are scraping together the weed and clothes on the floor into a thicker mound and piling on top together, like puppies.

I keep my voice low. "The children are not surviving to adulthood," I say, watching the Lioness for confirmation. "And I've traded our safe passage in return for some understanding of why that is." The Lioness's eyes glint in the firelight, but she says nothing.

"Tell her the story of how the under-city people died," I say to Aki, "in exchange for more information about the children."

"It is a trade," the Lioness responds graciously.

• • •

The Lioness is not impressed with Aki's story. The children listened with fluttering eyelids and are now asleep. The Lioness does not bother to lower her voice.

"I see no similarities to these ... pale ... under-city ... people," she says haughtily. "Your story implies that they're blind because they hid in dark. I understand this – there are fish that are the same – but we live in the light. You say they died from eating those round metal cylinders. We do not eat such things and never have. What possible use is your story to me and mine?"

I almost call her "Lioness" out loud, but stop myself. She hasn't given us her name. No doubt we'd have to trade for it. For now, I'll continue thinking of her as the Lioness.

"There's an older message in this story, one that Aki may not know," I say. "To understand, you need to know what was here before the ice."

"Before the ICE was the void," Aki says automatically.

I sigh. "Aki, can you not bring religion into this for a moment?" Now I've offended her too. I have to remember that she doesn't necessarily believe I've lived before the ice either. "Look, just show the Lion– ah, our hostess – your book. Please?"

Again we have a struggle. Why do objects need to have such importance? Eventually Aki takes the book from where it's hidden under her wraps and offers it "just for a look" to the Lioness. But then the Lioness won't take it until she retrieves something from under her bench, which turns out to be another book. The slim volume has no pictures. It's a book of poems.

"Yeats!" I cry out in delight. "And Frost, and …." Thoroughly distracted, I flip through quickly. The Lioness watches with an expression of disgust, but shrewdly notes my interest.

"Just for a look," she mimics Aki's words, "unless you will trade for that knife hidden in your leggings." Clearly she doesn't value the book as I do. I would have traded her all the knives in my leggings (I have about seven, and sometimes they can poke one most uncomfortably).

"Trade," I say quickly, and we bump fists.

"What use is it?" the Lioness asks with mild interest, as she puts away her new knife with a satisfied expression. "I was going to burn it."

"No. No! Don't ever burn these," I say excitedly. "Your children will value them some day."

"It is rude to brag about a trade," she says.

"I'm sorry, uh, ma'am. Let me trade you words from the past to show you why you mustn't destroy these when you find them."

And I read to her the words of William Butler Yeats, 1865 to 1939, writing, perhaps, about the aftermath of one war and the advent of another. I know that neither the words nor the context – but perhaps the concepts – might have meaning for these women, listening around a water-weed fire inside a rotting tanker, long centuries after the writer's death, and even after the death of his uncivilized wars and civilized fears.

"'Turning and turning in the widening gyre
The falcon cannot hear the falconer;
Things fall apart; the centre cannot hold;
Mere anarchy is loosed upon the world,
The blood-dimmed tide is loosed, and everywhere
The ceremony of innocence is drowned ....'"

I close the book when the poem is done, unshed tears warming my eyes. I've missed books so badly in this world. The two women are watching me with open mouths.

"It was not ... unpleasant ...," the Lioness says, eying Aki sideways.

"A good trade," Aki says firmly, nodding to the Lioness. They must both think I'm mad.

"Never mind," I say. "You'll get it someday. Now, for Aki's book."

• • •

It takes time, but the pictures help, and I eventually get across to Aki and the Lioness that, for the sake of argument, *maybe* once there was a time before ice when humans built cities around lakes of water. "Where else did this big boat come from?" I say, gesturing widely and almost losing them again. Because of course what we are in can't be a boat, it's too damn big. But the Lioness is intrigued by the pictures in the book and interrupts several times to try trading with Aki for it, before giving up in disgust.

"When humans built the cities," I tell my very resistant audience, "they were not careful about what they took from the earth to build them." I have a brainstorm. "Okay, for instance, there was this city called Rome, across the salt sea." (That was a mistake, because then we had to talk about the sea, but eventually we got back to my parable.) "This city brought water to its people through pipes, like these over here." And I pounded on the weird shapes protruding from the ice near what may have been a boiler once – also no help. "They took soft metal from the earth and shaped it into these hollow pipes, not realizing that the metal was poisoning the water running through it. It was a slow poison," I say sadly. "Later it was understood to be lead poisoning. It worked into their bodies slowly and made the people stupid, and aggressive. Eventually it killed them."

"All the people died?"

"Uh. Sure. I guess."

"What happened to the other cities?"

"Similar kinds of things," I say, realizing that it really was very similar. "The people didn't understand how each of the new things they separated from the earth was affecting them. Like mercury, a kind of liquid metal, which gets into shellfish and fish, causes shaking, and dizziness, and sometimes death if people eat too much of it." I nod toward the sleeping children. "People kept inventing new poisons, not understanding how they'd affect the people and animals around them. Sometimes they'd figure it out and stop using that thing. Once they stopped making a poison used to kill bugs –" ("I like bugs," the Lioness says, smacking her lips) "– and they saved many birds from dying." The women stare at me, unmoved, having never seen a bird. "The problem was, soon there were too many different poisons being released from the earth, and they couldn't tell which ones were causing problems, so they stopped trying."

"Thank the ICE," the Lioness says, nodding to Aki, "that we do not live on the earth, but on solid ice." And Aki nods in righteous agreement.

"Even worse," I continue, "was that humans didn't understand what would happen when all these poisons mixed together. Soon *all* the animals were dying. Frogs were the first to go, then the rest of the amphibians, then reptiles and sea mammals, any animals that lived in that place between water and air. Then birds. Then many kinds of fish." The idea of losing fish made my audience finally pay attention. "People also cut down trees and weeds that helped clean the poisons, and soon the air they breathed started to change, go bad, and parts of the world became very hot and dry." There's just no comprehension in their faces at all. "And other parts got very wet, and then very, very cold."

"Is that when the ice came to save them?" Aki asks, breathlessly.

"Sure," I say. "And the ice trapped many of the poisons within itself. Keeping them away from the humans who survived."

"Ah!" Now the women are starting to like this story. It's beginning to fit into their worldview.

"But there are places," I warn, realizing that the story as a parable could still work. "Places where many people gathered before the ice. The under-city was one of those. In those places the poisons still leak through, contaminating some foods, and even ice and air. And there's a prediction, a prophecy, that when the great Thaw comes, melting the ice on the lakes and warming the earth" – the Lioness is again skeptical, but Aki, probably remembering her dream of the wind on the waves, looks more uncertain – "it will bring warmth but also hardship, releasing the stored poisons from the ice."

"These children did not dig poison from the earth," the Lioness says grimly. "Why would the ICE bring this curse down on them?"

"It's no one's fault, Madam," I say, dropping all pretense of storytelling. It's just too hard. "But your children are eating shellfish and weed that store, and concentrate, poisons that were left here long ago. You live in an area that had one of the highest concentrations of industrial pollutants on the planet. The ice you melt is also putting those poisons in your drinking water. Are your children losing their balance? Unusually angry or aggressive? Developing oddly?" (*"Born intersex?" The mean little god in my head sneers.*) "Going to sleep and not waking? It may be mercury, lead, cyanide, cadmium, organochlorines (*hormone disruptors*) – or a mix of those toxins and more. NO! It is *not* their fault!" I realize I'm getting loud. The pile of sleeping children stirs and shifts. I lower my voice.

"But millions of people who lived before you went about their days the same way you do, doing what they thought was best for themselves and for their families. They're all long dead – buried under ice. They weren't able to change quickly enough to save themselves – can you?"

My head hurts. Now *I'm* preaching, frack-it. How did that slip in?

"Your children are dying. Is that so?" I ask. The Lioness nods slowly, digesting my words. Clearly trying to decide if I'm completely mad. "You don't have to believe a word I've said. But if you don't change *something*, then they will continue to die, and you will continue to grieve."

"What should I do?" she asks, faced with the mad prophet that is me. How should I know? What if I send them somewhere even worse?

"What *can* you do?" I ask. "Can you leave here? Can you go somewhere the fish and water are still relatively clean? Can you stop the children from eating shellfish and playing on rusted metal in abandoned ships that may have carried barrels of poison from one lake to the next? You need to get your kids out of this environment *now*. Even though ... for some it will be too late."

"I can't feed all these little ones out on the open ice!" she says angrily.

"You could with help," I say, turning to Aki. She's so very quick. Her face is shining and eager.

"The family ...." She grins. "Let's send Keycha a present!"

• • •

"Will you go back with them?" I ask Aki late that night. The fire has burned out, but the metal cabin is stuffy with the breath of so many sleeping bodies. The thought of going on by myself has me lying sleepless, staring into the dark. I don't want her to leave me.

"Hmm. But I've already been there," Aki mumbles. "Besides, with *her* around, there's no way I'd be leader."

I smile and turn over to sleep.

• • •

I dream of Keycha that night. He's standing out on the open ice, calling my name. I try to tell him I'm there, but I'm as insubstantial as the wind playing around him, ruffling his long hair. He can't hear me, but I tell him to sail north and something good will come to him. He shakes his head, and I see a huge dark wave rising out of the ice. It's coming in behind him and he doesn't see it. There are broken boats and ice sleepers, children and snapping fish tumbling in the wave. I call out helplessly as it curls over to consume him – and I wake, sweating in the close cabin. I wonder if I've started something that will have consequences I can't foresee.

I know that this has always been true.

• • •

We tell the Lioness that we'll leave first. I don't want her thinking we intend to trick her out of her toxic kingdom. From a massive container against the wall, she takes two adult-size foul-weather winter jumpsuits with built-in hoods and real sun goggles. The plastic cloth looks fresh off the production line, though I note that the insulation compresses too easily, crumbling a bit from age, no doubt, so I make a mental note not to discard our cloth wrappings. The Lioness also hands us each a pair of sturdy skates, the blades tall and sharp, with adjustable plastic boots. The inner padding has long since perished. She gives us patched-together backpacks for what's left of our dried fish and offers a small personal sled that can be dragged behind a skater to hold fishing gear, our skins, and our weed bales. We're stammering our thanks when she hands us two small triangular sails, colorful plastic stretched over a cross of light aluminum. They look like insect wings. My spears are tied to the struts on mine.

"What's this about?" I say, finally suspicious. All these gifts are just too far outside her own rules of trade – even if this stuff will be left behind anyway when the family leaves.

"I told you I would trade for your boats," the Lioness says easily, staring me down. "I've been more than generous."

"You're making out like a bandit," I say. But somehow I expected this. The rotting tanker reeks of illness and threat, despite the colorful baubles and childish voices. We were never going to be let go with our boats. We're lucky to get something useful in exchange.

"Thievery is also one of the rules of trade." The Lioness is pleased with herself. "Besides, you did well with your strange book." She's not wrong. But giving up our boats is like giving up our link to Keycha, and I can't imagine Aki without the ability to fly down the ice.

Aki looks stricken but resigned. "They need the boats for the smallest children," she tells me, pinching my arm to let me know she's also aware we have no choice. Might as well keep things friendly, or leaving might become even more difficult. So we spend half a day showing the Lioness how to run one of her own tarps between the hulls and replace the strut to make Keycha's boat into a catamaran again. That way she should be able to carry more kids. We never thought of using the curved hulls themselves for storage when it was one boat, but that gives them even more room on top. They have a few other makeshift boats, but ours is by far the best of the fleet. They don't have Keycha's clever designs – at least not yet. But they do have those marvelous insect wings and snowsuits from their own scavenging expeditions. The adults and those children who are still capable, including our young doorkeeper, are going to skate-sail, as we are.

We scratch a crude map on a plastic sheet for the Lioness and explain it as best we can. Aki writes the mile markers in days. Presumably, they won't have to beat upwind when they reach Lake Michigan, as we did. But if it continues for a while, the southern wind blowing now should let them fly up Lake Huron. This wind has the smell of thaw in it. We warn the Lioness about the possibility of wet ice, of the snapping fish, of the ice sleepers. They're the only landmarks we have to offer. The Lioness will bring food for fifteen days, but I caution her to stop and fish soon and often, and to ditch the food from this place the minute she can. Because I can't see her throwing anything away, I tell her she will be trading with the lake, unsafe food for safe passage. I should have known better. Her raised eyebrows let me know she doesn't appreciate being patronized.

In exchange for the map, the Lioness orders one of the other adults to sing us the passage to Lake Erie. It is a strange song-tale of moving through a landscape, of landmarks to fish by, of a tiny lake between rivers. Of reaching a body of water smaller than Huron, iced over of course, yet somehow warmer, shallower, with faster-running currents beneath. It sounds like a story of moving into Thaw. It's rhythmic and musical. One realizes quickly that the end of each rhyme is a place to stop and camp, and at each repeat of the chorus there's a new landmark: a river leading to a new lake, a bend around the lake toward morning light to get on to the next river, and so on. It's a fascinating verbal map. Aki repeats it several times to herself. I compare it with our plastic map as she sings. The song is far more detailed.

"We're gonna wish we had floating hulls yet," I tell Aki, thinking of the feeling of Thaw in the song. Aki is already panicked about leaving her boat behind. The boy who first invited us into the tanker gives us skating lessons and she concentrates with grim determination. It's harder than it looks, and more tiring. "Look at it this way," I tell Aki, "we aren't likely to get cold."

"I feel naked without my boat!" Aki cries. But she never really complains. And I stop grumbling after I see the excited faces of the children helping each other get ready for their journey. The Lioness forbids them to bring shellfish, and we tell them how yummy the fish monsters are, though one tiny boy starts to cry.

"Don't worry," an older child tells him. "I'll leap and yell and smack it, like Jack, and we can eat it together," which cheers the little guy right up.

• • •

Of course nothing is simple. My story of the past has stirred up the protectiveness of the Lioness, who is young and restless. The children in her care will follow her anywhere. But the remaining adults have, so far, survived the illnesses that are claiming so many of the children. Some of them are weak and ill, though a few, like the Lioness, are healthy. The weaker they are, the more they cling to the comfort of what they know. The strange man who tried to barter for half our goods when we arrived faces off with the Lioness. She's strong, but he has the backing of a small group of adults who gather around him.

"What is this madness?" he screeches, managing to cringe and challenge at the same time. "You hear a stranger's fantasy of what once was, and you wish to lead us all to a cold death on the ice? And what about our trade?"

"Don't be silly," the Lioness purrs. "It's just a raid to get more good boats like this one. You just stay here, if you like. Hmmm? Anyone who wishes can stay behind." The man and I both watch her with a kind of thrilled horror. (*Keycha, what have I done?!*) She turns and winks at me. It isn't comforting.

• • •

A core of adults do choose to stay behind, along with the weakest children. It's awful to see them hanging back from the excited preparations, looking gray and lost, but also stubborn. They believe they're doing the right thing. The children staying behind are those with no chance of surviving the journey, and the Lioness spends time with each one, gravely trading keepsakes, hugs, and tears. I'm distressed to see the quiet little girl who'd shown me her shellfish, bundled in a soft blanket, clinging to the Lioness's neck with thin, shaking arms, while tears trickle down both their cheeks. I shed a few of my own in the privacy of the dark. But the Lioness is a survivor (*like me?*) and preparations continue.

At the Lioness's request, Aki tells one last story to the group who'll be traveling. The women understand what I did not. My frightening story of the past has nothing like

138

the motivating effect of Aki's hopeful story for the future. It's the tale of her family, of the Aanak in the days when she mothered Aki and her brother, of grouped huts out on the ice and firepits under the stars. Of heroic hunters, male and female, working together for the good of the family. Of sailing from the huts to the fishing grounds to eat fresh roe in globes like tiny suns. Of Keycha's boathouse, where a clever sun god creates flying machines. When she finishes, she wipes her eyes, and I half-fear I've lost her again.

"Why did you ever leave?" asks one of the adults who will accompany the expedition. As the thrall of the story fades, I can tell the tale had its impact. The children can picture where they're headed now, and they can imagine their new lives. I know it will help motivate them when the journey is difficult. I know it, without ever having experienced this for myself. I can't remember why I'm heading east, can't picture where I'm going. But the Lioness looks both dreamy-eyed and even more determined now. She'll take the children into the west. They have their goal. How do I reclaim mine?

• • •

"Lioness," I say, intending to ask her to carry a note to Keycha for me. Lacking writing utensils, I laboriously scratched it into a small chunk of soft pink plastic. Just as well she can't read.

"What is it you call me?" she asks curiously.

"Ah. I don't know your name. A lioness was a giant cat, fierce and protective of her young."

"It is a good thing to be called?"

"Very good. Powerful. A strong mother/leader name."

The Lioness smiles. "Then I will call you Jack."

Everyone's a comedian.

Just in case the Lioness turns to raiding after all, my message to Keycha reads:

Here is a powerful Mother
And many children
To replace the Maiden and lost Crone.
She is strong, a pirate at heart, be wary!
Live with laughter and love

— your Akna. P.S. Aki says hi.

ICE SKATING

"...the direful monster, whose skin clings
To his strong bones, strides o'er the groaning rocks:
He withers all in silence, and in his hand
Unclothes the earth, and freezes up frail life ...."
— William Blake, "To Winter"

The tanker has been hiding the way. After saying our good-byes, Aki and I skate right through it and down a river toward Lake Saint Clair on our map. Our new sails are folded away into long wrapped bundles on our backs. I want to get this skating thing down before adding speed. We estimate we've got about 200 miles once we're properly on Lake Erie, west to east, which is far less than beating north up Lake Michigan and flying south down Huron. But skating is more tiring, and it's different traveling with a changeable wind that can come at us from any direction at any moment. We can see both shores of the river, which is exciting at first, then oddly claustrophobic. The wind bounces from side to side. Drifts of snow pile oddly and the ice isn't always smooth.

My teeth feel like they'll rattle out of my head from the direct line of impact from ice to skate to shinbones and up. When the wind does blow from behind, we can lean back into it a little, bend our knees and rest while it pushes. But that never lasts long.

Finally, Aki slides to a stop. She's already got this skating thing down and is almost as skilled as the tanker children. I never noticed before how graceful she is. Like Keycha. She offers to pull our sled, but I like the feeling it gives me of being anchored. It does make me slower and more unwieldy – or at least that's my excuse.

"Time for the sails, old man!" She grins.

"Don't ever call me that again," I say grimly. "I can't think of anything worse."

"Well, you're skating like an old man with a cane. Take a risk! The Aanak was braver than you!"

"Bravery isn't really a survival trait," I mutter.

Aki just stares at me, hands on hips, until I reach for her sail, unhooking it from her backpack, and hand it to her. She opens the wing on the ice and carefully sets the struts in place. She has to struggle back up from her knees onto the skates, and the wind catches the sail as soon as she picks it up.

"Whoop!" Aki does a sudden twirl that would have sent me crashing onto my butt. Being the sailor she is, she immediately turns the sail into the wind and stops. "Funny little thing," she says, tilting the sail slightly to catch wind again. She gives one kick and is immediately flying downriver, knees bent, feet together, letting the wind do the work, shrieking with delight.

I watch grimly. Speed has never been my thing. Aki tacks back up toward me.

"This is easier than the sailboat!" she cries, suddenly sitting down hard. But she's still happy.

"Jack, you have to try this." Aki struggles to get back up. She raises the sail above her head as she rocks to a kneeling position and suddenly the sail lifts her, not just to her feet but right off the ice for a brief moment. She lands with a stagger and quickly turns into the wind again. "Wow! I wonder if I could do that at speed?"

"Please don't!"

"Come on! Let's get you sorted out, Scaredy-Jack. You're gonna love this."

I sincerely doubt it.

• • •

We experiment throughout the day. At first I hold the sail in front and it yanks me along, blinding me to drifts and direction. Unbalanced as it is, I'm more comfortable holding the sail behind my back and letting the wind push from behind. It feels a little out of control, but after a while I trust the sail enough to lean back into the wind, guiding myself with slight shifts of feet and arms. But that doesn't work well when dragging the sled, and eventually I tuck one shoulder into the sail at an angle. That way, I can see where I'm headed, and still tilt the sail to catch wind. After a while I don't even notice the speed, except on lumpy ice. Even with a stumbling beginning, we make Lake Saint Clair in less than half a day by Aki's sun reckoning.

Then I discover a big problem.

I call out to Aki. She's always ahead. Whisps of the travel song the tanker folks taught her drifts back to me. She's singing the route. "We have a problem!" I shout.

She finally stops. I sail up and turn my skates into a sliding stop, showing off my newfound ability. I'm getting tired, though, and my feet ache.

"Aki, I'm soaked with sweat," I say, and her eyes widen in alarm. Being wet out on the ice is no joke.

"*Frack*! I am too!" We've stayed warm doing all this exercise in our new plastic suits, but the cost is a drenching sweat that could kill us when the sun goes down and everything freezes.

"How do the tanker people manage?" I ask, but the answer is obvious: they go back to their giant metal windbreak and their fires at the end of each day. How will they cope out on the open lake? I consider turning back to warn them, but I'm so tired. I know I'd never make it before dark. We'd freeze if we tried. We'll have to look after ourselves and trust them to do the same.

Our small sails won't supply the windbreak our boats created, but they'll have to do. We need to build a fire and get into our old wraps, see if we can dry out the plastic liners of the suits.

"We'll have to anchor the sails so they don't fly off without us," I say and Aki nods. We fit our sails together into a small triangle, point into the wind, one snakehead hide below, and one on top for the weight. It helps anchor the sails, but won't be enough if the wind shifts. Aki upends our trailer and tilts the box up over the triangle of our tent, then wraps both kites and skin roof with fishing line tied off to the trailer. It still feels light enough to fly away. Keycha made us stakes for mooring our boats, so I hammer one near each point of our triangle and tie them to Aki's line. Our makeshift tent shakes and rattles, but doesn't take off. We build a fire nearer to the opening than I'd usually like and take turns using the small tent as a windbreak to struggle into our drier cloth wrappings. They're a pain to get on, after the ease of the jumpsuits, but they're dry. We turn the suits inside out and use Keycha's tripod to hang them as close to the fire as possible. Then we scooch backward into our small tent together, feet at the apex, heads toward the fire, pull the last skin over us, and suck on dried fish. We're both exhausted and sore. It's still daylight. Even Aki is too tired for stories.

• • •

As the days pass, we develop our new routine. We discover that leaving a layer of cloth under our plastic jumpsuits makes them easier to dry out each night. Sometimes we just cram wads of cloth into the legs and torso. Then only the cloth gets wet, and it is easier to remove and faster to dry near the fire. We swap out the cloth, relying on our jumpsuits more and more. They're so much easier to move in while skating. We don't fish as often as we used to. I want to get as far from the tanker city as possible while we still have our dried food store (not knowing if it will help), but we stop more often to rest and collect weed for our daily fires. Aki is the one clever enough to think of drying weed as we travel. She drapes it over the rails of the sled, which becomes a long, shaggy green snake following behind, a line of pale yellow on the white fields of ice.

Despite having (extremely) sore muscles after the first day, we take only another day to travel downriver to Lake Erie, our newest wind-polished ice giant. Now, no matter whether the wind is northerly or southerly, we catch it in our sails and fly toward the east. The distance between our bodies and the ice has shrunk with each change of transport: catamaran to wind-sailers to skates. Our connection to Erie is up close and personal. Once out in the middle of the lake, Aki starts having the dreams again. They're always about running water.

• • •

Lake Erie is strange. Although she also runs beyond our visible horizon, Erie feels like the little sister of Michigan and Huron, perhaps even the neglected or abused little sister, since I know all the industrial waste from the cities around those giant lakes made their way down through her. Our map indicates that she's not as deep, and Aki says she dreams of a hum coming from the lake, as if massive currents are vibrating the ice.

"Do you realize," I say to her, "that we're finally heading east?"

We've traveled perhaps 600 miles or more, first north, then south, but not more than 200 miles east the whole time, like a huge tack upwind across the continent.

"Imagine if we could have sledded due east across land?" I'm only asking rhetorically. After my own climb up out of the snow-and-ice-covered city, I'm certain land travel isn't possible.

"My first family did that," Aki says matter-of-factly. "They used caribou to pull the sledges."

"What?" My face must have looked ludicrous with surprise.

Aki laughs at me. It's becoming a frequent event.

"Keycha didn't tell you?"

"But … caribou?"

"I'm sure they're long gone," Aki says sadly. "There was never enough weed for them to eat. That's what made my family take a chance with the heavy snows around the lake. They were after water-weed for the animals. Our animals were family." I can't tell if Aki is remembering for herself, or remembering stories Keycha told her.

"They were grand furred beasts with antlers like sails. We raised them, fed them, worked them, milked them and slept with them. When they died, we mourned them, ate them, and used their bones for the sledges, and their hides for warmth." Aki looks at me slyly. "Where do you think our skins came from?" My jaw is already hanging open, imagining – remembering – large herbivores. "Keycha told you these skins were snakehead eels, didn't he? And you believed him!" For some reason, Aki finds this hilariously funny. "Can you imagine a snakehead that big? It would eat your head! It would swallow you whole!"

I finger the hide covering us. It's not quite dusk. We've gotten in the habit of stopping early to dry our clothes.

We're no longer hurrying toward a destination. Just moving forward, traveling together, is enough.

"Feel that." Aki strokes the hide. "See how thick and flexible it is? Have you ever seen an eel skin that soft? I mean, eel is thicker than regular fish skin, but they'll always crackle and aren't nearly as warm as these."

"That bastard," I say.

"Oh, he never told anyone," Aki says, comfortable in the knowledge that there's something about Keycha I don't know. "That way, people were impressed he killed such a big eel, and didn't try to take them."

"You took them," I say, remembering.

"I left him one," she says. "We needed them." We did. And he didn't stop us.

"The one I left him," Aki says wickedly, "the bottom one? Had *fur* on the hidden side. "Did he never show you? I remember cuddling it when I was small."

We're silent for a long time, remembering the plush, soft warmth of fur.

• • •

That night I dream of massive herds of furry caribou thundering across the ice field of Lake Erie. There are so many they run into the horizon on every side with no ending. As I watch, one beast stops and turns to face me, its long sad nose huffing the smell of fresh-cut weed into my face. "Why did you leave?" it asks in Keycha's voice. The thundering continues, but when I look up, all the caribou are gone.

• • •

Aki dreams of thunder too. She sits up, just before dawn, pulling the warm skins off us both. "Water!" she cries out, clutching at my shoulder. "It's coming!"

We struggle out of our tiny tent into the dim light, but, as in my dream, there's nothing except silent, unyielding ice in every direction. No caribou prints. No water. But something is new. A warm scent is in the air, and the vaguest tremor underfoot, a buzz in the ice. I look down at my feet curiously, then grab for the map.

"How long have we been traveling since we left the river mouth?" I unfurl the map by our dead fire, wishing I had something to anchor it with. Aki reaches to hold one corner.

Neither of us have been keeping track, but we count back camps (and dreams), and it seems we've been skating five days since leaving the tanker. Isn't that too soon to be near the eastern shore? I know it won't be immediately, but I suddenly don't want our trip to end. I can't imagine a world anymore without Aki and I flying through a field of white. Not for the first time, I wonder what's driving me east. I need to sit down and think some things through, piece together some evasive thoughts and memories. But not right now ....

"It doesn't show clear details on our map," I say to Aki, "but here, at the end of Lake Erie, is a waterfall, and before that a canal. If we skate the canal, it'll take us southeast and we'll get to the salt sea much quicker."

"I thought we followed the ice?" Aki looks confused. "Here. We should skip your canal and follow the next lake up to this long river, the S-something Law-rence."

"That's a helluva lot longer," I say. "Look how far that is compared to how far we've come. Besides, you know what that last river was like to skate on. Canals tend to be flatter. Easier to skate."

"You don't know that," Aki says. "It could be covered in drift. Look, the blue of the ice goes east and north. I like north. And you said north is cleaner. Better fish."

"That's true, but we'll have to go past Niagara Falls to get to the next lake. We could skip all that on the canal."

"We got past Scylla and Charybdis no problem. We got past the sleepers ...."

148

"This is different, Aki. You know that hum you've been dreaming? I'm feeling it now too, and I'm awake. Think about the currents of water you heard under the ice of Michigan and Huron. Imagine all that water running down here, under the ice of Lake Erie. Imagine it all squeezing through a steep drop" – I point at the map, just between Lake Erie and Lake Ontario – "to get to the next lake down. Imagine that huge amount of water in that narrow space. Do you think even the ice could contain it?"

"But why?" she asks, frustrated. "Why does the water run under the ice? Why does it want to go to the salt sea?"

"Water travels downhill," I shrug, "just like me."

• • •

We keep arguing about where we'll go next. I hadn't realized Aki was so intent on heading north again. She has her mind set on the Saint Lawrence Seaway. It's the logical route to pursue on the map, following one blue waterway to the next. The Erie Canal looks thin and unlikely in comparison, a mere dotted line across a landscape of browning paper. But our short trek due east on Lake Erie has set up that longing in me again. If we could keep travelling east it looks like we could reach the sea in about the time it took us to travel Lake Michigan. In contrast, Aki's long river would send us north again, maybe beating against the wind on a lumpy river. Who knows how far? Our map shows only a portion of the river, and that's already the length of two Lake Michigans before it runs off the edge of our map into the unknown, without reaching the sea. I've had enough of the unknown. Water will eventually run to the sea; I know this. But I have a burning desire to stay within the confines of the map. To be able to visualize where we're going next. To head east into the sun. Who told me that was important? I can't remember. Perhaps I told myself in another life.

It's our first real fight, other than the one about having children, so long ago, in Keycha's home. We've come a long way since, but not so far in our need to out-stubborn each other.

"Saint Lawrence River."

"Erie Canal."

"River."

"Canal."

"North."

"East."

Every time she circles back, looping around me in huge circles (*I'm still the slowest*), Aki brings up the argument again. I know she's out here with me partly because she can't stand being told what to do, but *gah*! As we skate toward its eastern shore, the hum under the ice of Lake Erie gets louder and more insistent.

• • •

Aki takes to leaping into the air every few yards, sometimes tucking her legs up and gliding just above the ice, sometimes ten feet up, suspended in air. I suspect it's as much to get away from the hum underfoot as it is her sheer joy in anything related to speed and flying on the wind. Once an updraft takes her even higher and she shrieks and kicks, coming back down rather hard. That keeps her ice-bound a little while. But not for long.

It's shortly afterward that a winged shape glides high over our heads. At first I don't notice. I'm shocked to see Aki suddenly drop flat on the ice, clutching her sail over her body as if she's hiding. Then a shadow swoops overhead and I flinch violently, zinged by that primal fear of things hunting from above. But there haven't been wild birds on this iced earth for a hundred years before my last sleep – and none with a wingspan like that in my lifetimes. What is it? I peer into the sun, but the bird swoops high above us again, circling, wings yawing. Aki crawls from beneath her sail, expression sheepish (*and sheep were gone not long after the birds left, though their place in our language remains – for now*).

"I don't know why I ducked," she says.

Because your primate ancestors were hunted by things like those, I want to say, but my brain is spinning.

"How does he sail so high?"

"What?" I'm confused. The bird angles into the sun and I see two long legs in silhouette. I'm reminded of a flying dinosaur – a pterodactyl? Is evolution running backward, the earth spinning out of balance under its lumpy coating of ice?

"That skater." Aki points impatiently. "How does he sail so high?" Which is the first time I realize how much better Aki's eyes are than mine. Either that, or I just see what I expect to, because the next moment the pterodactyl flies out of the sun's glare and it is clearly a human. They're flying with a giant sail similar in shape to our own, circling overhead and dipping down to yell something unintelligible at us. The flyer doesn't rise as high again, but stops circling and drops northeast in a straight, descending line.

"Shall we follow him?" I think we're both too curious and confused not to.

• • •

He's waiting for us on the edge of the ice. Behind him are high drifts and the white mounds that delineate the shore. We've reached the eastern end of Lake Erie.

The flyer's hood is back and he's removed goggles, face bare to the bitter wind. His skin is brown rather than ochre; his black hair is curly and wild in contrast to the heavy straight hair of Aki's family. He's young, that age between boyhood and manhood that's afraid of nothing because it can't foresee its own end. The flyer is older than the tanker children, younger than the fishermen in Aki's family. Aki

151

eyes him with deep interest. Other than Keycha (*and me, in a way*), she's never been around males close to her age before. He looks back at her with altogether too much admiration. I shift uncomfortably.

"I saw you try to fly," he says, voice cracking a little. So maybe he's younger than he looks. He's wearing a jumpsuit of sorts but not a nylon one-piece made pre-ice like ours. It's coarse cloth sewn with fish gut. The suit is buttoned with what might be twists of hemp. It's possible his people actually weave. That implies a fair bit of tech. I eye him narrowly.

"I could teach you to go higher." He's talking to Aki.

"That's quite an offer," I say, feeling like a protective grandpa. "But what we want is to find the Erie Canal to the east."

"I don't," Aki says. "I want to fly like you do."

The boy's grin is almost as beautiful as Keycha's. I groan. Aki doesn't stand a chance.

"I'm in training myself," the boy admits. "I'm not really supposed to be this far down river." He eyes our skates.

"I don't suppose you have another pair of those?"

"No. We don't," I snap. "And what do you mean, 'river'? Isn't this Lake Erie?"

"Sure," the boy says. "But the river connects the lake to – Niagara."

His voice, on the last word, holds the passion of a zealot. I groan internally. I hate that sound. It's the hollow sound of belief overriding reason.

"Isn't that the way we're going?" Aki's challenging me, our daily argument resurfacing.

"I don't know of a canal," the boy twinkles at Aki. "Perhaps you mean the Erie River? That's where I'm headed." He points behind him. I can't tell the difference from the lake, but Aki has a listening expression on her face.

"The current is fast in the direction he's pointing," she says.

"Fine!" I say. "But only if we hug the southern shore, then at least we've a chance of spotting the canal."

The boy shrugs. "You'll have to slow down if you want me to guide you," he says. "My family will give you a warm welcome and food. If you had extra runners, we'd get there faster."

"Why don't you fly?" I snap. I know I'm being unfriendly, but he rubs me the wrong way.

"I need to start up high, or an updraft to get up there." He points at the sky. "And it's a good 20 miles to shelter."

"So you need us," I say.

"Yup!" He's unapologetic. "What if I borrow the runners on your sled, and you let the box slide on the ice?"

"Which would slow me down."

"I could pull it," he offers.

"Like I'm gonna let you skate off with our gear," I snarl.

"I'm sure you could catch me if I did," he says humbly.

And in the end we try it – taking turns with the sled. He's strong, but the long runners are awkward strapped to his feet, more like skis than skates. His sail is large, better for holding overhead than sideways. It gets in the way of the sled, slowing him down considerably. For once I'm not the slowest skater on the ice. But to give him credit, he adapts quickly. Aki slows her pace to talk to him. I skate on ahead, leaving them to share the dragging trailer for a while.

I stop at a place where the river forks. There's an enormous drift in the middle. Our map isn't detailed enough to show the river diverging, and I've no idea which way to go, though I'm guessing the right fork to the south since I want a canal that heads east – if it even is a fork. We've lost time in deep harbors and oxbows before. What confuses me even more is that where the wind has blown the snow into dips and crevasses, I'm sure I can see green. It's there for sure (*frozen or growing?*) bristling up out of the deep snow. It reminds me of the hint of green I saw at the intersection between Michigan and Huron. When the others join me, I wait for Aki to notice this latest forecast of her great Thaw.

"Which way?" I ask nonchalantly.

"To Niagara," Aki insists. Her eyes haven't spotted the green. We see what we expect to see, and right now she can't take her eyes off flying boy. I decide, rather spitefully, that I won't mention it.

"Left fork it is." The boy scratches his nose. We don't know him well enough yet to realize it's a sure sign he's lying.

• • •

We follow Flyboy north around the green, which might as well be invisible. I trail them slowly now, scanning the humped snow of the shore, looking for more signs of life. I start to imagine it everywhere, in every dip and shadow. Is that an old treetop showing? Or a bit of wild grass blown in on the wind? I picture whole forests in my head. I can almost see them, like brittle green X-rays through the snow. What happens to the frozen seeds of a forest? Could they germinate again, after decades under ice? Could any of the smallest mammals or rodents still be alive under there? Perhaps they feed off the frozen plants like the under-city folk fed off the canned produce of dead supermarkets. How long could they survive? The hints of green rekindle a small hope, a long-frozen faith in the tenacity of life. But without new growth the seeds would run out eventually, I tell myself. Nothing lasts forever.

I don't realize I've stopped until Aki comes back for me. I've been staring at the undulating hills without moving for a while. I'm amazed she even noticed my absence.

"Jack? Are you tired? Shall we stop here?" She follows my gaze. "What do you see?"

"I see green," I say finally. But of course there is none to be seen now.

She scans the shore, then frowns at me. "This is as good a place to camp as any." But it's broad daylight, and the boy has said 20 miles. I don't want to share Aki and our small camp with him. It's *our* space.

"I'm fine," I say. "Let's push through and sleep warm tonight." Aki links her arm in mine and we skate side by side for a while, sails folded, letting the boy struggle with the trailer on his own. Aki scans the shore now and again and I'm glad. Maybe she'll see the vision that I did. But she says nothing.

• • •

Twenty miles is too much after a late morning start. On the open lake with the wind behind us it would be nothing. But we're on a wide river again, the ice is rougher, the shifting wind less predictable. By late afternoon, Aki and the boy are spending half their time leaping into the air and gliding over rough patches and drift, while I slog tiredly below with the trailer, sail flat against my back. The most disturbing part of this river is the change in the hum of the current below. The further east we skate, the deeper and more resonant the sound. The hum changes to a deep thrum and, finally – when I'm exhausted and ready to stop – to a rumble that I expect to shift to the roar of open water at any moment. For the first time, I distrust the ice beneath our feet.

• • •

We never see an opening to the Erie Canal as we skate along the river, but no one could miss Niagara. It announces itself with a growing thunder I can feel now in my teeth.

The ice underfoot still seems firm but, as the sound intensifies, I imagine a raging current waiting to yank us underneath. The boy shouts back that we're hearing the voice of Niagara. The sound permeates everything. The rumble rises alongside a primal fear. I can't pinpoint where the sound is coming from; it's everywhere. My body doesn't know which way to run and hide (*and my mind is no help*). So I slide along slowly, unwilling to lose contact with the ice even for a hearty kick and glide – even though it's the ice that might betray us.

But the ice stays solid and we reach another fork – another island, so the boy says, though much smaller. The sound is overwhelming now. I just want to curl up in a ball and stress-sleep. Aki stays close, and we both look to the boy to guide us. After weeks in the immense silence of the lake ice, I discover sound can be a kind of terror.

"Is this running water?" Aki asks. Neither of us wants to go on. It's too much. If we'd found my canal, I'd have no trouble convincing Aki to turn down it now. I consider skating back the 20 miles to try the south fork of the river. Even though I'm bone tired, it seems more reasonable than continuing forward.

"This is where you need a guide!" the boy shouts at us, his words invisible, barely comprehensible.

"What is it?" Aki shouts back.

"Niagara!" he cries. And again, though his words have to weave through the rumble and roar, I sense a tone of divine passion. This is not the roar of a reasonable god. The boy, at least, is unafraid, but given his obvious religious zeal, that does nothing to lesson my fear. Quite the opposite.

Flyboy surprises me by hunkering down on the ice and pulling a red tube from his own small pack. Aki clings to my arm, and we both stand with our sails heaved to, automatically turning so the wind won't catch them. The boy fusses with a flint and steel, making a mess of sparks, until finally the end of the tube burns and he steps back. For the second time today we see something take full flight. The red cylinder flies into the air and explodes noiselessly in the sky, its bright flash lingering for a time as it drops back to ice. I support Aki so she doesn't drop flat to the ice again. The boy looks at us, as if expecting a reaction, but I just watch him coldly. I've seen these before (*though not in a very long time*). I know what he's done.

He explains flares to Aki. I stand a little away, trying to come to terms with the sound and vibrations around us, and to harness my fear. We wait for Flyboy's family to see the flare and come meet us.

• • •

When they arrive, I can see the boy's family members are not happy with him. It becomes clear that he was not to have flown so far, was expected home sooner, was not supposed to waste flares so close to home, and should, in fact, have set it off much sooner. Most of all, he was not supposed to have taken the north fork home.

"You know how long we were searching the south fork for you?" An older man, as fit and wiry as the boy, greets us graciously and thanks us for bringing home his wayward son. We follow them into the interior of the island, off the ice. It's the first time we've been off solid ice in a very long time. For Aki, it's probably the second time in her life.

When we leave the ice for an open tunnel dug through drift and snow, I feel suddenly heavy. We're no long gliding, but stomping, skates removed from our wrapped feet. Our movements are awkward and slow, our packs and trailer sudden burdens. The ice no longer vibrates and rumbles underfoot, though the overwhelming sound is still omnipresent. It doesn't feel any safer. Aki is way out of her element. After losing her connection to the ice she stumbles like a sailor landing ashore after months at sea, staggering and weak-kneed. While the dynamic currents under the ice were frightening before, they also energized her. This lack of connection is worse. I believe the feeling will pass for us both, but Aki has no experience to tell her this. I try to talk to her, but she's trying to take in too much at once, so I let her be.

The tunnels carved through the deep snow are open to the sky. We come to the end of the island and are proudly led up to a high platform chopped from the ice and packed snow. The land drops away beneath our feet, and we can finally see the spectacular ice-trapped Titan that has been growling throughout our approach – Niagara.

ICE FLIGHT

"Oh! I have slipped the surly bonds of Earth
And danced the skies on laughter-silvered wings;
Sunward I've climbed, and joined the tumbling mirth
Of sun-split clouds ..."
— *John Gillespie Magee, "High Flight"*

Niagara Falls. The falls are amazing spikes and laceworks of frozen water that sit on top, encapsulate, and, in bushy lumps and filigrees, decorate the massive currents flowing under the ice in cold slow motion, carrying giant lakes of water over the cliffs, under the ice. It's loud and glorious and almost too much to take in. Aki is completely enamored by the running water, hosing forth here and there, forced from underneath before running over the ice. We can barely get her away from it.

Eventually, we're taken into a series of underground rooms where we drop, exhausted. Despite our tiredness, we sleep uneasily with the floor and walls shaking and rumbling around us. We rise in the dark feeling unrefreshed and unable to tell if it's daylight or night. People come and feed us, ask questions, and leave again. It's like we've been transported back in time. The rooms are square; there is furniture Aki doesn't know how to use.

There are electric lights. We beg Flyboy to take us outside. He asks his father if he can take us on a pilgrimage, which I hope is just a tour.

Flyboy introduces us to a small group of people dressed in tightly woven plastics as soft looking as the memory of burlap. I stare at stitches so close together they could be machined. I often forget to look at faces. It's a failing, since expressions can tell so much. I do notice a few. Flyboy's ever-cheerful grin fills every space with energy. His father's calmer, bearded features seem to fascinate Aki. Almost every older male has a beard. I forgot that, like me, Aki's people are mostly hairless, except for the lush black hair of their heads. Flyboy's people have a lot more color variation in both skin and hair.

"Is it disease?" Aki whispers once we're out on the ice again, relieved to be in the open air and sun. It takes me a moment to realize she's referring to the father's grizzled beard. I consider teasing her but finally concede that no, this is hair that grows on the chins of some people and can protect from the cold.

"It is very ugly," she says, "but possibly useful."

• • •

We walk north, reveling in the sun but feeling ungainly without our skates. We've been on them so long I feel heavy and slow. To my dismay, Flyboy leads us back underground again into a narrow tunnel behind a wall of ice. We seem to be heading back the way we've just come, but this time we're inside the belly of the giant falls. The roof is low. The walls thunder and shake. The way is lit by the arc lights we've seen everywhere. These are set into the cement walls of the tunnel, electricity leaping between two bare points, uncovered by any glass or bulb. The very air buzzes and I feel my hair lift as we pass each light. There are so many threats in the sound, and now in the feeling of the air, it's

160

hard to concentrate on what the people are saying. After a while everyone falls silent. It's too difficult to speak, and the shaking of the falls makes all other concerns lesser.

Occasionally there are side tunnels that may have opened once under the falls, but little is visible even in the arc light. One seems filled with chunks of ice, another with thin frozen spears. We can hear, but not see, the water thundering around us. Which is more powerful? Running water? Or frozen ice? Wind whips water and slides off ice, but this water is pounding with a ferocity that makes the floor under our feet tremble, and my mind goes a little numb with fear and the need to escape. Like the under-city, this is not a place I can be in for long. I try to picture the ice fields we traversed for so many days: the blue skies and the way the light on the snow splinters away into the huge curve of the horizon. I try to hold on to that peaceful feeling, but the rumble of the falls turns the vision ominous.

We walk farther in, my mind screaming to get out, get up, find the sun. How can humans even *be* in places like this? Eventually we emerge on a slope of scree, so steep the snow seems to have slid off. The cliffs tower 100 feet above, with the ice river even farther down below. The frozen falls are an alien sculpture behind us. Spray swirls, blowing out from under and around the impossible frothy ice monument. The spray adds its substance to new stalagmites and stalactites as we watch. A path has been carefully beaten down onto the scree, though it's covered in black ice. We're given odd textured boot coverings, which we pull on before continuing along the path. A misstep would send us onto the rocks, but it's impossible not to stop and stare up at the dizzying height, or the glorious blocks and spires and bridges of spikes that make up the mighty horseshoe waterfall of ice behind us, curving away in a deep bow. We can hear the massive water, see the spray, and observe disturbed giant blocks of ice below. But of actual running water, that rumbling animal, we can see little. The fall is a frozen, trembling confection, waiting for a sunbeam or a single high note, to send fragments of itself crashing into the river below and set free the water beast.

We climb the treacherous path around the cliff, feet sliding on iced and frosted scree. Eventually, we see another icefall ahead, thinner, another frosted tribute to the terrible beauty of ice. Behind it, we find another cavern, open to the sky. The spray is worse here, billowing out in visible clouds, instantly turning to snow as it spews out from under the ice. We all turn frosty. Aki's brows and eyelashes have turned white, and I can feel alarm bells going off in my head; even my invisible mental mini god (*who does not always suggest options that lead to survival*) wants us gone from here. Getting soaked is death out in the open. The leader guides us to the very back of the cave. I keep telling myself that if they can stand it, we can. But I'm not entirely sure these people are sane. How could they be, living in this threateningly glorious place?

At the back of the cave the world turns from frothy blue and white ice to disappointingly flat gray cement as we pass an open arch that leads to a doorway into a small dingy room set deep into the rock. Inside a few people are tending to a machine. I can smell hot engine oil – and something more alive. Electricity. Which would explain the lights. I can see the machine is some kind of generator, presumably creating power from the falls. It seems there's far more produced than is used in the arc lights, for the air is greasy with potential energy. When it feels like the very atmosphere in the room will explode, one of the tenders throws a switch and there's a pop. The power rushes elsewhere, and the air calms a little. I take a deep breath and try to take Aki's hand. But she has them tucked under her arms, hugging herself. Her eyes are wide and she's pale. The machines look old and some parts mismatched. The people tending them look tired. We move on through greasy air and noise. I can only hope we'll find a quiet place soon. How can people live like this?

• • •

Thankfully we leave the room, but only to go deeper in, where the rumble and shake of the falls immediately over-whelms the shriller whine of the machines. Flyboy turns to us with the rapturous look of a man who has walked through nirvana. He may have expected us to reflect back his joy, because his face falls as he looks us over. Aki is hugging herself miserably. I'm fighting my own demons to stay awake and alert and alive. Neither of us have experienced anything on this earth with the power this unseen water-fall displays. If Aki's god is ice, and her gift to find running water, what does it mean to her to be inside this shaking, plummeting insanity? Focusing on Aki helps me cope.

"Aki," I say sharply, "even this water can become ice." But even as I say it, I wonder if it's true.

"I thought water was weaker than ice," she laughs shak-ily. "Guess I was wrong."

"Why look to compare when it's all one?" Flyboy's father speaks calmly. "Ice is water, water is ice. They can even make fire," and the man points to one of the arc lights set in the wall. Flyboy grabs Aki's arm as she moves toward the lamp.

"You can't touch it," he says.

"Water and ice made this?" Aki is confused. I can't clearly explain the process either. How in the world have these people kept electrical generators running all this time?

"The machines we passed," I say to Aki gruffly, since our guides aren't even trying to explain, "they turn the motion of the water into power, which makes light as it jumps between those two points."

"Very good," the older man says, looking at me with not a speck of friendliness in his eyes. Have I stepped on a religious landmine?

"I'm impressed that you can run them," I say.

"I'm eager to hear how you know what they are," he replies.

Whoops! "Ah. Big reader in my youth," I say. But I can tell he's not finished with me yet. "May we go back? All this raw power is making me dizzy."

"Please!" Aki begs. "Back outside!"

Instead, Flyboy takes her arm and pulls her farther in. "Now wait a minute!" I'm angry. We need to get out of here. "It's time for the tour to be over!"

Flyboy opens a sliding grate in the wall. Inside is a platform I recognize as a lift. I can't believe it. There's no way this should still be in operation. But the metal looks solid and Flyboy struts aboard confidently.

"Don't worry," he grins, "we are going back up."

I step past the gate and Flyboy's father follows. A few others crowd in, but some of the group stay behind. I wouldn't recognize one of them if I saw them again.

Flyboy shuts the gate and throws a switch. The platform is yanked upward and Aki falls to her knees. She has no idea what's happening. I can see from the father's face that I'm not supposed to either.

"Ooh, magic!" I say, reaching down to help Aki stand. He's not buying it.

"We will talk," he says. Then we step out onto an overlook.

• • •

Somehow we're back where we started. I understand that there are at least two falls, and we've walked between and behind one of them, and back to the first again before riding back up to the top.

"There's one more thing you must see." Flyboy is having way too much fun. His father addresses him sternly.

"You *will* show respect."

Flyboy looks shocked.

"Of course, Father! But don't they need to understand?"

"They can try," the father's tone is dismissive. He's looking at Aki, who does look overwhelmed. She's been a child of the open ice for so long, with only her fast sailing to challenge her in that empty landscape. But I underestimate her. She's also the child of travelers and almost, once, the leader of her family. She adapts better than I, who just closes down when life becomes too much. Aki doesn't have that option.

"Show us," she says firmly.

We walk again on top of the waterfall, moving inland this time, through the open tunnels of snow that let the sun in overhead. After a short while, we step down into a kind of theater pit carved into the ice, concentric circles that could serve as chilly benches for a crowd to sit and stare at the thing that dominates the middle of the circle. It's huge, man-shaped, and covered in black ice. For a moment, I flash to Aki's parents. Is this another sacrifice? But no, it's far too big.

Flyboy grins at us, and then his face turns rapturously to the dark, ice-coated figure of a giant sitting with a parchment in his lap, apparently reading.

"The great Nikolateslainventor," he intones, "'whose-discoveries-in-the-field-of-alternating-electric-current-advanced-the-world-into-the-modern-industrial-era.'"

"The wha?"

"The modern-industrial-era," Flyboy says happily. "You know. Now!"

If this is the modern industrial era, I'll eat my skates.

• • •

"So Tesla is a god, one ancient electrical generator an industrial era makes, and your people have hydroelectricity, weaving, and really good hang-gliding kites." I'm alone with Flyboy's father, the paternal leader of this family. The family is big, more than twice Aki's family, and they're eating well enough. Though I notice they seem to eat mostly dried rather than fresh fish – brought to them in trade. They also have engine oil, wire, generator parts. "Is this the height of civilization?"

"Tesla?" the older man says. "You mean Nikolateslainventor?"

"Uh, yeah. Him."

"Scientists may venerate, but we do not worship any god." The old man is dead serious. "We are scientists and engineers. We run the great machines. And yes, we are aware of being the pinnacle of civilization."

"And what civilization is that?" I say dryly. I'm going to get myself iced. But this guy fascinates me. I want to know what makes him tick.

"We are Niagararians," the old man says calmly. "We trade with lesser peoples who provide food and materials so we may continue our great works. We are above them both physically and mentally, trained from birth in the great art of Nikolateslainventor to run the generators, produce power, and light the darkness."

He turns his old gray eyes on me – eyes that have stared out at the frozen falls and listened to their internal roar since birth. This man has lived with the terrible shaking of massive currents in his bones every day of his life. He must be a little mad.

"And who," he says, "are you?"

Who am I? Good question. "I suppose I can tell you, since you're a scientist. You would know the theory of time travel."

The eyes never waver on mine. "Go on."

"I'm a time traveler. I did not know Tesla," I add quickly. *Don't mess with people's gods*. "But I've seen many of his inventions in use. I've seen the massive cities his generators powered." Nothing like the truth to validate a good lie.

"I've seen pictures of these," the old man breathes. "Niagara Falls and both sides of the river lit up with Alternating Current!"

"Yes. And more."

"There is no more," the man says flatly. "It is clearly written that Niagara is 'Top of the World,' its generators a 'Pinnacle of Engineering,' and its hydroelectric output a 'Testament to the Modern Industrial Era.' What *'more'* could you possibly be referring to?"

"Where is this written?" I ask hesitantly. My half-jesting explanation of my origins could become complicated. It's interesting that he didn't question its validity though.

That doesn't sound like good old-fashioned scientific skepticism to me.

"The sacred scientific literature," the old engineer says. And because I'm also, presumably, some sort of scientist – since I know what a generator is and have traveled through time in some fashion, no doubt knowable only to the great Tesla – I'm taken to see them.

Plastic lasts. Sometimes longer than metal, longer than oil and wood. Longer than most of the species that used to live on this cold earth. If alien anthropologists ever land on this lump after humans have finally given it up, they will dig down to a layer of plastic from the industrial age the way we used to dig for pottery and clamshell middens. If I ever want to leave a record of the incredible things I've seen humanity live and die through, I think I'll carve it into plastic.

The Niagararian leader takes me to an excavation in the ice full of lovely plastic, all with the name NIAGARA FALLS printed bold and legible. There are plaques and globes, spoons and dolls, mini-Teslas standing on tiny plastic generators. There are plates and plastic medallions and squashed water bottles. There are waterproof journals (which I lust after) and brief laminated pictorial histories. There are toy-sized Tesla coils.

It seems the Niagararian Scientists are basing their beliefs, their self-identities, and possibly even their engineering know-how on the Niagara Falls Souvenir Gift Shop.

••••

Keycha, who questions and tests every idea, is my idea of a real scientist. I dream that night that I really can travel through time, not just forward, as we all do, but also back. The rumble of the falls judders into my dreams and becomes a train rattling through a golden prairie.

••••

Aki and Keycha are by my side in the train car, murmuring happily about the massive herds of animals swooping beside, and sometimes through, the train. A herd of buffalo thunders past, turning to cut across the tracks and passing as white ghosts through the car. My caribou are back, running alongside in numbers so great, their antlers look like forests of trees. They fade into odder animals from other continents. Gemsbok, giraffes, then tiny antelope with sharp conical horns and even smaller jumping things, and finally packs of dogs and rodents flow over the landscape like waves. I try to turn to Keycha, to tell him it's like old movies I've seen of dinosaurs trekking through a drought-ridden landscape, but there's only a pile of old bones and scat sitting beside me on a rock. My companions, the train, and the running animals are long gone, but something gigantic passes overhead, casting a long shadow over the ground like the arched threat of a scorpion's tail.

"Banji wa yumé." My temporarily Buddhist, invisible godlet whispers in my mind as I drift awake. "All things are merely dreams."

● ● ●

Flyboy has more fun than his old man. He's a true believer in Nikola-Tesla-Inventor ("Slow it down," I tell him), but he doesn't let it ruin his day. Flyboy flies like Aki sails – with joy. They have a lot in common, so I make it my job to be monkey-in-the-middle. But I get tired of hounding him after a while. He seems like a good-enough guy. I'm a little worried about the flying lessons, though. They look dangerous. But Flyboy always takes Aki upriver, never toward the falls. They start on skates, but soon he presents her with a larger kite for longer flights, a sturdy thing of woven plastic on light aluminum struts. How he shaped the scavenged aluminum I never do find out. Much of the Niagararian gear comes to them in trade. Flyboy admires our smaller sails, which I'm quite sure were originally mass-produced for the purpose for which we use them, and then stored well somewhere near the tanker. They're just too good. But I can see a day coming when we'll need to replace the thin, aged nylon sails with the heavier hand-woven scavenged plastic that Flyboy has access to.

He really is the young prince of the Niagararian, and he seems to have set his sights on Aki, but she is thankfully oblivious to anything except learning as much as she can. So I'm not too worried – yet.

"Who makes these?" I ask him finally, fingering the fabric of a kite. I think I've been in almost every cavern and room I can find in my wandering, but saw not a single loom.

"We trade with the folk downriver for them," he says and shrugs. I wonder if it's smart for him not to know how something so important to his life is made.

"What would you do if you couldn't get any more?" I ask, and leave him thinking about that.

Later I hear him asking his father if he can learn to weave plastic. That gets me a trip to the principal's office.

"You and your companion may stay here as long as you need, but I'll ask you not to get involved in our family matters," the old man says severely.

"Why would it be so bad for him to learn?" I ask. "He uses his kite every day. Shouldn't he know everything he can about it?"

"My son has a higher calling," is all the old fart will say.

There are other young people in this family, and Aki enjoys the company of that group, though I soon tire of it. So I end up spending time with the leader and his gaggle of old men, often talking about the generators. He doesn't seem to have the same resistance to finding out as much as he can about *those*. All their talk about "science" gets me thinking about what I remember about electricity.

I have some memories about simple mechanics. I remember how to build a battery and rudimentary motor with scavenged nails, copper wire, and the magnets that Keycha gave me. (*Sort of. I only stole two and the Grandmother wasn't around to complain by then.*)

I show some of the younger kids how to create a basic vinegar battery with a copper strip (positive) connected to an old zinc-coated, galvanized nail (negative) stuck into a cup of fermented water-weed vinegar. We attach leads from the outermost positive and negative forks of three linked vinegar batteries and balance a wire bent into a coil in the middle. We center the coil above one of the magnets and watch it spin. It's a kids' game I learned long ago, before the crossing. But it gets me another visit to the office.

This time the old man wants me to show him how it's done. His willingness to learn seems to be a good sign, but when he finds my batteries are too weak to do more than spin the coil of wire, he loses interest. Again, I can't help comparing him with Keycha, who would have thought of a dozen applications for, and improvements to, my vinegar battery.

When I mention the use of batteries for storing electricity, the old man is dismissive. "If Nikolateslainventor had wanted us to store electricity …," he actually starts to say.

"But of course he did!" I say heatedly. "Everyone was trying to perfect the battery right up until …." I stop. Why go there? Didn't the industrial age create the pollution that changed our climate so it would fry and freeze the earth? Why reinvent disaster? (*It's the clever ones like Keycha that got the world into this mess,* my evil, internal little god snickers. *It's the clever ones like Keycha who allow us to continue,* I want to answer back – but that would just be me talking to myself again.)

"How do you trade power with the other villages if you can't store it?" I ask, and the old man looks annoyed. Perhaps Flyboy has been giving away secrets he wasn't supposed to again.

"We have … other generators," he says slowly. "We provide power for limited hours via conduits. We find that the closer the source of generation is to the user, the less loss of power. But if the villagers could store energy, who knows what they might do with it, where it might end up." Perhaps the old man is ethical, in his own way.

"Are you afraid people will misuse electricity?"

"It is very powerful," the old man says, sadly. "We've lost family members to it, when someone was careless, or there was a surge."

He wants something from me. He has that look.

"How … did Scientists harness it … in the past?" He sounds ashamed to be asking, which I can't figure out.

"I'm not sure I know how to answer you. Perhaps if I knew what was going wrong?"

"Nothing goes wrong," the old man says automatically, but he seems to have questions that he can't ask.

"In the past," I say, clicking and unclicking my magnets together, "scientists were all about asking questions and testing ideas – as objectively as possible."

"I find that highly unlikely," the old man says dryly.

Ah. He may have a point.

I leave, but something bothers me. The Niagararians venerate Tesla, who was famous for his alternating current, AC, which was used in households around the world before the snows. So why is the old scientist so worried about losing power, presumably to cable resistance, over what must be relatively short distances? What was Edison's complaint about alternating current? I know he and Tesla competed. I vaguely remember a story about Edison electrocuting animals using Tesla's AC to try and convince people it was unsafe, in order to promote his own DC (direct current) model. What was the issue? That DC was safer but AC could go farther? Maybe I should have another look at that one generator the old man allowed us to see. I wonder if I can even tell the difference between a DC and AC generator. AC should have a moving magnet, but .... Ugh, the information is so old and my memory so faulty. But I do remember that AC can be processed through a transformer to vary the voltage and current.

Transformers allow electricity to travel over distance by transmitting it at low current and high voltage, then reducing the voltage and increasing the current at the receiving end. This reduces the power loss from cable resistance (the main problem with Edison's direct current). So if the old man is looking for ways to deliver electricity over distance, and doesn't have batteries, and if he is indeed producing Tesla's alternating current, then he just needs some good transformers, which I vaguely remember being constructed using a particular formula for looping wire to change the ratio between voltage and current running through it. But that's all I've got. I'm no engineer, just a time traveler with a flawed memory.

What we all really need is a good library. I also want more information about how all this electricity is being used. Maybe limiting use isn't such a bad thing, though I feel a kind of optimism when I think about the possibility of improving the lives of the imagined people downriver. Maybe Keycha's ethics have rubbed off on me a little. Can I imagine Aki's family with electricity? No. It would have no place out on the ice. But in Keycha's workshop? Wow, so many applications. But my mind boggles when I suddenly picture Keycha lighting up the under-city. Not that he would. And would any of us want those gigantic, polluting cities to come back again, even if it were possible to feed all the people who used to live in them? All that fire, after all, led to all this ice.

I walk out into the sun to find Aki and the flyers.

• • •

Aki and her new friends are practicing lifts by running down a light slope – the built-up shoreline covered in meters of snow (another buried city?) – and lifting off upstream, away from the falls. The winds are enough to send the seasoned flyers spiraling higher, but Aki's new kite, gifted by Flyboy (*who does have a name, though I won't use it. Oscar or O'car, I think I heard someone call him*), seems to be giving her trouble. She nosedives into a drift shortly after lift-off. Flyboy pulls her upright, laughing, just as I arrive. Her cheeks are rosy and her goggles askew. She's happy. Three more flyers land to laugh with her and give her tips, and soon they're all off again, dotting the sky with spiraling bird shapes.

I'm so enthralled by the circling grace of the kites that I imagine, for a moment, that they are birds on a winter day. I can no longer remember the names of the largest of the birds-that-were, but I keep expecting the kites to flap once before gliding on.

A flyer thuds down near me in a swirl of snow, pushing up goggles and grinning from under a woven brown cap.

"Are you here to become a flyer, friend? The festival is coming up soon but there's still time to practice."

Suddenly Flyboy is there too. I never noticed him approaching. He's left his kite anchored on the slope.

"Father has other plans for this one," he says, thumping me hard on the back. It hurts. "He's got engineering talent."

"What about Aki?" I ask.

"She'll fly," he says, shading his eyes to watch her. She's lower than the others. I can just hear their thin cries of encouragement on the wind.

"Is that her choice?"

"Who wouldn't want to fly?" But he's not looking at me, so I turn to the newcomer.

"What's the festival for?"

The small brown flyer's mouth drops open, as if she's never heard this question before.

Flyboy waves her away and she trudges back toward the slope, struggling when the wind tips her oversized kite the wrong way. Flyboy turns to me.

"We fly to prove ourselves." His face is more serious than usual. "It's my chance to learn to be a real Engineer, to eventually take my place as a Scientist."

"What does flying have to do with running generators?"

He shrugs. "The first Engineer, Fatherbenfranklin, flew a kite to discover electricity in the air. Nikolateslainventor harnessed the electricity of the water. During the festival we ground one of the kites to include the electric fire running to earth."

"The four essential elements." I nod. "Earth, air, fire, and water." Aki would include ice.

"Air, fire, water, and earth," he corrects me, then grins. "Though my father would put water first."

"So you prove yourself as a flyer at the festival, then start your training as an engineer?"

He nods enthusiastically. "We fly off the top of Niagara Falls into a lightning storm. Those that survive study to become Scientists. Those that do not are given back to the elements."

That doesn't make any sense. "Wait a minute. Why wouldn't you survive? You all fly perfectly and it's what, 200 feet down? I've seen you go up higher than that. And who has seen lightning in ages?" I don't remember a single thundersnow since I awoke under the ice.

"Oh, there will be lighting. The falls demand their yearly sacrifice," he says, not smiling. "All of the villages send representatives to participate in the choosing."

Aki circles back toward the slopes, coming down a little fast. A couple of flyers track her from a higher elevation, hooting encouragement.

"What about Aki? Will she fly? Will she become a Scientist too?" I remember the dismissive way the old leader addressed her. "And will I be asked to fly?" *That'll be the day.*

"My father already considers you a Scientist; you have skills to share. You won't be asked to prove yourself – at the festival." But Flyboy is staring at me intently. "I do not believe my father will accept Aki as a future Engineer."

"So she won't fly."

"It will be required of her."

I stare at him. "Aki is the sacrifice?"

Flyboy says nothing, but he isn't looking away either.

"Why are you telling me? Did you just pick us up so Aki could save you and your friends by being the sacrifice at your dumb festival?"

"No," he says. "I'd hoped you would be."

That shuts me up.

•••

Flyboy and I agree to meet later and make a plan to protect Aki. Then we slog over to greet her on the slope. I'm not sure I trust him at all, but I trust his father less, if only because it's clear Flyboy has a thing for Aki. Let's hope he feels strongly enough about her to break a few taboos. It's clearly time for us to move on again.

The father's comment about needing to generate electricity close to where it's being used gets me thinking again about losing electrical power over distance. How could he run a generator and not use transformers? How hard could it be to make a transformer if he already understands the principles of a generator? And what is it about transformers, those coils that can hugely increase voltage, that make the old man cagey about information?

What was Tesla most famous for? The invisible friend in my head asks the best questions. It's why I let them stick around. And Flyboy has already provided the answer.

Lightning.

I decide to play devil's advocate with the old man again to see what I can get him to admit. I plan to mention the name Edison. That ought to bunch his Tesla-loving panties in a wad.

•••

Edison's name works like mentioning the Antichrist to the Inquisition. The old man spends way too long reviling the man who disrespected Tesla's alternating current in favor of his own direct current design. Then he decides to take me to the inner holy sanctum to *prove* Tesla's genius to me – in good scientific fashion. We take the elevator back down to the Cave of Winds.

Turns out that the old man has a transformer after all. It's the biggest fracking transformer I've ever even heard of. Hidden behind a door in one of the cave rooms, one wall completely open to the view downriver between the waterfalls, is a gigantic Tesla coil. At over 15 feet tall, it's horrifyingly big. If it works, it should be able to make lightning by drawing from the most powerful hydroelectric source in the Western Hemisphere, Niagara Falls. Which answers my question about how the fireworks will be provided for the festival. I suspect it isn't just electricity the old man trades for the food and resources provided by the lake villages. He's also trading in magic and fear.

I wonder why he doesn't use villagers for the yearly sacrifice – Flyboy said something about the villages participating. No doubt that's why Aki and I were welcomed in so easily. Maybe visitors are always encouraged this time of year. I'm a little surprised the old man showed me the lightning generator, though, if he's planning on sacrificing Aki. He should be smart enough to know he can't kill off my companion and keep my trust. I wonder if he knows that his prince and heir, Flyboy – who dreams of becoming a Scientist – may even now be thinking of running away with Aki into the icy unknown (*if I can believe his last urgent whisper on the slopes*). What a romantic. Just goes to show that hormones outperform intellect any day. Plus he's at *that* age. So am I though, technically. And I wouldn't jump off Niagara Falls hanging from a flimsy bolt of woven plastic – for anyone.

Let's hope Flyboy is smarter than I give him credit for. I'll work with him for Aki's sake. I need Aki. I've become pretty clear about that in my own mind. I miss her when she isn't around. I'm a little jealous of her friendship with the flyers. I'm looking forward to running away with her in the night, for both our sakes. I never planned on staying here this long. But Aki's been having so much fun learning to fly there seemed no need to rush away. Perhaps we both needed a break from each other's company, after weeks together on the ice. But now I'm eager to get back to our traveling life. To simplify things again, even knowing it will be harder to find food and exhausting to keep moving into the unknown. I may actually miss my conversations about the past with this old man. I wonder when travel itself became a goal.

The old man interrupts my thoughts.

"I need you here," he says, as if he can read my mind.

"What?"

"I need you here, during the festival. Will you stay with the coil?"

"No!" I say automatically. I can just imagine the filaments and streamers of voltage pouring out of that thing when it connects to a power source. I wonder whether the amperage would be enough to fry someone standing nearby. How would one know?

The old man frowns at me, then goes to the wall and opens a yellowed plastic tub. Inside is a pile of rubberized metallic cloth. It unfolds stiffly into a full body suit, with booties, gloves, and a hood. The lapel has an ancient Westinghouse icon: a "W" with three balls on top, and the word: "Lineman."

"Now will you?"

Well. No. But I don't tell him that. The ancient Faraday suit has given me an idea.

• • •

Flyboy and I talk far into the night. The festival is only a few days away, and he utterly rejects my plan to simply leave with Aki while everyone is asleep.

"We control all the towns along this river," he says. "They owe fealty to my father."

"So we don't stop." I feel irritable. It should be so simple. "We just keep ahead of them. How far do we have to go?"

178

"You need to get past the river and well onto the lake. There's a trading town about five days' skate from river's end along the south shore of the lake. It's called Oswego. We trade with them, but they're independent. They owe us nothing."

"So what's the problem?"

"You can't stay ahead of us."

"You can glide down the entire river length?"

"I can fly farther than you can skate in a day. You should have learned to fly," he says sadly, as if he can't understand why I wouldn't want to.

"So what do we do then?"

"You could stay and let Aki fly away," he says. "I could go with her. We could wait for you in Oswego."

This doesn't feel right to me. "But you want to stay, as long as Aki is allowed to. Right? So why would you leave?"

"I told you; my father won't let Aki become a Scientist. She has no aptitude."

"But if she survives the flight off Niagara, he has to let her stay anyway, right?"

He doesn't answer.

"Your father wants me to stay, but not Aki. You want Aki to stay, but not me. Have I got that right?"

The boy has the grace to blush.

"So we all go!" the boy says quickly. "Aki won't leave without you anyway. I asked her." (*Charming.*) "If we leave as seasoned flyers – if we complete the ceremony – no one can touch us. But You! Can't! Fly!" He glares at me.

I think about it. He's willing to give up a lot to help us. To help Aki. I have to decide to trust him – or not.

"Who will the sacrifice be?"

"One of the villagers … perhaps." He doesn't want to look at me, but it would be a hard thing to talk about. One of his friends and family, or one of the villagers, will die in Aki's place.

"What happens if there is no sacrifice? What if everyone lives?"

"Then the Great Thaw comes and washes us all into the sea." It sounds like he's quoting something used to frighten children rather than something he believes.

"What really happens?" I insist. "What if everyone flies through the lightning and lands safely?"

"It's not like that," he says. "Because we tether one kite – to the lightning machine."

• • •

"Are you out of your mind?!" I'm not angry, exactly. Just utterly gobsmacked. Does this guy think I'm a total idiot?

"I don't fly, so you want to put me in a kite 200 feet in the air. I don't want to die, so you tether me to a monster Tesla coil putting out who knows how many amps to fry me to a crisp. Do you think I'm gonna just nod and say '*duh*, okay' and let you kill off the competition?" (*And what are we competing for exactly? Aki?*)

"I want to put you in a different kind of kite! The one we tether is bigger and holds more air. Anyone can fly it. It's a bell shape that can stay aloft on its own longer and comes down slower. It's a little harder to steer, but much safer. If the wind is right it could take you all the way to river's end!"

"Except that I'll be TIED. TO. LIGHTNING!"

"So untie it." He says it like it's so simple.

Maybe it is.

"Do you always tether the sacrifice?"

"That's the beauty of it. You will already be sacrificed and then you'll float off, so no one will think to look for you. Aki and I will follow after you. If you get off track, just tilt the bell and land. We'll come down to you. I'll have our skates in a pouch."

"Great plan. Except for the sacrifice bit. And the flying bit. And the why-am-I-even-having-this-conversation-with-you bit."

"The lightning plays over all the kites. It doesn't hurt at all. In fact, often flyers will add bits of metal to their kites to attract it. Flying within the lightning is a sign of power."

"Then why does it kill the sacrifice?'

He hesitates, then leans close. "The sacrifice is tethered by a line wrapped in copper wire," he says softly. "But we'd swap it out!"

Dear god, not just a conductor, but a coil to increase amperage. They'd fry. *I'd* fry.

Not even I would come back to life after being hit with 2 amps or more. I've always believed that I *can* die, given the right circumstances. I've even considered it as an option. But you know what, I argue with myself, forget that. Even when things are at their grimmest, change happens – eventually. Things get better again – or at least different. And life is so very interesting. I'm just a freakin' billboard for the tenacity of life.

So of course I tell Flyboy to get stuffed. But I walk away thinking about that lineman's suit. It was essentially a Faraday cage and would distribute any electrostatic charge around the exterior of the suit's mesh, canceling the charge inside (and protecting me). It would make a great light show around a tethered flyer while keeping them safe from any increased amperage by re-distributing the electricity around the suit.

So who wasn't telling the truth here? If the old man wants me alive enough to lend me the Faraday suit, why stick me in the sacrificial chair – or kite – in the first place? If Flyboy wants to help me escape, why not tell me about the suit? They both want me in the hot seat for what reasons? Status? Acceptance? Escape? What's Flyboy not telling me?

I get the distinct feeling that Flyboy and his dad need to have a long talk. Leaving in the night still seems like the safest way out for me and Aki. We need to talk.

•••

I find Aki where I least expect. Inside, lying on our shared futon, staring into nothing.

"You tired?" I ask, plopping down beside her.

"Every muscle screaming." She sighs and rolls on her side to face me. "Jack, are we gonna stay here forever?" She surprises me.

"Do you want to?"

"I'm not sure," she says. "I feel like if we don't go soon, we'll build our lives around this place and be here for good."

"I'm ready to go."

"Really?" She looks happy for a minute, then thoughtful. "But I do want to fly off the waterfall with the others."

"Why?"

"Well, we've been working so hard for it. It's like, proof that I can do it, that I'm one of them?"

"That sounds like you really want to stay."

"Nooo." She draws the word out, as if to test it.

"Do you want to grow old here?" I ask bitterly. "With Flyboy?"

"What? No! What're you talking about?"

"He likes you."

"Maybe. But I'm not sure he … values me."

"Do you like him?"

"He's better than the fishermen."

"Argh!" I throw myself flat on the futon beside her. "*I'm* better than the fishermen."

"Yup!" She smiles at me.

"Am I better than Flyboy?"

Aki looks a little alarmed. "Why … would you ask that?"

"Do you want to go with me, or stay with him?"

"Oh! Go with you, dummy."

"Thank gods." I bury my face in the mat.

Aki touches my hair tentatively. "Jack? What's going on?" She pushes at my shoulder. "You saying you value my company?"

"Better than a poke in the eye with a sharp stick," I mutter, and she smacks me.

"You're my family," Aki says comfortably, which disappoints me a little, for reasons I don't care to examine too closely. "So. Is it time to move on then?"

"It is."

"Our gear is easy to collect, I think. Though I'll have to get my old skating kite back. And we'll need to ask for some food if we're leaving."

"Flyboy says they won't let us go unless we prove ourselves flying off the falls at the festival."

"Pshh. That's easy enough," she says. "Oh! But ... what about you?"

"He and his dad want to put me in a kind of kite, it sounds like a parachute really, that's supposed to pretty much fly itself."

"Can't see you doing that!" Aki says cheerfully.

"Plus, it's tethered ..."

"But ...."

"... to a lighting machine ..."

Which takes some explaining for someone who's never seen lightning. Fortunately, the arc lamps provide a simple example. I throw a piece of weed into the arc and we watch it burn while I tell her everything.

In the end, it's Aki who cuts through all the confusion by pointing out that whatever they're claiming, both father and son seem to want to kill me rather spectacularly. And it's Aki, former almost-leader of her people, who comes up with a solid escape plan.

•••

We play their game. I agree with Flyboy's plan to swap out the conducting copper-wrapped tether for a plain non-conducting line. I tell the old man I'll wear the lineman's suit to protect me from the electromagnetic fingers of lightning the Tesla coil will send out. It will be a grand show, I tell the old man. I'll cut the tether and escape downriver, I tell Flyboy.

Aki and I work far into the next few nights, careful to get at least a few hours' sleep so we don't wear out from exhaustion. We steal dried fish and weed from the kitchens and hide our packs and skates below the Cave of Winds, down in a giant pile of rubble. I really hope it will be possible to navigate those slippery rocks later, in the dusk. We have to leave our bulky sled behind.

We sleep on the hard stone floor while Aki – with me trying to help – turns the cover of our futon into two whitish cloaks. We turn the interior of the futon into something else.

When we're almost ready, I ask Aki, once again, to just leave with me in the dark. It's the night before the festival and the tunnels are full of travelers from the villages and nervous teens getting ready for their flights the next day. I doubt anyone would notice us missing with all the new people milling about. The kitchens are in constant rotation, and there are folks sleeping in the halls. I'm intrigued by the village folk. They're deferential to the Niagararians, but there's an edge to them too. They're here to compete, to give their children a chance at the life the Scientists have. But I also get a feeling they're as dismissive of the Scientists as the Scientists are of them. It's a mystery to me.

"Shtoopid," Aki tells me. "Don't you feel defensive when some jumped-up Scientist acts all snooty with you? I've seen it on your face. It's the same thing."

"Then why do they put up with it?"

"Maybe because everyone is given an equal chance once a year? And really, the lights and all are pretty impressive." The villagers, like Aki, like to stare at the many arc lamps, the kids sometimes daring each other to touch, which always gets them a smack. They villagers aren't allowed on the lift, but the Scientists seem to use it more when they're around, rising and sinking mysteriously to an "ooh-ing" crowd.

"Whatever," I say. "Let's just go already."

"Go where?" Flyboy is in our doorway, looking irritable. "Are you still on about leaving before the flight? You know the flyers will just bring you back."

"You being one of them?" I snap.

"Of course not." Flyboy is still saying he's coming with us. But I haven't noticed him packing up food or gear for the trip. "I'll be with you."

"Can you really give all this up?" I wave toward the crowded hallway, and Aki elbows me sharply. Why am I questioning him now? But I really don't understand what he's up to. I want to know.

Flyboy looks out the door, his face as haughty as any prince. Then he laughs at me and takes Aki's hand. "This is what I can't give up," and he kisses the back of her hand. She actually blushes and giggles.

I'm horrified. Who is this person and what have they done with my Aki?

But she treads on my foot as she leads Flyboy to the door, just so I know everything's okay.

"I'll meet you in the Cave of Winds before the flight," Flyboy says to me.

"Better not," I say. "Your dad plans to see me off."

"My father?" Flyboy pauses. "Why?"

"Don't worry," I say. "It doesn't change anything. Besides, I want you to be the one who releases my kite from the top of the falls." The tethered flyer will step from the cave containing the Tesla coil, already strapped into a harness, and hooking it to a rope let down from above – leading up to the parachute-style kite on the clifftop. The chute is too broad for the cave and needs the greater height to fill the bell. "I only trust you to make sure it's done properly."

"Yes," Flyboy says thoughtfully. "You can count on me."

"Oh, but then you won't be at my side when we fly off the falls." Aki pouts at him.

Flyboy looks slightly appalled. "This is a test of courage, not a time to flirt," he says stiffly. Then he softens his tone with an apparent effort. "We will have all the time there is – later." He smiles that boyish smile at her. Fortunately, Aki waits until he leaves to make gagging noises.

"You know what stinks?" she says later.

"What?"

"I did kind of like him. Before he decided to kill us."

"Hmph," I say. "What makes you think *you* were gonna die?"

"Have you seen the kite he gave me?" she asks grimly. "The handlebars are wrapped in copper." Aki is *such* a quick study.

• • •

I ask the old man to meet me earlier than planned in the Cave of Winds. He agrees so readily I wonder if I haven't misread him after all. When he arrives, he's in ceremonial dress: a flight suit embossed with icons of all the elements. There are three horizontal wavy lines for water, five stacked dots for earth, a lightning bolt for fire, and vertical curls for air. There's an extra one I don't recognize, a triangle with a ragged point.

"Ice," he informs me when I ask. Ha! A new element. Aki would be pleased.

He shows me how to turn the Tesla coil on and off. He hands me the lineman's suit, and then starts climbing into the kite harness himself. I see no sign of the plain tether I'm meant to swap for the carefully coiled copper-wrapped tether leading to the silent Tesla coil, which rises like an evil mushroom out of the middle of the room.

"What're you doing?" I ask and he looks at me oddly.

"Surely it's obvious? You will assist me by turning the coil on – there. You will help me launch once they drop the parachute tether from above. After some time has gone by, you will turn off the coil and pull me back in."

"I thought I was the one flying," I say stupidly. As if I had any intention of doing so.

"You? the old man laughs. "You're hardly qualified yet. This is the Head Scientist's moment of glory. It's traditional. This year I'll be wreathed in more lightning than any other flyer, thanks to my son's clever tether design."

The copper penny drops. Flyboy lied to all of us.

"Have you ever flown with that kind of tether before?"

"Never." He smiles triumphantly. I can just imagine the effect this show will have on his audience of lesser scientists and naïve villagers.

I hold out the Faraday suit to him.

"I think you're gonna need this more than I will. And – by the way? Your son is trying to kill you."

• • •

The old man refuses to believe me, right up until four young flyers burst into the cavern and accuse me of plotting against him. They yank my arms behind my back and shove me up against the cave wall. They argue while tying me to some odd loops of metal set into the wall. It could be the remains of a melted Faraday cage. Ugh. All I need is to be near more metal when this thing is turned on. I'm wishing I'd kept the suit. So I'm to be the sacrifice after all, the scapegoat for the old man's murder. The flyers kindly offer to help their leader buckle up his harness and tether. He's been standing back, watching events unfurl.

I nod toward the suit and he slowly picks it up. I nod again, encouraging him.

The old man takes off the flight harness. There's sudden silence in the room.

"If you suspect him of treachery, why not send him out to fly in my place?"

The four flyers seem stunned by the suggestion.

"But ..."

"Ah. I can see that you feel it's more fitting for the leader to fly the ceremonial kite, yes?"

Yes, they all agree, relief on all their faces. That's enough for the clever old man. He climbs into the Faraday suit.

"By the way, in what way was this lad planning to assassinate me?"

"There's a confused clamor while the four talk at once. I make out that they believe I plan to sabotage the Tesla coil.

"And which of you will turn it on and stand by while I fly?"

Again, there is silence.

"It *is* very dangerous," the old man says kindly. "Often the ones nearest take the full brunt of the lightning." More silence.

"Never mind. It is a simple switch after all. You four make sure this dangerous character is tied up well, and then leave me to turn the coil on before I jump. Go prepare for your own flights. Be sure to be well clear of the caves when the sun sets – or you could be struck!"

Why they don't notice the bitter irony in his voice I don't know. But Flyboy's friends add a few more knots to my bonds and skedaddle.

"I'm afraid none of them are really known for their intelligence," the old Scientist says sadly. Now that the others are gone, his face sags into lines of sadness.

"That coil around the tether," I say. "You understand that it could increase the amperage enough to kill you?"

"Not with the suit on."

"You'd better hope there are no breaks in the fabric."

"Indeed." He continues to stare at me thoughtfully.

"Are you gonna let me go?"

"Ah, that is the question," he says. "What if you *are* a danger to me?"

"I just want to leave this place."

"If you stay here without the suit, you may not survive."

"Then there will be no one to pull you back in afterward."

"Hmm," he says. "You came here thinking you were going to fly. Were you planning to leave *me* suit-less?"

"I planned to send out a dummy on the kite and run away. I had no idea you meant to fly. Your son told us the tethered flyer was a sacrifice to the falls."

The old man closed his eyes as if in pain. "That does sound like him. He's always treated science like one of the old religions." (*Look who's talking.*) "So where is this dummy then?"

I jerk my chin toward the shadows behind the bin where the lineman's suit had been stored.

The old man pulls out the dummy Aki and I made from the rags stuffed inside our futon. It's a little too small. He makes no move to untie me.

"To fly or not to fly," he mutters.

"To die or not to die," I quip back.

"I'll send out your dummy," he finally says, shoulders slumping. "And stay here in the suit to greet my son when he arrives." I hope he can get angry so that instead of one tied-and-fried scapegoat, his son finds one angry Scientist King.

"I'm sorry."

"You would make a good leader – after me." He still hasn't untied me.

"I would not. I have no interest in it."

"That's why you would be good at it." The old man sighs and finally trudges over and starts to untie my bonds. His hands are shaking.

We hear a hoot from outside the cave, and a rope drops down in front of the opening.

"I'll just get that," he mutters.

"Please! Please don't leave me tied. I'll get the rope for you."

He hesitates. "I chose you for this ceremony because I believed I could trust you."

How sad that somehow he knew he couldn't trust his son. "You can."

"Prove it." The old man angrily pulls at my bonds again. As soon as they drop free, I run for the dangling rope.

I hook the rope and grab at the harness on the floor. My own hands are shaking too as I hurry to tie the harness in. The old man hands me the dummy and we stuff it in the harness, tying them together with the dummy's own rags. I weight it with loose rocks from near the cave's rough stone wall, stuffing as many of them as I can deep into the innards. Outside, the light dims as the sun goes down behind the falls. Almost time. The old man has the copper coiled tether in his hand, ready to hook it to the harness as well.

"How will you get out? There may be someone waiting outside the door."

I stare at him. Will he really let me go?

"The dummy is still too light. I think it's gonna take both of us throwing it out of the cave to get it far enough away to give the parachute any balance."

"I'll have to turn on the coil immediately," he says. "You know that."

I look around the room. The only way out is the cave opening, or the door the flyers left through.

"What if I fly it away after all, but we just don't tether it to the coil?"

The old man shakes his head. "The show must go on or they will follow you. To live, you need to die." And he points at the dummy. If he only knew how true that always is in my life.

"Thank you for believing me."

"Thank you for my life." The leader of the Niagararians gestures graciously toward his heart before bending to hook the copper tether to the harness. We lift the dummy, one on each side, and stand near the cave opening, ready to swing it outside as soon as we hear the signal from above. Lights are shining all along the river below. I can't see overhead to the top of the falls. I hope no one can see us. I wonder how Aki is managing.

"Wait!" I say, and drop my half of the dummy to scrabble behind the tub again for my white cloak – my camouflage on the ice. I slip my head through a slot in the middle and belt it at the waist.

"Clever," the old man says. "Are you sure …?"

"I'm a traveler," I say firmly. "As I told you before." He nods. "What will you do now?" I ask, as we wait for the signal.

The old man sighs again. "Maybe I've lived too long."

"I don't think he will make much of a leader without your help," I say earnestly. "Maybe you just need to out-clever him …."

The old man starts to get a twinkle in his eye. "He doesn't know about the suit. And I do still have control of the coil …." He's about to tell me his idea when we hear a shout from above. Immediately we swing the dummy back once and throw it out into the air as hard as we can. The cable rattles on the floor as it follows, coil by coil, unlooping as it's pulled after the dummy. The parachute above swings into view as the dummy swings back toward us, and then they both swing outward again, away from the cliff's edge. Without looking at me, the old man turns back toward the coil. I take a breath and slip over the cave lip, letting go just as I hear the crackle and hum of the giant Tesla coil sending out its first lightning forks into the night. As I slip and scramble down the rocks, a double-fingered filament buzzes overhead, searching for a conductor for its symphony of fire.

• • •

Aki finds me with my foot wedged and completely stuck between two rocks, not 20 feet from our packs. It was slippery coming down from the cave, but I couldn't help myself from looking up at the lightshow. Between the fire and ice, I missed my footing.

While waiting for her to arrive and unstick me, I've been watching the play of lightning over the kites, the most powerful bolts lingering on and petting lightly over our dummy, which finally burst into flame, consuming the entire parachute above. I wonder what Flyboy will think of that. I wish I could see his face when he opens the door to find his suited father running the Tesla coil. I wonder if he will find a forgiving leader or a tongue of flame. I decide I'm better off not knowing. We need to leave, and fast. But I feel sure the old man will be keeping Flyboy's mind on something else for a while at least.

Aki's working on freeing my foot. The rocks are hard to move. "How bad is your ankle?"

She had to come down the elevator and across the black ice in the dark. Her rigged kite was flung off the cliffs on its own and is presumably broken on the rocks below us.

My ankle hurts like hell. "I'll be fine by tomorrow."

She glares at me. "We don't have until tomorrow."

"I know!" I've really fracked things up. I won't be able to skate if my ankle's sprained.

"You idiot." I hear a sob in Aki's voice. One of the rocks she's trying to move slips back down, scrapes my leg, and suddenly her hands are covered in black.

"That won't kill me," I say firmly. Then ruin the effect by spinning out.

I guess I fainted at the sight of my own blood.

ICE SLEDGING

"Two vast and trunkless legs of stone
Stand in the desert ....
And on the pedestal these words appear:
"My name is Ozymandias, king of kings:
Look on my works, ye Mighty, and despair!"
Nothing beside remains. Round the decay
Of that colossal wreck, boundless and bare
The lone and level sands stretch far away."
— Percy Bysshe Shelley, "Ozymandias"

I must be well anchored now to this time and place not to continue into regression. Or perhaps it was because I felt so cheerful before I fainted, so pleased to have escaped, to have helped that grand old man, to be found by Aki and to be on the run with her again. I'm also happy Flyboy turned out to be an evil prat. I never did like him.

When I come to, I think we're back in the caves again. And we are, but not the ones I feared. Aki has dragged me and both our packs, using her cape and mine as a skid, over the slippery shale pathway to the tunnel under the second falls. Shades of Keycha dragging me out of the under-city. At least the distance was shorter.

Aki's eyes are red and puffy. She's been crying. It must have been difficult and scary getting me hidden away after I fainted. Sometimes I have to have it thrown in my face that I'm not so tough after all. I reach for her hand in the arc light, but she pulls away.

"You okay?"

"Why did you come with me, Jack?"

"Uh, because they were gonna kill us, maybe?"

"No. I mean why did you leave the lake. And … and Keycha?"

I'm lying flat on my back. Aki is crouched under the arc light, her face shadowed. Our packs are nearby and Aki has covered me with her cloak. I'm lying on one of the caribou hides. We'd agreed we shouldn't – couldn't ever – leave those behind. I'd brought my book too, as had Aki. We are away and we have everything we need.

"What's up, Aki?" I'm so happy to be here with her. We've barely had any time together since we arrived at the falls. I know we have a long way to go, but I feel oddly content, despite the throbbing in my ankle.

"Sometimes you talk in your sleep."

This is news to me. "What do I say?"

"You were talking to Keycha. You asked him why he didn't make you stay."

For once I don't remember my dream.

"Are you sure it was Keycha?"

"You sobbed. You begged him. You were … fawning on him!"

She's really upset.

"I'm so sorry, Aki." I try to take her hand again. "It was just a dream. I don't remember."

"Were you in love with … are you in love with my brother?"

I don't answer. I've lost so many people I cared about. I don't really know if I can allow myself to love anyone anymore. Perhaps my dreaming mind thinks differently.

"You're the one I need right now," I finally say. "I woke up so happy to be here with you."

Aki lets out a sob and throws herself at me, her face tucked into my shoulder. She's matured since we left the lake. Her shoulders are broader, hips rounder, and she's taller than me by at least three inches now. She's all muscle, yet feels womanly as she curls beside me. Aki is maturing and I'm still in this adolescent body; a teenage kid waiting for his voice to break. I'm a little pleased that even after our weeks of rest, my own skating muscles don't put me entirely to shame. But has she noticed yet that she's moving on without me?

"I've missed you," she sighs. Her body is so warm against me.

"Aki ...." What do I say? Ask if she loves me? Tell her that I love her? All I want is to sail with her out on the ice under the sun. Cuddle with her in the firelight after dark and tell stories. Squabble over our route, and share this life with her. Is that love? Aki is life in action. Keycha was ... something else. Something more visceral. Something I don't really want to think about too hard, or a feeling of unbearable loss wells up in me and closes my throat.

"I missed you too," I finally say, my voice thick. I hug her close. If she feels the tears running down my neck, she doesn't ask what causes them.

• • •

I heal fast. But it's still two days before we poke our heads out of the tunnel, partly driven by our diminishing food supplies. We need to have enough left for the trip down-river.

It's disturbing to see a number of flyers plying the winds over the falls and downriver. It's not a place even the seasoned flyers used to go during training. They look like colorful vultures circling.

There's also movement at the base of the southern falls. The villagers from downriver still have their tents up. I realize there are far more of them than I'd noticed before. The caves had been full of festival participants, but it looks like whole families have camped below the falls.

"How long does the festival last?" I ask Aki, who's staring up at the flyers.

"Could they be looking for us?" she mutters. "I don't see O'car ...."

"Hmph." I'm a little put out that she's looking for Flyboy at all.

She jabs me with her elbow. "Don't be stupid. If he's up there it means they may be hunting us."

"We should have had your kite go up in flames too," I say grimly. "I thought we'd be long gone by now. I'm sorry."

"Clumsy oaf." She jabs me again. "Who told you to get stuck in the rocks?"

"And we're still halfway up the face, in plain view if we leave the tunnel."

"I have an idea," says my clever Aki.

• • •

We backtrack, trekking north inside the tunnel until we come out the end as far from the flying Niagararians as possible. This is the entrance we came in on the second day, during our tour. We climb to the top of the Horseshoe Falls and set off west upriver, the sound of the falls receding like a crowd roaring in the distance. I'm not convinced by Aki's plan yet, but at least this way we should have a few drifts between us and the flyers, and maybe be able to fish before we move on. But we're going in the wrong direction, as I mention to Aki more than once.

"It isn't far," she replies patiently, each time.

"It" is what worries me most.

"At least this way you can finally see whether one of your precious canals is staying drift-free."

Aki isn't talking about the Erie Canal, but another canal just a short way back along the north side of the river used, once upon a time, to divert water around the falls for shipping traffic. It should parallel the river. There's something else there too. Aki heard from Flyboy – and she told me about it. There's a gigantic tunnel circumnavigating the falls and running underground all of the six-plus miles downriver to a huge generating station, where it dumps into the western end of Lake Ontario.

I remember, in one of those bubbles of memory that surface from nowhere, that the tunnel was one of those hopeful human endeavors before the snows came. Ontario (the province) had allowed itself to see, earlier than most, how its coal fires were tipping the climate toward a new Ice-Age. It shut down all of its coal-burning electric-generating plants and built a massive hydroelectric tunnel project. It was a heroic, visionary move. Sadly, too little too late – though if other provinces and states and countries had followed suit, things might have been different.

I have clear memories of other visionaries with good intentions. Norway subsidized Guyana, putting hundreds of millions of dollars into an effort to slow deforestation. When Guyana had started sinking below sea level, it acknowledged that uncontrolled carbon emissions led to global change, glacial melt, and ocean rise, and it worked hard to keep as much of its land in forests as possible – until the richer country's funding ran out and all aid stopped.

So many people came up with imaginative ways to save the world. There was replanting in the African desert. Alternatives were found for undersea mining. Voices rose up in protest on one continent against oil fracking, and

on others against coal. China developed a way to seques-
ter at least one greenhouse gas by turning carbon dioxide
into liquid and injecting it into limestone. Several South
American countries asked the North Americans and other
First Worlders to help save the Amazon basin by providing
subsidies so poor farmers could stop chopping trees and
taking the last fish out of that river (and in other parts of
the world, reef fish) to provide just one more day of food
and life for their children. They argued that if given alter-
native ways to eat, then the hungry could afford to care
about the long view. But most of the wealthy preferred to
sit on their piles of gold until, like Midas, it burned them,
drowned them, or they froze to it. (*I have to acknowledge that
is also my belief: to protect myself first. Could Keycha be right? Have
I missed the bigger picture all this time?*)

Water and air quickly became more important than
gold. The buildup of gasses released from the earth by
coal fires and burning fossil fuels for power – and the lack
of trees and healthy, diverse ecosystems to bind carbon –
ruined the balance in our small earth terrarium and sent
the environmental seesaw first one way, toward heat (*fire*),
then the other, into ice. Aki and I are just lucky that the
Great Lakes we skate on didn't dry up entirely before the
ice came. I remember so many species of fish dying in
droves in every body of water after the water warmed up
just a few degrees. Looking back, it seems incredible that
there is any life left on the planet at all.

(*A comforting thought: Life is tenacious. If humans die out, life
will continue to exist; in bacteria, insects, and on the many other
rocks orbiting distant suns. So many possibilities. And yet I hope
not to see my own kind fail utterly. What individual of any species
wants to face that grief? The fear of it happening is bad enough. And
yet one lives on, and life is sweet.*)

I remember reading about the Ontario Tunnel project,
how exciting it was. How people cheered the cutter, Big

Becky, on her five-year journey through the rock. It was one of those projects that let you know our big human brains were useful after all, that we could anticipate our own self-destruction and actually do something to stop it, like when the Americans passed the Clean Air Act and the air actually got cleaner for a while. At least we try. But then, when one climate disaster after another hit the planet – in the form of massive floods, fires that burned for years, and winds that nothing could withstand – each nation (*and then each city and town and family*) narrowed its focus on its own crises, and any hope of working together on a global scale was lost, as was civilization-that-was.

The industrial age that had given humanity so much changed our environment so radically that humans could no longer survive in it. Or they could only barely. I'm amazed every day to be alive, to find people living along the frozen waterways. Life truly is tenacious. I wonder what more I'll find when we reach the salt sea. I'm greedy that way.

I tell Aki nothing about my fragmented memories of disaster. My sermon back in the tanker showed me how little it would mean to her in the here and now. But it feels like a step forward. I need to remember, in order to put the puzzle pieces together of who I am and why the east beckons.

• • •

Now that we're actually standing at that massive tunnel's lip, I wonder what Flyboy knew, or thought he knew, about this place. The tunnel itself is big enough to drive a bus through easily, maybe two buses. (*What's a bus? I imagine Aki asking.*) It's as tall as a four-story building. (*What's that?*)

"O'car says this tunnel goes right to the mouth of the river." Aki says as we stare into the dim light.

"He's been down it?"

"Um ...."

"Has he known anyone who actually went down it?"

"*Ah* .... Well, he showed me a drawing. A map of it. And he *said* people could travel inside."

We're standing in a tunnel mouth so large it seems unreal. It's unbearably dark and deep, as if it drops into the earth's core. The outside edges are softened by icefall. It's above the current level of the frozen river, though there's ice inside as far in as we can see. There are no arc lights here. From the outside light, we can only see that it dips sharply downhill into darkness.

"Why would they? Who would go in there! That's just nuts."

"We haven't found any sign of a canal," Aki says hesitantly. I can't believe she's even considering this. "The tunnel's only six miles long. We could be at river's mouth before the villagers even return home. We'd be invisible for the whole trip!"

"We'd be dead when we arrived. Aki," I say in what I believe is a reasonable tone. "You know I have a particular aversion to dying, yes?"

"So does every living thing, Jack."

"The only thing that would be worse than dying would be waking up again stuck deep inside that giant gullet. I will not do it."

"Yes, Jack," Aki says sweetly. "So let's just explore inside a little. O'car said he found sledges in there."

Sledges. Aki's people traveled by caribou sledge once. Maybe she's hoping to find some sign of them. I agree to explore and we dig out our crank lights and step inside. Maybe if we stall long enough the flyers will give up and stop looking for us – if that's even what they're doing. We haven't seen them since we backtracked upriver.

The tunnel is a wonder of the world – better than the pyramids, since it was built to serve the living. At the top, as far as we can see, there are catwalks along the sides. Cables run along the roof. *Maybe* it didn't fill completely with water – but any water inside would obviously be long frozen and could be blocking the tunnel somewhere along its length. It would be suicide to go down there.

Aki goes inside farther than I'm comfortable with at first, but the tunnel mouth is wide. She does find sledges, stacked against one wall. Most of them are concreted to each other in a mushroom explosion of rust stopped only by the ice that now covers them, sealing them away from the corrosive oxygen in the air. They've been there a long time. But there are signs of more recent occupation too. There's a firepit next to several heavily oiled sledges in better condition, and a long black plastic-covered cable that looks like it was minted yesterday, snaking way into the darkness. Aki follows it back up to the mouth of the tunnel, where it disappears under a drift.

"I know something you don't know!" Aki sings, turning around and racing back along the cable, into the tunnel again.

"Aki, don't mess around! It's dangerous in there!"

I can see her light bobbing around, though she's still visible in the half-light of the open tunnel. She's looking for something by the firepit. I hear the sodden thunk of punky old metal.

"Aki, don't cut yourself on that stuff!" Tetanus vaccines are long ago and far away in time. Then there's another sound. A click and a hum. Crap. Does the old man have generators all over the place?

A series of loud clicks and pops echo through the tunnel over the hum, the sounds fading into the distance. Aki comes running back to me, grinning and bright eyed.

"What did you do?"

"Wait," she says. "I just want to see something." The clicking sounds are coming back toward us again through the dark of the tunnel, getting louder as they approach.

I want to run but Aki is holding my hand, still looking excited and expectant.

"What were you doing?" Is it time to panic yet?

"Stealing electricity," Aki says happily, just as the lights come on.

• • •

It should have occurred to us that the Niagararians might notice such a huge draw on their generator. Or at least it should have occurred to me. But Aki and I were having too much fun exploring the now lit tunnel. The breaker Aki threw lit up a string of lights that stretches around the first bend of the tunnel and out of sight. Now we can see that the drop isn't nearly as steep as it seemed in the dark, and there are marks of runners along the ice at the bottom of the tube. Someone has sent sledges down into the depths. But how did they get them back up again? Or did they?

"O'car told me the flyers have been exploring in here. He told me about the breaker for the lights, and the sledges. He claimed that everyone says riding them is even more of a thrill than flying."

We find a huge winch just where the slope drops away, which *might* explain how the sledges return to the top, but not entirely. Not for a six-mile slope. There's no rope or chain on it. And anything other than a bungee cord attached to a sled would likely stop the sled so abruptly when they reached the end of a tether that the passengers would go flying. So I'm guessing the sleds don't return.

"Very nice," I say. "Now let's go make camp and figure out how we're gonna get past the flyers tomorrow."

Aki looks disappointed. But I can't believe she's really imagining that the tunnel would be clear and open all the way to the river mouth. Not after all this time.

We find enough weed stacked around the old firepit to make a good blaze. It's eerie sitting inside that giant pipe with the lights still blazing. Our camp is about 40 feet wide. I wonder what the monster-fish will make of all these lights once it gets dark. I feel very exposed. Aki opens her pack to get some food started. I'm about to suggest that we turn off the power when the late afternoon sun lowers enough to glare directly into the tunnel mouth. I squint into the glare just in time to see the silhouette of several flyers cross the light. They've found us.

• • •

I wouldn't have run if I thought it was the old man. But the old man wouldn't have come after us. Flyboy is the one I'm afraid of. If he beat the lightning of the old man's Tesla coil – if he's taken over leadership by force from his own father – then he's too scary to face. Chasing us down is not the action of a man willing to negotiate, not if he's already turned down what the old man can teach him. He can only be after us for revenge. We messed with his plan, and he wants to hurt us.

Or maybe I just react as prey. When chased, it's time to run. So when Aki throws my pack at me, I shrug into it, and when she shoves a sledge over to the drop in the tunnel, I follow. It must be the adrenaline surge from being hunted. Why else would I do something so unconditionally stupid?

• • •

We slide down into the tunnel, on our stomachs, holding to a bar at the front of the sledge. The lights flash by far too quickly as we pick up speed. The scrape of runners echoes in the round space. We can hear yelling behind us. But by then nothing matters as much as our increasing speed.

"Is there a brake? Can you slow us down?" My voice sounds weak, torn away by our forward motion. We're starting to rattle and bump and I'm feeling queasy. I can't help wondering when we'll hit a wall of ice, or a roof-fall.

Maybe it will happen so fast we won't feel anything. Aki's laughing beside me. She has her flight goggles on. My eyes are streaming so I struggle to pull mine down with one hand. I'm not about to let go of the sledge with the other. The lights blur past us, faster and faster. The noise is incredible.

"Aki!" I shriek. "The brake!"

"If we brake …." She stutters, her words left behind as we race forward. "We won't make it up … slope at the end …."

She's got to be kidding. Could this get any scarier? It could. We rattle around a corner, barely hanging on, see a vast slope stretching away from us, miraculously clear of rubble, but oddly narrow in the distance, as if the ice is deeper down there, filling more of the tunnel.

Then the lights go out.

• • •

We scrape through pitch black. I can feel our speed, but can't see Aki beside me. I'm terrified, but after a few moments sound overwhelms almost every other sensation. There's a feeling akin to sensory deprivation. The very lack of control and sight means there's nothing we can do. With responsibility removed, without being able to anticipate each bend and bump, I'm resigned to just hanging on. We will make it, or we won't. I lie prone beside Aki, my hands clenching the sled's railing in a death grip. The side of her hand presses slightly against mine. She's not letting go either, but the light touch is comforting in the rattling dark.

"Stay low," I say, barely able to force my voice above the noise, thinking about that narrowing path of ice below us. Hoping our packs aren't sticking up too high. I feel pressure from her hand in response. Even speaking is too much. Better to just embrace the darkness – and endure.

We scrape swiftly over the ice. It goes on and on. Only when an irregularity in the ceiling rips past us, clanging against the sledge, do I know for sure that we're being squeezed up against the top of the tunnel. My stomach drops when we slow a little, rising upward. I can't stand the thought of the sledge stopping and slipping backward, and I urge her forward. Our bodies seem to float for a moment and then, with a crack, we break free into light. We slam down out of the tunnel so hard the wind is knocked out of my lungs. The sledge skids out onto the open ice of a canal lit deep orange by the setting sun. I've never seen anything so beautiful in my life.

The sledge continues to slip forward. Aki and I sit up dizzily. She's laughing with relief. I feel limp and boneless, a noodle person. But the sledge doesn't stop. We continue down the canal at a fair rate. I'm looking for a brake again when Aki gasps. Ahead of us the ice disappears, like we're about to drop off the end of the world. Forget the brake. I grab Aki and we kick off the sledge, slamming into the ice hard, rolling and slipping another 20 feet before drifting to a stop. The heavy sledge never slows but continues on over the edge, sailing off the top of what must be the old hydroelectric dam like an iron bird, disappearing silently from sight. I never hear an impact. I lie there, bone weary, and stare at Aki, shocked and so relieved to be alive and in the light. There are just no words left.

• • •

We eventually manage to creep away from the cliff edge and hide in the lee of a drift. We lie between our hides and drape the white cloaks over us, hopefully camouflaging us from any flyers passing overhead, just another white lump in a world of white. We don't build a fire. We don't bother with food. It takes hours to calm down, our bodies jazzed up and buzzing from the danger and vibration and fear. We're warm enough, cuddled together. There is really nothing to be said about what we've just done, and we simply lie there staring at each other under the stars. It's enough that we've survived. Neither of us is ready to comment on the event. It isn't time to make more plans yet. Who can move on after that experience? After a while I see Aki's eyes closing and her breathing slowing. Once she's asleep, I lean in to close the narrow space between our faces and touch my lips gently to hers, holding them there for a heartbeat, breathing her breath. How can I not love her? We've risked dangers together I could never have faced alone (*or stayed awake through!*). We help each other survive – and more. It's been *fun*, I realize suddenly, laughing loud enough that Aki's sleepy eyes open for a moment, frowning before she drifts off again. I hug her to me, and she mumbles in her sleep. I can't believe I'm even thinking it. But that was actually fun!

• • •

The next morning, we're both stiff and bruised. There are no signs of flyers, so we make ourselves get up at first light, groaning and complaining. We still don't talk about our slide down the tunnel. It's too soon. It's a thing between us, but it will wait. I feel more energized and alive than I have in some time. I wonder if near-death experiences are good for the depression longevity seems to bring on. It's a beautiful day.

The only problem is there's no obvious way to get down from the massive dam we find ourselves atop. We can see our river below, stretching toward Niagara in one direction and the villages and Lake Ontario in the other. There are no lovely ice-forms flowing over this dam, or even rubble, just a pitted cement wall, pretty enough with steep buttresses curving down to the river below.

"We could fly down," Aki says, the first words I've heard from her all morning. She also looks hyper-alive and alert in the bright morning air.

"With what?" I'm startled. She can't be hiding kite cloth in her pack. We needed the space for food and Keycha's hides.

"With something to brace them, our cloaks might work." She says it, but I don't believe she's serious. Though I didn't believe she'd sled us down that tunnel either.

"I think we've had enough near-death experiences for now. Can't we just walk around it?" But the drifts are deep here too. "Besides, the cloaks might work for skating, but kites for real flying are a lot bigger, *neh*?"

Oh, what the frack. If Aki thinks it will work? I'm feeling pretty pumped up. If we can survive that wild ride through the tunnel, why can't we fly off a damned dam?

"Okay, let's do it!"

"What? Really? No." Aki sounds amused. "Feeling invulnerable now, are we?"

"We are!" I grin like an idiot.

"Yes, but no." Aki grins back. "You're right, we wouldn't get enough lift and you don't know what you're doing anyway. You might as well jump down."

"Whatever my lady commands." I step toward the dam and Aki grabs my arm.

"Don't be a doofus ...." She's laughing when a single flyer comes in fast from the west and lands in a spray of snow not 20 feet away from us.

"Well now, there's a kite," I say, hearing a new and dangerous note in my voice. I'm done running away. Aki's hand tightens on my arm.

It's the brown flyer. The woman I met the day Flyboy came up with his whole ridiculous plan. Or at least the day he made me part of it. She's clearly one of his, so I brace for conflict. But the woman has a huge grin on her face as she walks toward us. She's anchored her kite, I notice. Could it hold both me and Aki?

"I can't believe I found you!" she calls before she reaches us. She sounds delighted. "Did you really do it? Did you go down the tunnel?"

"We did," Aki says shortly. Watching the other woman suspiciously. "What do you want?"

"Isn't that ride like nothing in the world?"

I can't believe it. Has this maniac actually ridden the tunnel by choice?

"I did it once." This gal is just way too cheerful to be an assassin. "It was awesome. But I hope never to do it again."

"So?" I'm feeling a little deflated now. Our terrifyingly grand experience reduced to a joy ride.

"You left too soon. You missed the festivities. I was sent to bring you these." She swings a long pack off her back and thumps it down in front of us. "Heavy, aye?" She tips the pack and a slew of trinkets from the Niagara gift shop pour out. "Welcome to Niagara" plaques, a snow-globe, a miniature Tesla .... "We use these for trade in the village. A present from O'car for your help during the festival."

Aki and I look at each other. For a brief moment, all I can think is that we didn't have to sled down the tunnel after all. But then why did they turn the lights out on us? I picture the old man with his sad face in the Faraday suit, waiting with his lightning. He would never have been able to turn it on his own son ....

I turn away from Aki to face the brown flyer, my mouth open to say ... something ... when another shadow passes low over us, and this time, that instinctual urge to duck from an overhead predator sends me flat onto the snow. I hear a thud behind me and roll over to see Aki being dragged over the ice, struggling in the grip of a flyer who's headed right for the drop. I leap up but the brown flyer is in my way, grinning triumphantly. She has a long blade in her hand and is between me and Aki.

Why do people think that just because someone is small they can't fight? I have 200 years on this stupid girl. Time moves slowly. I can see Aki being dragged toward the dam, skidding and kicking. The flyer's wing is tipping. She may bring him down before the drop. The brown flyer steps toward me and I leg-sweep her down onto the ice. I don't try to disarm her. I just slam the heel of my hand into her throat. No holding back. I need to get to Aki fast. But when I straighten, the kite is at the bitter edge of the cliff.

Aki and the kite drop suddenly below my sight. For a bare second I hesitate between running toward them (*too late!*) and veering left toward the brown flyer's kite. A sharp pain in my leg tells me I should have disarmed her. She's choking for breath but has managed to stab me in the shin with one hand. The blade doesn't go in deep, and I kick her in the head with my stabbed leg (*same fracking leg I sprained!*), then run for her kite. As I reach it, the knife falls free, so I use it to slice her anchor lines. Then I'm staggering to the edge, struggling to control the kite, which yanks one way and another as I run, trying to break free. I've got almost no air under her as I reach the edge. I'm angled all wrong. There's no time to think. I launch, only just remembering to push the bar forward and tip the nose up. And then I'm in the air, nose too high, fighting to straighten. When I do, I see the other kite spiraling below me. It's sinking fast. I can only hope it's dropping because it's still holding the weight of two. I hear Aki shriek in anger and suddenly I'm no longer seeing through a white fog of panic. She's still alive.

The worst part about flying is landing, so I've heard. I never learned. I've skate-sailed enough to have a feel for the air under my wings, and I don't have too much trouble turning, but the wind keeps pushing me back up. I can't get down to the other kite. I consider a nosedive but can't tip the front downward. When I lean forward to dive, the nose pops up instead. I keep my eyes on the fast-descending kite below me and cry out in frustration. I can only circle slowly, inches from the dam on my inside turn, hanging almost always at the same height in the air. It isn't nearly as frightening as I expected it to be. I'm being held by the kite, so there's no feeling of falling (*yet*). But when I finally manage to tilt the wings, I get momentary blasts of adrenaline as I drop.

The other kite vanes and wobbles and – no more than 10 feet from the ground? – it turns a sharp right directly into the side of the dam. Its wings fold up like paper. I hear yells, but the wind pushes me up again and I lose sight of them while turning back into my circle. I swear, yanking on the bar, until I finally drop down a little in stomach-lifting jolts. From 50 feet above the crash, the other hang-glider looks like a crumpled butterfly on a wide cement platform just above the bottom of the dam. I circle overhead, swearing, and a single figure crawls out from underneath the wreckage and stands, shading their eyes to look up at me.

I manage to drop down a little more on the next turn, and it's Aki standing on the platform, waving at me, yelling something. I think she's calling out directions for landing, but a second figure emerges from the wreckage, rearing up behind her back.

It turns out that staring at something is a good way to aim for it. I come in at a rate of knots right at Aki. She drops flat and I hit the flyer dead-on with the aluminum-framed kite, pushing him into the wall of the dam with the full force of my speed and body. He probably cushions me from quite an impact. Maybe I should thank him – when he wakes up.

• • •

"I meant to do that," I say grumpily. But Aki doesn't buy it. We've made camp right there on the buttress. The platform is an easy 10 or 12 feet above the river ice. I mention rolling Flyboy off the edge about once every 10 minutes. But Aki wants to patch him up before she kills him. Or so it seems. I have to admit, I'd like him to wake up and answer a few questions too, but he hit his head pretty hard when I took him down, and that was after Aki already made him crash into the dam.

We're in pretty good shape, despite my newly re-damaged leg and a raft of new scrapes and bruises on us both. We were both wearing our backpacks (*or we'd be in real trouble*), so we can make a fire and have food left, and we *are* at the bottom of the dam. Almost. So it could be worse. The broken kites work as a windbreak for now. I'm thinking about folding the sails on their bent frames and seeing if I can drag them like a travois in the morning. I'll take them with us either way. The cloth is good. The real question is what to do with Flyboy.

"Why can't I roll him off?" I complain. "He was trying to do it to you."

"Well, that's the thing," Aki says. "He could have dropped me, and he didn't."

"If he'd planned to just give us a ride down he could have done it more politely," I mutter. My shin is aching from the knife wound. It's small but still nasty. It's close to the same place I'd scraped my shin on the rocks under the falls. I was just starting to get less gimpy from the sprain too.

"Honestly, why in the world are they all after us anyway?"

"They aren't all after you." Flyboy is face-down on one of our precious skins, his voice muffled. "They're after me."

It takes a while to get the story out of him. The old man isn't dead, I'm relieved to hear, but he did banish Flyboy from Niagara. It's the worst thing that could happen to a Niagararian, according to Flyboy. I can see sympathy on Aki's face, which pisses me off. Didn't this guy just try to kill her? But I remember that in her family, banishment means death out on the ice. Flyboy doesn't seem to have it that bad in comparison, and I tell him so.

"You brought this on yourself," I remind him. "What did you think would happen when you tried to lie and kill your way to the top? You couldn't just wait a few years and inherit?"

"My father has a lot of children." He still hasn't turned to face us. "He's named my younger sister the successor now, since she made a successful flight at the festival – and is willing to learn."

"So all this is because you weren't willing to learn?"

"I can't understand it!" He rolls on his side with a wince. He'd taken quite a hit to the head up against the dam, and he'd landed hard when Aki crashed them. He'll live, though.

"None of it makes any sense to me. You," he says, pointing to Aki. "You picked up a lot in just a few weeks. The old man talks and talks about positive and negative poles and about coils and cathodes and anodes and – what the hell does it all mean? I don't even really understand what electricity is." His voice drops to an ashamed whisper. "Flying is something I can throw myself into. But the rest ...."

"So all those flyers out over the river earlier in the day?"

"Were after me. The old man told me to get out. So I stole some of his sacred literature and stuff. I thought I could trade it for food and shelter in the village."

I remember the trinkets the brown flyer dumped on the ice to distract us. "And your friend?"

"Dolores came with me. She's the only one who cared."

For a failed killer, this guy sure is having himself a pity party.

"Why turn the lights off on us in the tunnel?"

"Really? Wow. You guys did that run in the dark? That's pretty bad." He looks impressed. "That wasn't us. Maybe the others thought it was me in the tunnel – *bastards*."

"Do you ever think about anyone but yourself?" Aki finally chimes in. "What about your girl, Dolores, up on the cliff? She's up there with no kite, no way down, and a bag of your stolen junk." Anything she can't eat, use to keep warm, sail, skate or fly with, is junk to Aki.

"Now I've got nothing," the stupid boy says. I can tell Aki is about to hit him.

"What about your *friend*?" she says through gritted teeth.

"She can take care of herself," he says sullenly. "Save your sympathy. She only helped just now because I said I was gonna drop you off the cliff."

"What?! Why?"

"She knows I like you. Jealous bitch."

"Let me get this straight," I say. "You attacked us so that you could carry Aki off into the sunset? Are you completely insane?"

"You!" he spits at me. "It always comes back to you. If you weren't around, Aki wouldn't have wanted to leave. My father wouldn't have – he was even considering *you* as the next leader! Did you know that? Over his own son!" He's panting with rage. "I just can't stand you. You're just ... *fracking* weird. There's something wrong with you. I wanted you and Dolores to fight it out. She wanted me and said she'd distract you for me. I don't care about her. But I was never gonna drop *you*, Aki!"

"I know." Aki says this with such calm. I'm ready to deck the guy. "You could have, but you didn't. So what is it you want from us exactly, the weirdo and me, that you'd abandon your only follower and wreck your escape plan?"

"I'm just angry!" the boy cries out suddenly. "I want you, and you only look at *him*. My father only looks at *him*. It's his fault I was banished. I have nothing now. No one. I hate him!"

"And yet you always smiled in my face," I say, as lightly as I can. I've had people hate me before, but usually with more reason.

"I hated you as soon as I met you," he says tiredly. "You were both so happy, so … complete … playing out on the ice together – as if you didn't need anyone else in the world. I could have taken you to that canal you were looking for, the day I found you. It's there, on the south fork of the Erie River. I just wanted to … make it harder for you. And look where it got me."

"Yes. Look at that," Aki says. "Does that mean you're actually taking responsibility for your actions? Do you not see how you've brought this on yourself?"

"If you'd loved me, I would have been a different person," he says.

"Don't blame Aki for your fracking mess," I say. "Or me." I sigh. I'm trying so hard to be reasonable when what I want is to kick him off the buttress. "Go to the village. Learn how to be less of an asshole. Then maybe your father will take you back."

For a moment his face looks hopeful, then suspicious again. This kid has a long way to go. "You aren't gonna leave me here to die?"

"Oh, for crying out loud. Melodramatic much? The village can't be more than two or three miles downriver. You could crawl it in a day if you had to. Your flyer friend up top is gonna have a longer hike out than you. And she's got all that explaining to do once she gets back to the falls."

"But I'm hurt."

"She's hurt too," I say grimly, wondering how badly. But Flyboy just looks at me sideways and drops the subject. Caring sort of guy. Aki isn't done, however.

"I hate you," she hisses into the boy's face. He looks shocked. "You don't care about anyone but yourself. You have friends you just abandon. You try to kill your own father and blame my friend for it .... What's *wrong* with you? And don't you dare say you love me. You were planning to get rid of me too!"

"No!" he says. "You're wrong!" But he knows what she's talking about. "Your kite was Dolores's idea. The wrapped cable too. She's smart with electricity. I knew it wouldn't hurt you, though. You just would have drawn more lighting, gotten higher status! With you at my side, maybe Father ...."

"Your father, who would have been fried by then? Let's be very clear about this. I do not respect you. I do not like you. If you ever try to hurt my friend again, I will kill you with my own hands."

"You might as well kill me then, if you can't love me."

(*Oh puleeeze ....*)

"Don't tempt me," Aki says. "If we even help you get to the village, it will be because of this guy." She takes my hand. I feel awfully flattered. "Because *I* think we should leave you to crawl there on your own."

In the end, we decide to drag the banished prince of the Niagararians downriver on a travois made from his own bent kite. His leg is broken, and maybe a couple of ribs. He likely has a concussion and ends up throwing up anything edible. So Aki suggests we don't waste good food on him. He gets the message and is remarkably quiet as we horse him down off the abutment. It probably hurts.

We leave the base of the dam and I point out a figure standing at the top. Flyboy ignores me, focused on his own pain. But Aki turns back to look, shading her eyes, and then, surprisingly, waves. At first the figure doesn't move, and then there is a half-hearted flutter of one hand. I'm a little relieved. If Dolores is still standing after all that, she should be able to get home.

"Did you know Dolores means 'sadness'?" I say.

"What a horrible thing to name a girl-child," Aki says, mildly enough. "What does 'O'car' mean – 'idiot'?"

"Oscar means 'dear friend.'" I'm surprised to see Flyboy's eyes well up. "There's still time to learn how to be one, you know – to someone else."

"It's just … m'leg hurts," he mumbles, keeping his face turned away. Maybe there's hope for the idiot boy yet.

• • •

When we arrive at the village, the headman takes O'car the Flyboy off us, treating him with great deference. Despite a feeling that the festival happened weeks ago, it has only been four days. Given the headman's attitude, I assume the villagers who attended have not returned yet with the news of the prince's banishment. Flyboy looks a bit panicked as we part ways. But Aki just shakes her head at him and he slumps and lets himself be hauled away. Maybe they'll patch him up before the news catches up with him, but that's his problem. We're on deadline too and ought to restock and get out of town before the posse arrives. One thing I will not do is go back to the falls. I'm so done with those people. Why does it seem like the more people have, the less they look after each other? I don't miss the Grandmother, but I miss the ethic of Aki's family. I liked how they felt responsible for each other. I surprise myself with that thought.

• • •

There are more signs of thaw in the village. I wonder if Aki notices. She seems a bit jittery when we walk near the egress of the headwaters. Aki doesn't trust running water anymore. The village is a lovely place. It's several villages really, spaced out around the curve of the river mouth. Both sides of the river are backed, north and south, by the usual drifts and mounds that delineate the river itself. The homes lining the banks and spreading across the river – all built on top of the ice – face east, over the lovely pristine ice of Lake Ontario. Surprisingly enough, most of them are made of scavenged wood and corrugated plastic. Clumps of homes are grouped back to back, perhaps for warmth, but then there are wide spaces between each group. The effect is open and homey. (*To me. This building style is all new to Aki.*) Near the river mouth there are places clearly marked for fishing, wide-open ponds of rushing water, so large an iceboat could never span them, no matter how long its runners. I suppose that their size helps keep the ponds ice-free. Villagers with rakes haul weed up out of the water, stacking it in mounds around the edges. There are racks of fish drying in long rows between the houses; some are probably for trade with the Niagararians. The ice looks solid out on the vast expanse of the lake, but my nostrils quiver with the smell of running water and the earthy scents of fish, weed, mud, and the faint, teasing smells of spring. There is no doubt about it. Thaw is coming.

Despite the bustle of the villagers and the rushing currents in the ponds, it's so quiet here compared with the rumbling falls. I have a pervasive feeling of well-being I didn't know I was missing. The energizing ozone scent of the falls is absent, but it's calmer and more serene here. I like this place. I hope they move the houses before they fall in the river when the ice melts. Aki likes it here too. As we walk around, folks nod cautious greetings that turn to welcoming smiles when we stop to talk.

The fish racks create an ongoing marketplace, unattended unless a stroller stops to look them over, then whoever happens to be nearby suddenly pops up to haggle, as if the village is a hive with a shared purpose. Using

Flyboy's broken kites, we buy enough dried fish and weed to last us across the next lake. The folks are more interested in the frames than the cloth, and for good reason, since all the cloth originally came from this village. On the southern shore we're shown a longhouse made of ice and scavenged lumber housing huge electric looms. Outside its doors, tunnels of ice lead under the drift and we see folks emerging with armfuls of ancient plastic bags, tarps, dreck. The plastic goes into the longhouse where it's sorted, sliced, twisted, and folded into lengths for weaving on looms made for giants. Two people stand on either side of the loom feeding plaited cords of plastic across the width, others twisting new plastic into the end of the cord as fast as it's fed out. The result is a loose packed weave like a very coarse burlap. There are several smaller hand-looms around the large room, producing a finer weave.

The woven plastic is stored by density and strength of the weave. There are no arc lights in this building (and I've seen them in the public house where we're staying). The weavers' building is lighted only by a scratched and frosted roof of once-clear corrugated plastic, and by huge double doors at each end. I suspect the arcs are too dangerous near the flammable "cloth." Most of the looms are electric and I notice they kick up a lot of plastic dust.

The weavers are intrigued by our small nylon skating kites, and more than happy to replace the nylon for their own weave, with the nylon itself as trade (our nylon is a bit like silk, in comparison to their rougher plastic weave). The head weaver is disappointed that we won't trade the frames as well. I'm happy to have the new, heavier sails. The winds blowing in from the south are warmer than anything we've experienced yet. If my patchy memory serves, a warm wind hitting cold creates storms. We may be getting even bigger winds soon, and I don't want our sails blowing out.

•••

In the village pub that evening, we try a new kind of weed beer that's been fermented and distilled into a strong, clear alcohol. It's as close to a sake as anything I can recall, and I end up trading my smallest dagger for as much as we can drink. I plan to get stonkered. There are just too many things right now between me and Aki that haven't been worked out. I don't know where to start. It's wonderful to be with her again. I really missed her in Niagara when she was always off with the flyers. In the weaver's village, Aki shows a real gift for getting a good trade. She seems to enjoy negotiating. We work well together, agreeing on almost every deal, collecting what we'll need to head out onto the ice. We've done this traveling-together thing for a while and, now that we have a chance to plan, we know how. I feel us moving in step with each other. It's familiar and comfortable. But more and more I wonder what Aki is getting out of all this. What does she want from me? The smells of thaw make me a little restless, despite the relief of being in this friendly, open place.

In the pub, we eat fresh fish (*so much better than dried*) and tender weed salad with a vinegar dressing that is to die for (*I trade for a small carafe that's almost as good as salt*). The cook has sprinkled the salad with some kind of crunchy, roasted insect, which the amused villagers tell us are called ice beetles. Despite their proclaimed lower caste, I can't help feeling that the villages live far better than the Niagararians do in their rumbling, arc-lit caves.

When the stronger weed sake is brought out, Aki and I toast everyone we can think of. Keycha first, then the Grandmother, the Tanker Lioness, even the old man – leader of the Niagararians. When we get to the last one, our village drinking mates fall silent for a while, then ask us careful questions about the falls. I get a feeling they're not exactly fans of the Niagararians – and yet there's some connection there. When we ask why they grumble, the most they'll say is, "They are not fair in trade."

This seems like a pretty big thing for a trading town, so I keep asking.

"What're they doing that isn't fair?"

Our fellow drinkers tell us that Niagararians do provide electricity, which is useful some months of the year, but at other times, like now, there's plenty of sun, so who needs it? They do not hunt for, scavenge, or *make* the electricity, so that's unfair. And what seems to bother these kindly folks most is that the electricity is invisible, so how do the villagers know if they're getting their fair share?

Furthermore, they're looking forward to the old man turning over leadership to the young prince, whom everyone adores. He's friendly, has practical skills as a flyer, and isn't snooty with people. They can't thank me enough for bringing him here after his accident (*I wonder what Flyboy's told them*). They intend to shower gifts on him before he returns home, in hopes he'll accept more of their young people as Flyers and Scientists in future.

I decide that the Niagararians really *aren't* being fair in trade. Electricity is more tangible, perhaps, to me than to the villagers. But the villagers are giving up their children to a quality of life worse than what they have here. When I try to say so, the villagers laugh. It's hard for me to understand how they can look up to the Niagararians while still feeling hard done by them. Everyone has an opinion.

Aki is snoring on the table by this time, but my arguments have drawn a deep chuckle from an adjoining table. I look over to see an incredibly tall, rather handsome man in, I swear, what looks like buckskin clothes sewn from eel skin. He's like Daniel Boone without the raccoon hat. He doesn't seem like one of the villagers. Turns out, he's not.

He comes over to join our table, handing a rope of shells to the landlord in trade for more weed sake. I can't take my eyes off the shells. Are they old? New? Freshwater? Or could they be … ocean shells?

"You like these?" He puts several in my hand and closes my fingers around them. "I'll give you these and more if you'll spend the evening with me."

"What?!" The villagers at our table all talk at once, telling the man this is not something to ask from a respected guest. That Aki and I have brought the prince from Niagara and are to be treated as honorary Niagararians. They're very emphatic, but also seem maybe a little scared of the big man. He just throws his head back and laughs that deep laugh again.

"An evening of conversation only," he says, kindly enough, squeezing my hand around the shells to make sure I know I'm to keep them. Then he releases me and pulls his own oversized cup off his belt and holds it out for his sake, which makes the Landlord groan that he's made a bad trade.

"But it's a shame," the man says, gulping back the strong drink. "You really are a lovely girl."

I tense instantly. I can see the folk at our table suddenly looking at me askance, trying to figure out exactly what I am. I haven't run into this kind of reaction in a while.

"How old are …" he starts to say, when Aki's head lifts up off the table and she glares at us blearily.

"Don't be shtoopid," she says to the man.

"Oh! Another beauty. Your older sister?" He eyes Aki's breasts far too avidly.

"He's *my* older brother." Aki scowls, and thunks her head back down on the table again. Out.

"Ah," says the man complacently. "So you *are* related. Good to hear. And my comment stands whatever your gender. You really are lovely." And he runs his thumb from my cheekbone to my chin. I shudder right down to my toes, which I'm sure he notices. He doesn't miss much, this one. He laughs again.

The landlord thumps my own jug of warm sake down between us rather hard, and wanders off, muttering.

One of the older villagers jabs me with an elbow. "That young'un's a trader from Oswego," he says, raising his eyebrows as if that explains everything. "Not one of us." He looks at the man disapprovingly.

"I'm not really one of 'us' either, I suppose," I say. The villager looks surprised.

"Well, an' that's true enough, lad. But don't say I didn't warn ya."

"Warn me of what?"

But the man just nods meaningfully at my new drinking friend and turns to his table mates to talk about the southerly and wonder, yet again, how long it will last.

"So you've been down the lake," I say to the Daniel Boone look-alike.

"I have, and I can talk about more than the weather," the man says, jerking his chin toward the villagers, who ignore him. "The name's Harken."

"Hark, Hark, the Dogs do Bark?" I must be a little drunk.

"Dogs?" he says. "Oh, we really must talk."

"Tell me about these shells, *ah*, Harken," I say, rolling them in my hand. They're small and compact, like cowrie shells. Did this kind of creature ever live in freshwater? They're glossy too, as if they recently housed living beings.

"They come from a great salt sea to the east," the trader says, and there's no way he can miss the reaction I have this time. He's definitely got my attention for the evening.

• • •

223

We talk, and drink, far into the night. I have a good tolerance for alcohol, much to the Landlord's dismay, so I hold my own against the bigger man (*much to his?*). We spend a fair bit of time being cagey about where our information comes from. I try the time-traveler shtick on him, but he just laughs. I finally admit I've seen a dog, but long ago, being eaten for someone's dinner – and that it was the last dog I'd ever seen (*true enough*). He admits that he hasn't seen the salt sea himself, but that he'd traded up the Saint Lawrence as far as the beginning of the Hudson Bay, and heard tales of giants that once swam those waters. He's seen their skulls. He's quite a storyteller. I'm not sure how much he believes himself. I swap him some of my own tall tales. Toward dawn, when the drink is finally getting to me, I ask him if he knows the meaning of his name.

"'To listen,'" he says, wrapping a very drunk me in his arms and carrying me to the room I share with Aki.

• • •

When I wake, I'm sure we're back in Niagara. The futon is rumbling and shaking. My head pounds as if nails are being driven in. When I finally manage to open my eyes, Harken is lying beside me, snoring like the falls themselves. We're both fully clothed, thankfully. Aki's on the other side of him. While I watch blearily, she rolls over until her head is on his shoulder. Ugh. This guy is too much. I poke at her over the bulk of his body and her eyes open. When she finally manages to focus on who she's hugging she rolls away fast enough, then crouches on the futon, holding her head – and she'd had only one mug to my two shared jugs.

"Make it stop," she whimpers.

"If I move, I'll throw up," I whisper back. Harken stops snoring. His eyes are still closed.

"Who th' hell is that?"

"He followed me home. Can I keep him?"

"Gotta stop picking up stray … whatsits." Aki tries to smile, but winces.

"Definitely a whatsit. But he knows the route to Oswego. And …." I hesitate. Do I want her to know this? "He's been up the Saint Lawrence."

Aki straightens up too quickly and regrets it.

"Ouch. Ugh. So he's a human map?"

"Kinda. He's pretty interesting." I notice Harken's eyes don't seem completely closed anymore. "Even if he does look like a particularly ugly pigfish."

"Hey!" Harken's eyes open wide.

"I knew you were awake!"

• • •

When the three of us stagger into the pub's main room the landlord's wife gives us the stink-eye. So much for friendly villagers. I congratulate her on the strength of her sake and she smirks, then gives us some kind of weed stew so close to miso soup I could cry. I beg her to tell me the secret to making it, and she warms up enough to let us know that everyone is gathered to welcome the festival-goers home and hear who's been chosen to stay and study in Niagara.

I kick Aki under the table and mouth "time to go" at her, but she's got her head in her hands. We won't get far in this shape. Maybe it will be okay to risk another night in town.

"Hair of the dog?" Harken hands me a very small cup with sake in it. I pour it in my soup when the landlady isn't looking and sip slowly.

"How do *you* know about dogs?" I ask, belatedly.

"Don't drink hair," Aki whines. "I can't cope with that."

"Poor Beauty." Harken says, reaching into his pack. He pulls out a soft-looking bag that smells heavenly. "Lean back and rest this over your eyes. See if that helps."

Aki lies right down on the floor near the low table, with her head near Harken's knee. He gently places the bag across her eyes. "Better?"

"Smells nice," Aki sighs. "Nice trader. We can keep him ...."

I'm a little surprised Aki feels that way too. I really like our trader, and he's proved himself mostly harmless by not taking advantage of our drunkenness last night. Plus he'd be awfully handy to travel with.

"Where you headed?" I ask.

"Oswego. Then the Saint Lawrence River," he says. "A new trade route for me. I'd be pleased to have company for a change. Especially two such delightful folks as yourselves."

"Stop," I growl.

"Keep talking," Aki says from under her perfumed eye bag.

Harken laughs.

I'm torn. I've been looking forward to the easy days of just Aki and me out on the ice. But Harken is entertaining and, because he knows the route, I wouldn't have to worry about our direction. The prospect of passing on the responsibility of being in charge (*at least of the route, Aki being who she is*) is compelling, to say the least. It has never been a role I cherish. I picture trusting ourselves to this big capable man. It isn't hard to imagine.

"Aki?"

"*Frack*, yeah," she says. "But make sure you buy some of that sake for the trip."

• • •

We're packed and ready to go. Aki's found a small travois for me to pull and overpacked it with supplies. We have only one knife left each and new heavy-duty outer suits that breathe in place of the sweaty nylon gear we got from the tanker folk. I have my jar of vinegar, and Aki, a newly hatched glutton, is carrying way more sake than we need. The landlady gave me a block of powdered weed for making faux miso, then only charged me a morning's labor in the kitchens for it. But now I know how to make more. I feel rich.

Harken has his own trailer, which slides on the smoothest runners. They even swivel. I bet it hardly drags at all. His skates look like they have the original uppers and brand-new blades. I wonder out loud why a trader doesn't have a boat for carrying goods, which makes him look at me oddly. I haven't seen a single iceboat since we left the tanker folk. Could it be no one here uses them? But they have skates – something we should discuss around the fire one night out on the ice.

We're heading toward the lake, Aki in the lead, when Flyboy steps in her path. He's moving pretty well for someone with a splint on his leg and probably very sore ribs.

"Come to see us off?" I ask dryly.

"Don't go." He's addressing only Aki of course, and his voice cracks. He's got it bad.

There are three young men flanking him. I suspect they're flyers from Niagara but I've never been good with faces. It doesn't seem like his reputation's suffered since the festivalgoers returned the day before.

"Dolores made it back, then?" Aki asks him.

"What? I don't … I don't know."

"You still don't care about anyone but yourself." Aki lets the disgust show in her voice. "Fix that."

"If I do, can I go with you?" The young men attending Flyboy shift restlessly.

"No," Aki says firmly. "You can't." She moves to step around him. He grabs at her arm and suddenly Harken is there, pushing between them.

"The young prince of Niagara!" he says. His voice is even kind. "I think you have other places you need to be."

I can only see Harken's back, but Flyboy's expression is awesome. He stares up at Harken's face with something like horror. Does he think Harken wants to steal Aki away? Well, he could be right. I wonder why that thought doesn't make me jealous.

"What? Why are you …? You can't!"

"Can't travel with my friends to my own home?" Harken's voice is still gentle, but there might be some threat in there. I want to see his expression. Something sure is upsetting Flyboy. I remember that Harken is not one of his adoring "subjects."

"No!" Flyboy is staring at me now. "You can't go with *him*. For gods' sakes!" But Aki pushes past while Harken stands in Flyboy's way. I follow, looking back in time to see Harken flash a decidedly evil grin at Flyboy before he walks steadily after us, his swaggering posture daring Flyboy to interfere. Wow. Having that kind of presence would be handy now and then. The last words I hear from Flyboy are also the first time he has ever used my name.

"Jack!" he calls after us. "Look after her, Jack. I'm sorry, Aki. I'm so sorry."

ICE THAW

"The cold wind burns my face, and blows
Its frosty pepper up my nose ...
Black are my steps on silver sod;
Thick blows my frosty breath abroad;
And tree and house, and hill and lake,
Are frosted like a wedding-cake."
— Robert Louis Stevenson, "Winter-Time"

"I'm gonna call you 'Helen of Troy' from now on," I say to Aki while we're making camp that evening, finally together out on the ice. The village was good, but this is better. I'd almost forgotten the joy of those quiet, bright stars appearing overhead after the sun sets.

Harken almost spits out his miso soup. So he knows The Iliad story too?

"Don't hate me because I'm beautiful," Aki smirks at me. Stealing my line.

"Just what do you suppose a face looks like after it has launched a thousand ships?"

"Why you!"

"Hey, you two." Harken interrupts as we roll on the ice in a mock battle. "Don't leave me out ...."

Aki shoots me a look and I grin. How can we ignore an invitation like that? She counts to three under her breath and we leap as one to take the big guy down ....

• • •

I haven't had so much fun since the last warming period. Harken doesn't fit inside our makeshift tent, so we move quite happily into his tepee. The shafts of his trailer and a couple of spears serve as uprights. The villagers custom-fit the plastic fabric. It's roomy, but stays warm. It has the same problem in wind as ours, so he hammers iron pikes into the ice each evening when we camp to tie it down. When he's alone he lights a fire inside, but I don't like that idea after seeing how careful the villagers were with the arc lights near their looms. The nights are balmy enough (*relatively speaking*) so an outside fire with a windbreak made from chipped ice is enough. Our combined body heat keeps the inside of the tepee plenty warm at night. Usually Aki and I fall asleep together on Harken's wide chest. He's warmer than caribou hides.

Harken's a terrible flirt. I decide the reason I'm not jealous of him flirting with Aki is that he never leaves me out, and he never takes it too far. Aki is "Hey, Beautiful," and I'm "Sweetie!" This may be the first time I've trusted a grownup in decades (though he barely qualifies – he's just big). He doesn't hide his admiration, and he takes care of us. I feel the stress of Niagara Falls dropping away the farther we skate out onto the lake. With Harken, I feel safe. I don't worry about what will happen next.

With all the flirting and play, Aki and I once again manage to put off the conversation we should have had long ago, about just what we are to each other. We flirt with Harken, we flirt with each other, and it's exciting. But one day, while Aki and I are fishing – more to put off the inevitable arrival in the next village than because we need more fish – I notice I feel very small sitting next to Aki. She's just slapped my hand for stealing her bait, as if I'm a kid. It doesn't hurt, but I realize she's grown again. Aki no longer hides in her wrapped mummy bindings. Her uni-suit is open to her cleavage in the sunlight and her hood is thrown back. Her luxurious hair flows down her back. Womanly curves fill her suit. I look down at my own stick figure sadly. I don't know if I'm her friend, her boyfriend, or ugly little sister. I'm afraid to find out.

Harken ambles over and must have caught the expression on my face. He puts his big warm hand on my head (we don't wear gloves as much as we used to).

"Don't be sad, Sweetie," he says, petting my hair. "You're beautiful too." I tilt my head back to look up at him just as he leans down to kiss (I assume) the top of my head. He smooches me full on the lips. We both freeze in surprise. Then he looks me straight in the eye and says, "Yum."

He waits for a long heartbeat to see what I'll do, but a sound from Aki makes us both straighten. She's watching us wide-eyed, face flushed.

"Don't … don't do that," she says.

"Why don't you come try it too?" Harken's voice is rich and deep with invitation. He leaves me and steps around the fishing hole to Aki. It feels like all the warmth in the world goes with him.

Harken crouches down next to Aki, who refuses to look at him.

"Don't your people kiss, Beautiful?"

Aki shakes her head, still not looking up. He takes her chin gently in his hand and tilts her face toward him, moving slowly enough so that she can avoid him if she wants. Harken kisses Aki, while she stares at him like a stunned mullet.

He laughs as he releases her chin, then hugs her to him with one arm, stretching the other out to me. "You know

I love you both," he says. I actually hear a slight shake in the usually confident voice. He's taking a chance I've never had the guts to take.

I stand, but I don't move toward him.

"Aki," I demand. "Come here." As if Aki would ever respond to that kind of tone. But at least it knocks her out of her daze and she frowns at me.

"You can't," I say to Harken. My whole body is shaking. "You hardly know us."

"Everything I know I like," Harken says. "A lot."

I lock eyes with Aki. I'm being left behind, punched in the stomach by my own inaction. "To Aki, I ... we ...."

Aki pushes away Harken's arm and stands. She glares at me, waiting for me to say something, but I can't.

"Jack is not my brother," she finally says. Harken watches us both silently, but says nothing.

"Jack is not my lover," Aki continues, but there's a question in her voice this time. She pauses again, but now I'm the prey, frozen in fear on the ice.

"What exactly is Jack?" she finally asks me, cruelly direct.

My knees fold. I crouch on the ice and hide my head in my arms like a child being scolded. I like them both so much. I was having so much fun. But I don't know what I want – or what I am. Will they leave me now? The vastness of the ice surrounds us on all sides. It feels too big and empty to be real. There are only the three of us left in all of space and time.

"I left my home for Jack. I left my brother. My family. To help Jack find out who he is."

I look up at Aki, startled. Her voice is softer now. "But Jack? I need to do some things for myself now too. Things I don't think you can give me. Let me have this one, Jack."

Aki turns back to Harken. "Will you kiss me again?"

He doesn't hesitate for an instant but pulls her to him roughly. I watch Aki melt against the big man as if she belongs there. She matches him with a grace I didn't realize she'd matured into. They're heartbreakingly lovely as they kiss against the sunset.

I walk away awkwardly, trying to figure out what to do with myself. After staring at the sky for a while, I set up the small tent a ways out on the ice, taking two of the skins with me. I know they won't need the warmth as much as I do.

In the night, I wake, sweating. Wondering if I could be with them both now if I were braver. Wondering if I invited him along because I knew this would happen.

• • •

Harken treats me the same as ever, though he can barely keep his hands off Aki. She looks plush and satisfied, a cat-and-cream look I've never associated before with the girl who always thought speed was the best thing since Laker roe.

I'm still "Sweetie," and he still pats my hair, and sometimes even gropes me, though I swat him away tiredly. The playfulness has gone out of it for me.

Aki notices though, and our relationship becomes strained. We don't tease each other anymore. But she forgets soon enough when her attention shifts to him. I watch her, and she watches Harken.

One night, as I'm about to leave the fire to them, Harken grabs my waist and pulls me into his lap. "Don't go," he says, hugging me tight. "It's lonely thinking of you all by yourself out there."

"Gah!" Aki swats his massive shoulder. "Greedy pigfish. You'd go for Jack too given a chance, wouldn't you?" I wonder for a moment if she's trying to protect me, but the look she gives me is anything but friendly. My stomach hurts.

I struggle to get up but Harken laughs, "Of course!" and nuzzles my neck. It feels so good I go limp for a moment. I miss cuddling with them at night. I miss being touched at all. But I remember that it's Aki's turn to get what she wants, so I grab his nose until he lets me go, seeming reluctant. Aki not so much.

She gives me a dirty look and drags him to the tepee where I hear them arguing late into the night. In the morning no one is flirting or laughing. We all skate far apart from each other, keeping our distance.

Something has to change. I become certain, as I skate, that if we don't talk candidly before we reach Oswego then I'll lose Aki and everything we've meant to each other on this journey (*in this lifetime*). Fear is a powerful motivator. I still can't figure out what I want from her – or Harken. How can I when I don't know what I want from myself? Aki will eventually leave me, one way or another. She's already more mature than me. (*Will I stay like this forever?*) If we don't talk soon, she'll leave with Harken. How much do I need to be with Aki? I ran from something even more compelling, at the time, with Keycha. Maybe it's why I ran? I'm comfortable with Aki now, I love her, but I always lose everyone I love. How can that not affect us both? Perhaps it's time for me to be on my own again, terrifying though that is. But the one thing I'm sure of, is I don't want to be alone because I've lost Aki's friendship.

It's time to bring out the sake.

• • •

Everyone is quiet around our fire that night. After we've eaten, as the sun sets, I rummage through Aki's pack and pull out a jar of sake. She purses her lips but doesn't stop me. Perhaps she also realizes this may be our last chance. Oswego is less than two days away, even if we drop sails and just skate.

"We need to talk," I say. "But I'm not sure how to start."

We're all silent for a moment. "Maybe it's time to know more about each other. About what each of us is thinking. About what we mean to each other. It's hard because ... I think I'm really quite angry at both of you. And I want to let that go, because ... in my own way ... I care about you. So much." I rush the last part, mumbling. I take a huge swig of sake, and pass the jug to Harken while I cough from the fumes.

"I fell for you when I first heard you giving the villagers a hard time," Harken says to me. "And when I saw Aki, she just knocked the air out of my lungs. I still can't believe I found people like you two in the world, who I can really talk to – and play with. Who want to be with me. When that Niagararian princelet wanted to make you stay, my heart almost pounded out of my chest. I wanted so badly to knock him down. He knew it too." Harken chuckles a little. "But you don't really know me. I'm a little afraid for you to know me." He drinks and passes the jug to Aki.

Aki drinks before she speaks. Several times. Then she slams the jug on the ground. "I *hated* you, Jack, when you looked at my brother the way you did. Sometimes I've blamed you for having to leave home." My face flames hot, and even Harken stretches out his hand toward Aki as if to ward off the heat. Aki drinks again and sighs.

"But ... Keycha sent *you* away too. And sometimes you looked so sad. We got along after that, didn't we? I started to see what Keycha saw in you. You're kind and smart. It was best when we were alone together on the ice. I started to believe I was special to you. Would be, in time, once you forgot Keycha. But you never seemed to want anything from me. I was so relieved when you asked me to leave Niagara with you! I thought, perhaps, when we reached the salt sea, we'd find a cure for that scorpion's poison of yours. For whatever it is driving you. I liked that drive once. It was exciting. But it isn't enough now. I know you need me, but it's a child's need. I want more than that."

Frack, but Aki is beautiful. So hard and bright and cruel.

"I want you to tell Harken what you are," this cruel woman says. "You started this. Let's get it all out in the open." She pushes the jug at me.

I stare into the jug. I know she wants to see Harken recoil from my body. She wants to establish her claim on him. But being intersex, while it may (*or may not*) go along with being immature, to me isn't a problem in itself. I like my body. It becomes problematic only as a symptom of my other dual nature, a long-life paired with the inability to live for long in one timeline, with the people I care about. I really am a time traveler, always out of sync in body and time. I need her to understand this.

"I am nothing. I am no one. I am cursed by nonexistent gods for crimes I don't remember, to walk this earth while it burns and freezes and the people I love crumble to dust. Someone long ago told me there are answers for me in the east. But as long as I've traveled to find them, I cannot die. I cannot grow up. Perhaps I can't really love, either."

"Well, you sure can't drink," Harken says, taking the jug out of my hand. Aki snorts. Is she actually laughing? *Huh*.

"I'm a bad man," Harken says. He gulps thirstily from the jug. "I'm not ready to tell you how bad yet. But please believe me, I would never do anything to harm either of you. You two are such a gift. Sometimes I felt like there was not another human being in the world. That people just talked and said nothing all day long. I chose to be alone because of that. To spend my life on the ice instead of listening to the chatter of silly people with nothing to think about other than their weed haul and their endless fishing stories and …. *Frack*! But, meeting you two …. I realize I need people too …." He passes the jug to Aki.

"Sometimes I think I left the lake just to take you away from Keycha. And to pay him back for choosing you ...."

"*Gah*! Who's this Keycha?" Harken shouts suddenly. "Isn't this about *us*?"

"My turn, Harken," I say, taking the jug. "I wish you could choose me," I say to Aki. "I've never felt closer to another person, not even Keycha. You stayed with me. You and I have traveled under the sky with just each other, shared life and breath. You're a part of me .... But maybe I can't give you what you want. I think I figured that out when Harken kissed me."

"It was hot, right?" Harken says.

"Straight to the groin," I say, passing him the jug. I'm really toasted. I need to be drunk for this.

Harken lets out a hoot. Aki grabs the jug from him before he can drink.

"Don't you dare do this to me again," she hisses at me furiously.

I hide behind my hands. I don't want to see her angry face. "Don't you get it! I can lust after him, but I love *you*. But I can't be who you want. I'm neither one thing or another. I'm male. I'm female. I'm too old. I'm too young. Can you even begin to imagine what it's like to be me? Why did you save me that day on the ice? I could have just frozen until the thaw. I could have missed all this living. I hurt! Living hurts. *You* make me hurt!" I'm wailing. I can't help it. I'm a wounded animal, the last of its kind, howling in pain. "The worst is, I'll still be hurting and missing you when you're dead and gone and I'm still this horrible, hateful whatever-I-am!"

They close the distance. Aki pets my hair and makes soothing noises. Harken hugs us both in his big arms.

"You *will* leave me." My eyes are painfully dry and my body is limp. I need them so badly to just be here with me right now. "And I'll be the same as I always am. Just more alone. I will miss you *so* much, Aki." I take her face between my hands. "Live a good life. Make every minute count. I'll never forget you." I think Harken's crying. Gods and fishes, this sake is brutal stuff.

"Harken, you're totally hot. Aki, you're smart and beautiful and my other heart. I love you both, but I'm gonna leave you in Oswego." There, I said it. I'll let them get on with their lives and I'll travel on to the east. I'll do it for them. That isn't just me running away again – is it?

•••

The one who never really spilled his guts was Harken. But at least Aki and I are talking again. We're painfully kind to each other in the morning after we all wake with splitting headaches. Harken builds up the fire and makes us a "hair of the dog" using my block of faux miso and the sake dregs. We even laugh while explaining the phrase to Aki, who's still disgusted at the thought of drinking hair. It's late afternoon before we're in any shape to skate. But the fresh wind on the ice helps clear our heads, so we have a short day of travel, and by our evening camp, the mood is calmer than it has been for days. The easy camaraderie is back, though it has changed and is more subdued.

Aki and Harken sit touching, but they aren't grabbing at each other. I stick around after the meal is done. Harken tells us a bit about Oswego.

"It's a rough town," he says. "Not like the weavers' village. It's bigger, for one, and the first families mostly run things. Lot of traders come through. Lots of strangers. No one looks out for each other, and everyone hustles to get what they can, to make the best trade. You'll be robbed if you aren't careful, or if you walk down the wrong alley at night.

"It's a funny kind of place, Oswego. There isn't much that's scavenge-worthy nearby but, maybe because it's sort of midway between the Niagararian weavers and the Saint

Lawrence – and that old canal to the south – it became a trading center, the first stop for traders from the west and north."

"How about east?"

"Not much trade from there these days. I think that southern canal turns east after a while, or so they say. It isn't used much now. People do head down it now and then, but not many come back. It doesn't look like the easiest path to travel; narrow with lots of drift." Harken looks at me anxiously. He's already heard I'm dead set on trying the canal. But Aki doesn't try to talk me out of it anymore, which sort of hurts.

"The Saint Lawrence heads northeast," Harken says, not for the first time.

"And is it narrow with lots of drift?"

"Well. Yes. It can be quite rough. But it's traveled more these days. And I hear the Hudson Bay is … well, it's supposed to be a big lake, like this one. I didn't go farther than the mouth that one time, but I heard tales of big ice and rumors of open water. One trader I met said he'd sailed in a boat that floated – instead of skated."

Aki hangs on his words. I wonder if she's remembering her dream of the drowned sailors.

"Our map doesn't show past the bay. What happens after that? Is it the salt sea?" she asks.

"Don't know," Harken admits. "But a man with coloring like you two gave me those trade beads I carry. He said the shells were from critters that lived in saltwater.

"Oh! I got something else from him. Take a look at this." Harken roots around in his trailer, finally pulling out a small fish bladder. It's full of something that looks like coarse sand. "Taste. Go ahead."

I pick a small brown rock and hesitantly put it in my mouth. Aki does the same. Her face falls and she makes a pucker. Then she starts sucking in earnest.

"Don't bite; some of those rocks will break your teeth. Good though, aye?"

"You bastard! You've been holding out! You've had *salt* all this time?" I'm practically drooling for more, but Harken moves the bag out of reach and carefully ties the top closed again.

"Sorry," he says, "this stuff's worth more than I'd get for you two on the open market."

"More!" Aki says, grabbing at the bag.

"What?" I say.

"I said this is worth a lot."

"More than us?"

"Well, more than you'd sell for ... if ... I mean ... uh."

"You trade in kids," I say flatly.

Aki's still trying to grab the arm with the bag of salt. She has no idea what we're talking about.

"I did tell you I was a bad man." Harken sighs.

• • •

Harken and Aki both try to explain to me that trading in human beings is not such a big deal. Weren't Aki and Keycha sold to the Grandmother? It's usually children, Harken explains (*as if that makes it better*). Many adults can't conceive, so they pay for children to raise as part of their own families. I know all about the epidemic sterility that hit most species before the snows. There was a gigantic drop in human populations long before the ice.

"Is that what happens to all of them?" I ask Harken. "The ones you take from their homes and trade for profit?" I feel so betrayed. So this is what it feels like to meet the perfect friend – kind, intelligent, playful. Someone who likes you back. Then find some rot underneath, a terrible flaw in their basic outlook on life. How big a flaw does it have to be to ruin a friendship? A partnership? People being allowed basic rights and freedoms should be primary.

Children being abused is not something to compromise on. This is not small stuff. (*Could this be how Keycha felt, when he understood how completely my beliefs differed from his?*) How can I ever look at Harken the same way again? Trading in kids. It's worse than discovering he's a wife beater. Maybe on par with being a serial killer. And here is Aki, acting as if it doesn't matter. As if it's expected. That hurts even worse.

"I assume that's how the Lioness got all those kids." Aki peers at me with concern. "Weren't you sending them as trade to Keycha?" My stomach drops. Is that what I did? I'm so horrified I can't even think about that right now.

"Do they cry when you take them away, Harken? Are they always treated well? Do you also trade children – human beings – to people who abuse them, force them to work, treat them badly? Tell Aki. Tell her it isn't all about finding happy families.

"And you!" I turn to Aki. "Wouldn't you rather have been with your own parents, your people? Isn't the real reason you left the lake because you wanted control over your life? What if the Grandmother had forced you –?" Aki puts her hand over my mouth. Tears are running down her face.

"Stop. Just stop."

I pull away. "Harken," I say grimly. "I believe you're responsible for every heartbreak, every broken life, every abused child, every human being driven to hurt itself or others, as a result of your actions." (*I get it now, Keycha.*)

Harken looks aghast, but I don't hold back. "You like the two of us because we challenge you? Make you think? Well, have you never considered what it is you're doing?"

"That's … that's why I said I was a bad man," he says softly.

"So you *know*, and you keep doing it? What's next? You gonna trade us too?"

"No! Never. I … I skipped Oswego after my last trip up the Saint Lawrence. I was going to see if I could sell

the salt. The Niagararians do a trade with the villagers ...
that I used to get involved in; but the kids want to go! And
I didn't do it this year. I was late arriving for the festival,
and then I met you two, and you were so keen to leave ...."

"Did it cross your mind to sell us off?"

"Never. I thought I'd try trading salt for cloth – which
we need in Oswego. If it worked, I thought maybe I'd just
keep trading in cloth and salt – if folks want it. That's what
I thought."

"Do you take the kids who don't make the Niagararian's
cut to Oswego?"

"Sometimes ... I used to."

"What, do you tell them you're taking them to new
families and then just sell them to the highest bidder?"

Harken doesn't answer.

"Then you *are* a bad man," I say heavily. "Aki, I can't
leave you with this guy."

"No one is going to tell me what I can and can't do *ever*
again," Aki says. We both stare at her. I've never heard this
tone in her voice before. She sounds very – strong.

"Harken. You have the salt. Are you going to continue
trading kids?" Aki says.

"I left my iceboat back in the village, because I didn't
do that trade."

"Harken!"

"No! I'm saying I'm already done. It will be a little
harder – but I have the salt, and I hope to get more in
time."

"Are you saying this just because Jack doesn't like it?"

"No. No ... I ...."

"Are there any children you need to make amends to?"
I add.

"None living," Harken says, hanging his head. "Which
is why I've been thinking this way for a while."

"Someone died?"

"Yeah."

"You were responsible?"

"No! Not … yeah. In a way.

"I never really got along with people," Harken goes on, not looking at us. "My own family all trades in … kids, fish, scavenge, whatever. I grew up around it. I was a trade kid myself. Everyone looks up to my father. He's a big man in town. But at some point I just started to hate everything and everybody. I was the one who wanted to do the long-distance trade routes. I loved being by myself up on the river. Then I didn't have to deal with people – or trade kids. I thought I could find something new, not just a one-off trade, but something that didn't run out, but was necessary, like the cloth. Maybe I could please my dad and not have to be around people so much. I was going to test the salt in Niagara, see what it was worth before I bragged about it to my father. Then I met you two. I don't care so much about what my family wants now. If you two are with me, I can face him without the cloth … or the kids."

"Salt." I say, firmly. "You will make a fortune if you have a regular source of salt."

"You think?" Harken looks pathetically hopeful.

"Trust me. I've been around a while. Salt used to rule the world. The only thing that could even compete was sugar … and …." *(Oh, how I miss hot pepper!)*

"What about your mother?" Aki says suddenly. "Or grandmother?"

"Uh, they don't really have much to say about it, I guess?"

"Now, see, that's a big problem for me," Aki says. "Because I've no intention of being a hanger-on in this business. Will you be an equal partner with me, if I help you trade for salt with the man who looks like me up on the Hudson Bay?"

"Yes," Harken says, with admirable simplicity. "I will."

"Good." Aki turns to me. "Anything else?"

"No!" I say, surprised.

"I have your approval to love Harken and build a life with him?"

"You do," I say. And Aki grins at me, that wonderful, wild grin she has when she's being yanked down the ice at high speed, her sail just barely – and yet completely – within her control.

• • •

Oswego makes me imagine we've stepped back into the Wild West, and not the cute one from the old movies. Unlike the weaver's village, Oswego isn't on clean ice. Somehow the wind has scraped the shore clear here and the shacks and ice houses are built on hard frozen dirt, churned to mud and refrozen. Everything's dirty. It's obviously a trading town. There's an amazing mix of stuff everywhere: boats more diverse even than Keycha's experimental fleet, and far less ice-worthy by their look. Houses are made of rock, dirt, dirty ice, wood, corrugated plastic. The main street is the market, with everyone selling something. It's overwhelmingly stinky. The clean spring smell of the weaver's village is in the air here too, somewhere in the background, behind a smell of cess and rot. There are just too many people, and the ground is like iron. Far too hard to dig decent latrines.

There are food smells too, some better than others. A dozen fires dot the market, where folk are selling cooked fish and weed cubes on fish-spine kabobs. There are strange orange and white fish I've never seen before, and cauldrons of ice beetles, some roasted, some live. There's scavenged plastic, iron, needles, fish-skin cloth, broken mirrors, skates, kites. Everything from trash to old jewelry is being sold. One seller has a few tired-looking books, most coverless, the pages rolled and held together with plastic strapping. Others are just single pages, or collections of several pages carefully sandwiched between yellowed plastic sheets. I stand staring at his stall so long Aki has to pull me away.

"What have we got left to trade?"

"Leave it!" she hisses. "You can look later."

The book vendor nods at me, but doesn't push his wares like some of the others, who grab or yell for buyers. I don't imagine he does much business, but he knows I'll be back.

It's noisy here, dirty, crowded.

I want to return to the clean, open ice. I mention sleeping out there to Harken and he vetoes it instantly.

"You think my family's the only ones trading in pretty faces?" he says. "You wouldn't make it through the night." His tone softens. "Do you read, Jack?"

"I do."

"I do too – a little. Do you ... could you teach me a bit more? I have some writing I just can't make out ...."

"You have books? No wonder you know the old tales. You bet! I'd love to!"

"What're you two going on about now?" Aki says grumpily. She's been scanning the crowd like a pro. Once this town would have shocked her into speechlessness. She really has changed since leaving home.

"Books, books, books, books, books!" I sing and skip a little. Oswego is worth it for the books alone. "And you know what books mean, Aki?"

"*Eh*. What?"

"Stories! And I *know* you like stories." I throw an arm around her shoulder and leer up at her. She seems taller again. When did that happen?

"A matched set!" A stranger's voice cuts into our banter. "Harken! Good to see you still have an eye for the lookers. Mama Jia will want to see these two before they go to auction."

"Walleye," Harken says, his face flaming red. "You know damn well I don't sell to Mama. You can tell her these two are freemen."

"Which means you don't plan to trade at all." The stranger is an odd-looking man. He may be around Harken's age, which I put somewhere in the early twenties, but his hair is patchy and his skin bad. "Your daddy ain't gonna like that."

"That's between him and me," Harken says grimly.

"Well, welcome home and all. You got any trade for me, Harken? Anything at all?" The man's voice shifts to a whine. "For an old friend? Times is hard, what with the Thaw bringing sickness and all."

"Got no trade 'cept family business, Walleye. What you mean, sickness?"

"You been gone a long time, Harken. Can't you see on people's faces times is hard?"

"Well, you look like shit, Walleye. That whatcha mean?"

"Ha ha. Funny guy. But I got news for ya. Buy us a pint o' weed beer and I'll bring ya up to speed."

"Later, Walleye. I gotta check in with my old man. You know how it is."

"That's right, that's right. You see your dad. You'll see. Then you'll come find me. I'll tell you what's been going on, all right."

"We'll see, Walleye. Might not be tonight."

"I ain't going nowhere," the man says bitterly, and wanders off.

"What was that about?" I ask.

"Ah, nothing good. Look, I'm probably gonna have to go talk to Walleye for a bit. It sounds like something's up. Let's get you two introduced to the family first, though. *Gah*, this ain't gonna be easy."

Aki has wandered over to a vendor selling kebabs and comes back with one for each of us. "The woman selling these says there's a fever coming in on the warm winds."

"More likely it's coming in from the lousy latrines," I say. "*Frack*, this place stinks."

Harken sniffs the air. "It's not usually this bad," he says curiously.

"Well, shit don't smell so bad when it stays frozen," I say. I can already hear myself mimicking the lazy speech pattern Harken was using with Walleye. It has its own musical quality, in a way. "Ya know, Harken, this Thaw's gonna change more than just how you travel. The ice and cold protects folks from disease, from their own garbage, and from the garbage left by olden people in the cities-that-were." I'm thinking about the tanker children again. "At least this town is on solid ground."

"Useful but ugly," Aki sighs. "Like whiskers."

• • •

Harken's family home seems to be a gigantic warehouse. Or the remains of a warehouse, the jagged corrugated sheet metal at the back is sealed from rusting and held together by ice and drift. The front, which is what we see first, is a long room lined with real wood planks and warmed by a fire with an actual chimney – made of blocks of earth as best I can tell, cured by the fire until it's hard as pottery. It's clear they're rich, even by Niag-ararian standards, and certainly for this town. Harken tells us they keep a room at the back cold to store their goods.

Harken takes us to his mother and father, who stand in front of their storehouse door like royalty. The father's wearing robes of fur that I stare at hungrily. On close inspection, they may be faux fur. I'm dying to ask. (*Skins and fur always make my heart leap. What if? Could there still be populations of any fur-bearing species out there? Could animals come back with the thaw?)* I tear my eyes away to see Harken's father staring at me disdainfully. I'm messing up the introductions.

"... I have not brought wares into the house, Father," Harken is saying angrily. I haven't heard him sound so young before. "These are my ... friends. No. Aki is my partner. My ... wife." Harken takes Aki's hand and tucks it into the crook of his arm. "Please welcome Aki and Jack as you welcome me."

"You're joking." The father's face is stern. I look at Harken's mother, but she stands quietly beside him, a pillar of respectability. Her own clothes are equally rich and stately, and a graceful hood covers her hair and most of her face. I can't tell if she's even looking at her son.

"You return after months away, after promising riches if I allow you to make this new run. And you return with ... what? I see no cloth, no goods. And no trade kids? Have you fallen in love with your own wares?"

"They came with me willingly, as freemen," Harken says hotly.

"That hardly matters."

I poke Harken. "Show him the salt."

Both men turn to stare at me. They're like competing bull elk crashing horns. What they clash over hardly matters. I reach into Harken's pack and throw the bag of salt at his father's feet. "He hardly comes empty-handed," I say. "Trade in *this* will double – quadruple – your fortunes – if you let *her* handle the negotiations." I can see he'll need to be convinced of Aki's worth.

"The female speaks," Harken's father says mockingly. He nudges the bag with his foot. I hope my impulsive throw hasn't split the bladder.

"Father!"

"Tell us your name, child." Harken's mother cuts through the tension like a cool wind. She's addressing Aki.

"I am Akiak of the Western Lake People." Aki says, which gets Harken and his father into an immediate argument about just where his recent trade route lay. The mother steps forward and leads Aki over to a bench near the fireplace. They bend their heads together while the men argue. I'm left standing by myself between the two groups, fidgeting. I've just made up my mind to go pick up the bag of salt, which is close to being trod on by the two men, when Harken's mother gasps and stands. Her husband and son stop arguing to stare.

The mother throws back her hood, revealing long, thick black hair.

"Mara!" her husband barks, as if she's broken some kind of etiquette. His wife turns and I finally see her face. She looks enough like Aki to be her sister – or mother. Her face is older, haughtier, and her cheekbones are more severe. But the resemblance is stunning.

"Do you see it?" she asks her husband icily. "Even you can guess what this means. Look at this child. You were wrong. The children lived!"

• • •

Harken's father moves to his wife's side and stands with an arm around her, staring down at Aki, who looks totally confused.

He whips around to me. "You're her brother?"

"No," I say. "I'm her … friend." It's too bad that I let him hear the regret in my voice. This is not a man to show weakness to. He dismisses me absolutely and turns back to Aki.

"You had a brother?"

"I do. His name is Akycha. He stayed behind to take over leadership of our village."

"Ah," the father says with satisfaction. As if that's what he would expect. "Leadership is in his blood." He slants his eyes slyly at Harken.

"What's this about?" Harken has finally picked up the bag of salt and tries to step closer to Aki, but his parents are in the way.

"Let me introduce you to your long-lost cousin." His father's tone is derisive.

It takes a while to cut through the rivalry between Harken and his father to get to the meaning of his jibes. Aki finally moves away from all of them to sit beside me. I put my arm around her, and we face Harken and his family across the fire. I see the mother's hands flutter toward her, as if she doesn't want to let her go even that far. But her posture remains bolt upright, and her face composed. She's a woman with much control. She cuts through the father's needling effortlessly.

"I will tell it." Her voice rings out like a professional storyteller in the marketplace. "So listen," she says to her husband, who sits back with a huff.

"We were on pilgrimage," the mother says. "Five families, all related. We crossed the deep snows by caribou sledges, hunting, but mostly trading, as we traveled east." I feel Aki twitch. "Like many, we were heading to the fabled salt sea. In time, we lost too many of our beasts. We heard of a land of smooth ice to the north, where there was weed for the animals to eat, and fish to trade for. But before that land could be reached, there were piles of drift higher than could be believed, and the crossing was terrible. We lost many of our family." She looks at her husband. "And some were left behind so the rest could move forward." He flinches this time.

"By the time we reached the ice we had few caribou left and only two sledges. We took shelter with the people of the lake, hoping to trade with them for fish. My youngest sister, my dearest – and her husband – strayed into a strange place where many people had died. They took ill. They ... died. My husband judged that their two young children had also caught the illness. He felt it was not prudent to take them with us. But he got a good deal for them, nonetheless." The cool voice held no hint of bitterness, but the father stared at his boots. "We traveled on, eventually stopping in this place, our supplies exhausted, our caribou long gone. This is as far eastward as I'll ever travel now." Her voice holds longing – for a moment.

"But our children have followed us home." The regal lips curve in an actual smile. The hooded eyes gleam. "I welcome you, niece."

"One child has followed us. A *girl*-child. And don't forget we wouldn't have made it this far without those supplies I traded for. Do you remember ...?"

"I remember everything," the mother says, her eyes nailing him to the bench.

"And I found you a strapping young son," he says. I remember that Harken said he was a trade kid himself.

"Harken's not blood-related, then?" I ask, not thinking how that might sound. It's my turn to be nailed by those hooded eyes.

"Harken is my son," his mother says. "He will take over his father's business, in time." The look she shoots at the father hints that time might not be far off. "But it must be the gods who brought you home, sister's daughter. You are most welcome here." It's clear there will be no more talk of Aki being merchandise.

"He can hardly marry his cousin," the father mutters, but the mother's eyes slice at him again.

"And why not? As our young guest points out, they're not related by blood." She turns to Harken. "Now you're my son twice over."

I'm beginning to like this old gal. Harken grins at her and dumps the bag of salt directly into his father's hands. "I think this will make you feel better, Father."

The father looks like he'd like to find more to argue about, but instead he opens the bag and stares inside curiously. "Sand?"

"Taste it."

The man picks out a rock and licks it. "Gods! Is it …? But it's been years …." He holds the bag toward his wife and his eyes are actually moist with emotion. Perhaps family doesn't move this guy, but the prospect of a good trade sure does. "Mara, try this. Do you know what this is?"

Mara's cool face creases into a wide grin and her eyes sparkle. She looks 10 years younger and even more like Aki.

"It means we both get what we want this time. Family *and* riches."

• • •

That night I have to slip away from all that family tension and warmth. It's like stepping from Christmas into the sewers when I slip outside to wander the filthy streets of the village. But it's good to be alone for a while. I pat the thin book of poetry that never leaves my breast pocket and wonder if the knife still tucked in my leggings might buy another book or two, once daylight comes. The evening wind is warm and stinks of cess. There's also something sickly sweet on the breeze that reminds me of something my brain just doesn't want to identify. I veer away from it whenever it drifts my way. The stars are out and the night is velvety black. I let my mind freewheel while I walk. Aki's found her place and her people. With his mother's help, Harken will obviously persuade his father to let them run the Saint Lawrence trade route. Such a small world when people can find long-lost family just by traveling long enough down the Great Lakes Waterways. I wonder if Aki will go back to visit Keycha someday. My throat closes a little at the thought. It never occurred to me before that I could actually go back. I must ask Harken's mother why they were traveling east on their pilgrimage. What were *they* seeking?

An urge toward the salt sea wells up in me again. So long ago that I can't remember who I was, we crossed an ocean that could no longer support life. We were escaping something. Running from some invisible death. We were all heading east – before I was left behind. (*Who was left behind?*) Am I hoping that, like Aki, I'll catch up with my past if I follow the waterways? There have been too many lifetimes since I came out of the west. There's no hope anyone will be waiting to call me daughter, or son, when I arrive finally at the last river mouth at this land's end. And yet the salt sea signifies hope.

I see a figure up ahead, holding a lantern. In its light I see the face of Harken's friend Walleye. I'm about to call out to him when another man joins him. The second man has what looks very much like a body slung over his shoulder. I keep quiet and edge deeper into shadows.

"Don't touch it so much!" Walleye says loudly. His companion's response is too low to make out.

They shuffle away into the dark. For no good reason I follow. Wasn't Walleye supposed to meet Harken tonight? He said something was going on in the village. I don't want anything to mar the perfect life I'm envisioning for Aki. So I get nosy.

I keep to the shadows and follow the men south through the village. The streets are a maze of rickety shacks, so it's easy to hide. The constellation of the great bear is at my back, Orion to my left. There's no sign of the scorpion, but I know it's there, hidden by the curve of the earth. The men ahead are noisy, shushing each other constantly. It's as if the whole town is holding its breath.

I want to hold mine as well. We're moving toward the sickly sweet scent that's been bothering me since we arrived. It's overwhelming. This isn't latrines. It smells more like ... an abattoir. I have the sudden, horrible impression it's the smell of raw blood and bone. What are these two up to?

We reach the end of the shantytown. A hard-packed embankment lies ahead. I hear a trickle of running water. (*I must tell Aki.*) The men walk out onto a corroded cement bridge. I follow as close as I dare. There are no buildings, no cover. I duck below the bridge abutment where it melds to the frozen bank, thinking to get close enough to hear their muttered conversation. But the stench is so bad underneath I gag. For a moment I can't focus on anything but not throwing up. But I can hear voices overhead.

"Somebody gotta do it, don't they, Walleye? Or we'll all get sick. Harken's dad said ...."

"Shaddup, ya idiot." The second voice is Walleye's. "Ya huggin' that thing cause ya wanna be next?"

"You said to check the pockets."

"Well. Don' wanna waste any trade."

"She's kinda pretty ...."

"Just chuck her over, ya moron."

There's a scuffle above and a large object drops down, thudding onto the ice below. I hear a slosh, as if the ice plate below the bridge is no longer frozen to the shore. Could this be the Oswego Canal? I'm pretty sure that was a body just tossed from the bridge. From the smell, it isn't the only one down there. Are these people stupid enough to throw their dead into a thawing canal? *Gah*, people are pigfish. I wonder if a few monster-fish could clean up this mess for them. I start to trudge back up, no longer too worried about being seen. I remember Walleye telling Harlan that Thaw Fever had come through town. It sounds like Harlan's dad assigned the village idiots as grave diggers. My desire to travel down the Oswego Canal wanes sharply.

Hand over my nose, I'm in a brief and happy daydream about staying with Harken and Aki after all, one big happy family traveling the ice to the north – or maybe even back west to see Keycha again – when I come face-to-face with Walleye and his companion. The second man is huge. They're very startled to see me. They also are not pleased.

"Wa'll, if it isn't Harken's little boy," Walleye says. "Ya out looking for some fun?"

"She's pretty," the big man says.

"Ain't picky are ya, moron?" Walleye says. "Whatcha see out here in the dark, boy?"

"Not feeling so good," I mutter. "Just looking for th' latrine."

"Mama Jia'd say she's pretty," the big man says.

"What kinda not feeling good?" Walleye says suspiciously. "You got Thaw Fever, boy?"

"Feel like I'll barf if I have to look at you much longer," I say. *Gah*, I'm so stupid.

"Oh!" the big idiot says, stepping forward. "Ya sick! We'll take care of ya." And he swings something toward me.

"Wait, ya moron!" I hear Walleye yell, just before something whams hard into the side of my head.

I'm on the cold ground. A hateful voice is yelling words that are difficult to understand. I remember what "idiot" means because I've just been one. I hear a voice say: "Harken's gonna kill ya ...." Harken. That's a pretty word. "Gotta get rid of the sick ones. Ya said so." Am I sick? Maybe I am. My head hurts bad. "Think he'll pay for hurting his favorite? Ya moron." Who's favorite? Harken's? I want a Harken. But what is it? The word sounds pretty, like the color red. I'm hurting. Sparks are swimming behind my eyelids. Zooming around like fireflies. Are they stars? I try to focus on – Orion? Can he help? But instead a huge sparkly scorpion rears up and jabs at my head again and again with its spiked tail. My head hurts so bad. I can't move. "Harken?" I try to whisper. "Aki?" What's that?

"If we just dump him, they'll find out ...."

"Gotta hide ...."

I'm being dragged, my head thudding along on the frozen ground. Every thump brings new sparks of pain.

"She's pretty ...."

"He's got a squashed skull, ya moron. Roll him up. We'll hide him in that."

More dragging. More sparks. More swirls of red "Harken" and deep yellow. Yellow must be "Aki." All the colors and sparks are smearing together into an ugly bruised purple. Purple is pain.

"Harken. Aki." My voice flies away in sparks.

"Sheeit. He ain't even dead yet. Mebbe hit him again."

"She's pretty."

I'm falling. It lasts a long time. Falling is better than pain. The purple swirls in eddies. I hear water. The scorpion jabs at my head. Harken and Aki have skated away on a long ribbon of pain. I don't want to be alone. I land with a thud that knocks all the sparks out of me in a brilliant shower of white. The world rocks and shatters. Keycha's face swims up out of a deep blue puddle. "It's okay to sleep now," he says. I trust Keycha. But it hurts.

"I don't want to!" I try to tell him. Why won't he listen? "I want to stay with you!"

"Sleep," Keycha says. So I do.

ICE EULOGY

"How like a winter hath my absence been ...
What freezings have I felt, what dark days seen!"
— Shakespeare, "Sonnet 97"

Rocking wakes me slowly to a memory of pain while wondering how I can feel so *good*. I stretch luxuriously, thankful my arms aren't bound to my sides. (*Why should they be?*) I want to laugh out loud, but my throat is oddly dry. Wait 'til I tell Keycha my crazy dream .... Oh! But we left Keycha in the west. And – my head was really hurting a while ago. I put my hands to my skull but all seems well. Must've been a hangover. Maybe a little hair of the dog? But I don't hurt anymore, though I can almost feel the echo of it. What happened last night ...?

There's a sudden, dizzying, sideways slip. A hollow pit in my stomach tells me there's a missing chunk of time somewhere. I wasn't drunk last night. That was ... long before. I open my eyes to blue sky. I'm lying on something that's rocking. Water slaps on wood. I'm in the bottom of a very old, punky wooden boat. Slimy bilge water sloshes in the bottom. I'm still in my plasti-weave jumpsuit, which cracks in two places as I shift, like dry leaves. The boat is rocking on water. I sit up fast and my head spins. The memory of a brownish purple smear of pain sends me dry-retching over the crumbling gunnel.

Beneath is clear, blue water. There are no corpses floating past. (*Why should there be?*) I had a bad dream, maybe. A warm breeze lifts my hair. It's very long and tickles my neck. The wind smells sweet. (*Why shouldn't it?*) My reflection ripples in the water, shifting and changing. I'm afraid to look too closely. The boat drifts with the current into a long shadow and something touches my head lightly. I flinch and stare. There's a branch overhead, with real leaves. Insects are chewing on them. I sit up to a view of strange spiky bushes and willowy trees lining a shallow, free-flowing river. Everything is gentle green and blue. There's no sign of ice.

I've slept through the Thaw and the world has changed again. I lift my face to the friendly sun and howl out my sorrow and despair.

• • •

The bank is a dense tangle of green brush. I tramp downstream, struggling through the undergrowth, until the mouth of what used to be a canal dumps into a once-frozen lake. I had to see for myself. Blue water stretches out in front of me, begging for long-gone flocks of birds to disturb the still surface. There are plenty of insects though, buzzing in the bushes, dimpling the water. Fish as well, to judge from the sudden sucking that yanks an insect under. Of people, there is no sign. Oswego has been swallowed by time. There's not one stick left to tell me I'm in the right place; that a busy, smelly, trading market once thrived here. There are green trees, brush, tangle. I stare out over the water until my eyes blur. But there are no patchwork sails billowing past to welcome me into this time.

• • •

I walk alone, turning back to the southeast, trudging through the mildest land I've encountered in centuries. But it's the hardest traveling I've ever done, sorrow rolling over me in waves. The punky boat I woke in was derelict. I left it half-sunk in the reeds. I think I've been walking now as long as I traveled with Aki. Who knows. I've walked right through my leggings and my feet have become hard calluses spotted with painful lumps where I've picked up the odd thorn and failed to remove it. The plastic suit is too hot in this muggy world, so I draped its remains around my waist, where it chafes. I'm not ready to get rid of it yet. It works well enough as a cover at night. I carry only my flint and steel around my neck, a fishing spear that doubles as a staff, and my book, carefully sandwiched between layers of my suit and tied off. I air it daily and scratch off any mold with a fingernail. Fish are plentiful, though they're ugly, gray, eel-like things that taste horrible. I have no complaints. I have no feelings. I'm numb to it all. I usually don't bother to cook my catch. I find I don't like the heat after all. When I dream, I dream of ice.

My bare shoulders burn and peel. As I trudge forward, whole movie-reels of memories run through my head, over-laying the heavy scented trees and high bushes buzzing with insects. Eels leap high out of the water in aerial leaps to eat the insects. There are still no birds. I daydream of Aki, of Keycha. Even of Harken. I fly over the ice in Keycha's iceboats, my friends by my side. When I sleep, sweating under my plastic cloth, I conjure the sensation of Aki's legs entwined with mine, our heads together on the caribou hide. Then ... I can't stop it .... My friends' faces disintegrate in front of me, rotting, crumbling into the ground and blowing away as dust.

I know they're long dead. I cried my eyes dry many weeks back. I walk on painful feet. I daydream of ice. My night dreams always end in horror and grief.

The relentless sun and green, the slap of the water-way that I still follow, feel inappropriate. How dare the world be so gentle when I'm grieving? Aki would have been intrigued by this free-flowing stream (*which once ran with corpses*). Keycha would have missed the under-city salvage to make his boats. Harken would have no villages to trade with. There are no people in this gentle world. Just the trees, the river, the fish and insects, and me, walking forever forward on painful feet. Each day I tread heavily forward, making little headway. (*Oh, how we flew over the ice!*) Sometimes I think I might find the salt sea after all. (*And if I don't? What else is there to do but to move forward?*) When I do, I'll throw myself into it. Just what does it take to kill this body? Will I find my friends then? But I picture their faces in the dust and shiver. When my grief was new (*it's always fresh, every day*), I practiced. I threw myself face-down in the river and let the eels twine around my legs and arms. But the urge to breathe overwhelmed even my sadness, and I merely turned over and let myself float until the nibbling of the eels became irritating and I climbed back on shore.

Fortunately, my book stayed dry in its pouch.

I find a praying mantis and let it ride on my shoulder for a day. I watch it decapitate and devour numerous smaller insects, spearing them with its wicked prayer hooks. When it eats one of its own kind I leave it gently on a branch. It's too full of life and ferocity for me. I want only to fade away.

The insect's praying posture, both hooks together and big eyes upward, reminds me that I used to have an invisible god I talked to. I poke around in my own head for a while, making conversation. But even that comfort has forsaken me. I'm caught between past and present, like I'm caught between everything else. My invisible friend is finally gone for good. Was his name Coyote? I hope he's found his family and is partying even now in the Valley of Death. Is it odd that it makes me shed tears?

I trudge on through a gentle world of hurt. When the thorns start emerging from my feet on their own, I know there's no hope for me. I'm doomed to live. Why did Aki and Keycha and Harken have to die? It's a while before I realize that I have that backward. They most likely lived their lives, moving on without me.

I wake one morning from my dreams of ice, shivering in the muggy heat. It is bright morning. It's always bright here. There has been no reason to rise early since I woke to this world.

The scraping runners of my dream boats have given way to the slap of water on wood and the rock and hollow creak of what can only be a water vessel. I debate whether I should open my eyes. I'm not ready for something new. Let whoever it is assume I'm dead. Let them steal my spear and flint. What else have I got? But not my book! My eyes open and I'm looking down at a pretty little sailboat rocking against the bank. A husky voice says, "Finally awake?" and laughs.

A wrinkled face peers from the stern. She's tan as old leather, and her thin white hair flies in the breeze. She's the first human being I've seen since I woke.

"I got transport for them as can pay." The voice is younger than the face, which holds a lifetime of experience. "Oh! What's wrong, young'un?"

I realize that hot tears are once again rolling down my face. I don't know where they keep coming from. "I ... I lost my friends."

"Well, I ain't seen nobody on the river, and I come from quite a way back."

"No. I .... It's okay. Just haven't seen people in a while."

"It can hit a body that way," she says calmly, pulling out a clay pipe and packing it while she watches me from the boat. "Ya ain't crazy, is you? Ain't having no crazies on m' boat."

"Where you headed?" I ask, feeling silly. Where is there to go except eastward?

"Wa'll that depends. You kin pay?"

I look down at my meager possessions: a spear, a flint. "I can catch eels," I say.

"Any idjit kin catch eels," the old woman says, snorting and starting to busy herself with the lines. It looks like she's leaving.

"Wait!" Um, I can ... I can tell stories like you've never heard."

"So kin I, lad." She laughs in my face. "You think you got more stories in you than this old head?" She's really going to leave me behind! Suddenly I just can't stand the thought of being alone again.

I stand bolt upright on the bank and start reciting one of the poems from my book. I rarely turn the fragile pages. I've memorized them all.

"'Let us go then, you and I

While the evening is spread out against the sky

Like a patient etherized upon a table

Let us go through certain half-deserted streets

The muttering retreats of restless nights in one-night cheap hotels

And sawdust restaurants with oyster-shells:

Streets that follow like a tedious argument of insidious intent.

To lead you to an overwhelming question.

Oh do not ask "what is it?"

Let us go and make our visit ....'"

The old woman stares up at me, jaw dropped. "Well! I don't rightly understand it. But it has a nice sound. Musical-like. Guess I could stand to hear some more." I grin and grab my spear.

• • •

The old gal sure makes me work for my passage. I do all the fishing, cooking. She won't eat eel raw, she says. "What are ya? Uncivilized?" I scrub the boat daily. I even do the sailing, since she'd just float with the current otherwise (*"What's yer hurry?"*). But in any case, my hands itch to work the lines. Her ropes are something like twisted hemp, the sails a rough woven weed, basket-like. No plastic here. I forget about everything for hours at a time. But sometimes, during the moments when we're drifting quietly to the sound of water slapping the hulls, then everything, everyone I've lost, comes back and hits me in the gut and hot tears roll down my face and drop into the river. The old woman never comments on it, but she will kick me awake at night when I'm caught in a nightmare. The first few nights, I kept dreaming I was swimming in a river of cold corpses. Their faces, as they rolled toward me, were Keycha's, Aki's, Harken's. A bitter wind blows through my dreams.

It's tough for me not to equate that kindly face with kindness. But she's a hard old gal. She's lived through a lot and "ain't nothing free," as she says. She demands poetry every evening, but isn't picky about what, and doesn't mind repeats. During the day I can sometimes get her to talk about what she's seen along the river, but she's another body who hasn't spent much time with people, and she likes her silence. When we start seeing other people on the river, I begin to think she's taken me aboard for reasons other than my poetry.

Our small river is starting to move faster and widen out. We pass a few settlements, mostly muddy patches along the shore, where people stand and stare at us. But the old woman doesn't stop.

"Ain't safe. Not worth th' bother," she mutters, swinging out to the middle of the river.

Once someone followed us in a dugout for a few miles and she panicked, screeching for me to get the sails up and some speed on. We left the canoe behind easily. It made me realize I haven't seen any other sailboats. So I ask her about it.

"This un's special," she says, grinning to show more than a few teeth missing. "Ya won't see a Jackboat often, and no one lets 'em go once they sail one."

"Jackboat?" She spends the next hour pointing out her precious boat's features. The high bow that slides so smoothly through the water, the careful joins, the single upright mast and forward jib. To me, it has elements not unlike our mix-matched transforming iceboat, but simpler and streamlined for a single purpose: sailing fast on water.

"Don't no one make 'em like this in the south," she mutters. "Traveled north with m'dad to get this un. Had her ever since."

I feel a little dizzy. "Do you know the name of the boat-maker? Did you ever hear the name Keycha? Have you been as far as Oswego?"

She just shakes her head. "Mebbe the makers mark?" And she points to the side of the bow. I lean over to look at the crude eyes I thought she'd painted on either side of the bow. One eye open, one asleep – or winking.

"Why's it called a Jackboat?" Even my lips are shaking. I imagine I can see Keycha's clever designs in every particular of the boat.

"Dunno," is all she says. She's silent for a long while, eyeing me. "Yeh cain't have her!" she says suddenly, her voice hard.

I reassure her as best I can. "Just wondering if an old friend was the boat-builder," I say. But she remains suspicious for a long time, barely sleeping that night to keep an eye on me.

I lie awake as well, mind spinning far into the morning.

The next day I ply her with questions. I know it's danger-ous. She's a crank, and can't stand too much attention.

She'll likely get sick of me and kick me off the boat. But I have to know.

"*Obaasan*," I say, surprised at how easily the honorific title comes to me. I've used that language so rarely of late. "Can you tell me anything about ice?"

"Whatchu call me?" she says sharply.

"I'm just saying 'grandmother.' I don't know your name."

"Ain't never had no kids," she says firmly, and is silent for a while. "What's *yer* name?" she finally says, eyes slanting at me slyly.

"Jack."

She hoots with laughter. "Like m'boat!" Then: "Still cain't have her!"

"I don't want her," I say firmly. "I want to know whether you ever heard stories about this river being covered in ice."

"In winter?"

"Yeah, but all year long. With no summer in between."

"I wouldn't like that. Wouldn't like it t'all," the old gal mutters, falling silent again.

It's almost half a day of traveling to the sound of insects buzzing on the bank, and the eels slapping the water to get at them, before she suddenly says: "Me Gran said it used to be colder."

"*Obaasan*?"

"That word again," she huffs. "Speak real words. Me GRAN said winters was a lot longer, and they caught their fish through holes in the ice. Dangerous, she said. You could fall through and freeze, she said."

"Where was your gran from?" I ask.

"Never asked," she says. "I were just a kid, weren't I? Then there was the big fight and people we thought we knew, they just took everything. Even me mum. Left the rest dying on the ground. It was just dad and me after that."

"I'm sorry," I say.

"What fer? You didn't do it – did ya?" She shoots me another suspicious look.

"You're like me," I say. "You've lost everyone."

"Ain't no one like you," she snorts and my shoulders knot up. How does she know? "Ain't never seen a kid for spouting rubbish like you. You sorry? Everybody dies. I'm dying one day. But you still cain't have my boat!"

I grin at her. "I'd rather have you around than your boat, Gran," I say and she snorts again. But she looks a little pleased too, her brown ears blushing red.

The river gets wider and we see more people and more boats. Gran won't anchor anywhere we see signs of people on shore, and one night, when we hear crashing in the bushes, we scramble aboard in the dark and just keep sailing until the light pales to morning.

Once we see another Jackboat tacking upriver. I can't help waving, but Gran hits my arm down and then smacks the back of my head.

"You crazy, boy! Just 'cause they look like you don' mean they friendly."

The only response from the other boat is to swing a little farther away from us.

I realize along the way that I'm having fewer nightmares, daydreaming less often. Life is getting in the way. The ice is starting to seem long ago, and I panic a little, replaying my memories so I won't forget. Gran finds me, in the middle of the night, rocking and clutching my head. She pokes me in the ribs and I cry out. "I can't remember their faces!" I wail. "I can't see them!" My throat closes and the tears come again. As I rock, I feel her crabbed old hand petting my head. It feels like a bundle of dry twigs.

"Sussen, sussen," she croons.

"Why did they have to die?" I sob.

"Mebbe they did better," she mutters. "Mebbe it's the ones still living as is unlucky."

I picture Aki and Harken living out their lives as traders along the river, getting old like Gran, but with children around them; Keycha, building his boats and sending them downriver, remembering me. To them, I died.

"Maybe I'm the one who didn't get to live," I say.

"Mebbe."

"They left me behind."

"That's so. But didn't that poem-thing of yours say it? I cain't orate the way you kin. The one about death kindly stopping fer the lady as wouldn't make time fer it?"

"'Since then 'tis centuries, and yet each / Feels shorter than a day,'" I quote.

"Dunno about that," the old woman says. "Feels like a long dang day to me."

"Yeah," I say, calming. My dearest ones didn't die. They just lived without me. I'm the one who missed out on life. The old woman continues to pet my hair with her claw-like hand until I finally sleep without dreaming.

• • •

I know Gran is worried about me. I only recite the poems about death lately, and I don't pester her with questions. But she's familiar with loss and loneliness and lets me be. We're companionable enough, and are also increasingly busy dealing with ever more unpredictable winds, avoiding other boats, and finding safe anchorage. Even fishing has changed. The eels have given way to some kind of large, toothy bass that have a tricky way of slipping off my spear. They're delicious when I do manage to catch them, but I lose more than I land. I ask Gran for rope to make a net, but she says I'll have to wait until we make the traders' market downriver. So now I know where we're headed at least. It sounds like up ahead there's a bigger trading town than Oswego, and more dangerous. Gran gets tenser the closer we get.

I'm intrigued by the changing river. It's so wide now we can only just see the opposite bank. In the evenings, the wind shifts upriver and is sometimes stronger than the current. We actually have to tack downriver at times just to make any headway. Gran knows – but I have to learn – that the height of the river also starts to change daily. Sometimes the muddy banks are exposed; other times we step from deck into deep brush when we want to land. Gran laughs and tells me not to be a fool. Everyone knows this is a tidal river (*I didn't*). The tide is rhythmic evidently, but I have trouble figuring out the pattern, and Gran doesn't care, as long as we don't ground her Jackboat in the night.

With the tide comes the smell of rotting weed on the shore, and something else. The faint taste of salt in the water. Gran makes a face when we boil river water to drink and calls it brackish. I've never told Gran I'm heading for the salt sea, and these small signs raise that deep restlessness in me. I can tell I'm close. But nothing's changed. I can find no epiphany about who I am or why I'm here.

• • •

We approach the big trading town in the dim early hours of the morning. Gran has been clear that we're to be well gone by nightfall. I'm not entirely sure why she wants to stop at all, given how nervous the place makes her. But she just says there are some things we can only get from other people. I know now that she picked me up as a guard, someone to stay with the boat while she goes ashore. She's so tense I don't tease her about stealing away with her precious sailboat, but I do offer to trade places with her. She just pats my arm and says, "Good lad, good lad." But continues with her plan.

It's an eerie place. Our river narrows again, and on either side gigantic piles of rubble and derelict buildings rise up through the brush, so old and damaged they're often no more than barren patches showing on the skyline. I'm reminded of the under-city, yet these are out in the open, and the ghosts of this place have been long washed away. That's not what's been scaring Gran.

We follow the line of deterioration for hours. I'm reminded of a very old poem called "Letting in the Jungle" and try to tell Gran, but I can only remember a few disconnected lines: "'Veil them, cover them, wall them round / blossom, and creeper, and weed/ Let us forget the sight and the sound/ the smell and the touch of the breed.' Um, something, something and 'the blind walls crumble ... and none shall inhabit again!'"

"Yeah," the old woman grunts. "'Cept folks do 'inhabit.' If you kin call 'em folks."

"What're you nervous about, Gran?"

"People," she says shortly. "People is dangerous."

"I'm people?"

"And it's an amazement ta me you've lived 'til now."

Truer words were never spoke. That being the longest sentence I've heard from her in days, Gran lapses into a tense silence again.

• • •

I've been waiting for Gran all day. She told me to sit offshore and watch for her signal. I dropped her on a massive crumbling pier just as the sun came full up. We need rope and tar, I told her. I know she's also after needles and patches for our sail. She left with a bag on her back of rolled eel-skins she's sewn carefully into cloaks (*beautiful needlework*). She's given me instructions to sit off a ways, but to watch carefully for her. When she waves, I'm to sail in as fast as the winds allow, and paddle if I have to. "So don't be too far! And don't you go to sleep!" She told me to expect her before the sun reached midday, straight above. It has been hours since then. I'm getting increasingly fidgety.

Only one other boat comes in, a canoe with two big guys, who tie up at the dock. They turn to stare at me. I've drifted in until I'm only 30 yards off by then, anxiously scanning for Gran. They leave their boat by itself and walk inland. I wonder if Gran was being a bit paranoid. But if so, where is she?

People are moving about on land. I must be seeing the edge of a marketplace, but as dusk falls the place empties out suddenly and completely. Even the men in the canoe leave, staring at me as they pass by a little too close. But there's no sign of Gran.

I've had enough. I paddle in under the pier. The tide is out, so the dock is far over my head, hiding the Jackboat from easy view from above. I tie up to a flimsy ladder and test it with my weight. It creaks and wobbles, and I give thanks I'm light. A few tentative steps up, I notice iron spikes hammered into the old wood on the inside of the pylon, so I swing around and climb those instead. I come up under the pier and then have to climb around to the ladder again, but it feels like a safer route, more hidden. Someone's added some extra pieces of wood for handholds right under the pier at the top.

I creep up onto the pier and trot down it fast. I'm exposed while moving along it, and Gran's paranoia has gotten to me. As soon as I reach the end I duck into the shadow of an empty market stall. I'm surprised folks don't just sleep in them at night; they look sturdy enough. But the entire marketplace is deserted. The only things left are empty shacks, a few rough tables, and some odd fruit or vegetable rinds on the ground. I scoop one up and I try chewing on it. It's bitter, so I spit it out. I try calling out for Gran a few times, but the sound of my voice makes me think of things listening in the dark, so I stop.

I've walked the entire length of the market when I hear a sound from a deep patch of darkness a little away from the open ground. I really don't want to go in there, but I call once more, "Gran?"

"Good lad." The words are so soft, so gasping, I wonder if I've really heard them, but I scramble down in the dark into a ditch that edges the tamped ground of the market-place. I can barely see a thing, but I hear a light rustle, and finally find what's unmistakably Gran's hand, twig-like, and very cold.

I peer into the dark, trying to see where she's hurt.

"Gran! Can you stand?"

"Heh. Couldn'ta stopped me if I could. Shoulda known. Just too old. Makes me ... look weak. Won't trade if they can just take it. They took it all. So fast. Just took my gear and threw me down. No one t' stop 'em. No one ...." She's drifting, and I clutch at her hand. A rustling from the dark makes her cold fingers twitch in mine. "Gotta run, boy. Run, boy! Run!"

Her voice is weak but urgent, and it terrifies me. I grab her by one arm and sling her across my shoulders. She's got something clutched in one hand that bangs my chest but when I try to pull it away, she won't let go. I stagger up the bank, and as soon as I'm on flat ground, I run.

Wee but wiry, that's what I am. Gran weighs nothing. Not with all that adrenaline pumping through my body. We hit the pier just as I hear shouts behind us in the market and the sound of feet pounding. I don't even know if they're after us but I'm not about to stop. When I climb down the ladder, I'll have to trust that Gran can hold on. I swing around under the pier and stop to catch my breath. Gran is in an awkward position. I'm afraid she'll slide off, so I brace against the handholds and swing her to the front of

271

me. I finally get a look at her. In the dim light, I can't see anything obviously wrong, but her breathing is labored and her eyes closed. She's still holding on to that damn bag though, so I know she hasn't passed out. I'm wondering how to get her down to the boat when I see a canoe tied up next to our Jackboat.

The two big men from before are working my lines loose (they haven't seen the one underwater). They're stealing our boat.

"Gran, I gotta leave you here for a minute," I hiss. "Can you hang on? Gran! Hang on?" She just nods silently, which I don't quite trust, so I tuck her arms into the handhold crosspieces and brace her in as best I can between the overhead pier and the pylon. When she's as secure as I can make her, I climb quietly down the inside of the pylon until I'm about six feet above the head of the nearest man. He's looking anxiously toward shore, telling the other to hurry. They've found the last line and the second man is head and shoulders underwater, trying to untie it. I'm so angry, so pumped up with adrenaline, I don't think about what I'm doing. That boat is our survival, Gran's and mine.

I swing hard and leap. There's a crack as I come down on the first man's head with both feet. We both fall into the water with a gigantic splash. The other man is leaning out over the gunnel, head up and looking confused when I come at him from the water. I rear up as the boat rocks down toward me and grab his neck and drag him under. I'm lucky, and he hits his head squarely on the pylon, my full weight yanking him into it as he goes down, heavy and inert. (*Look, Keycha. I'm not running away now.*)

I tug the sailboat under the dock, treading water as I look up at Gran, 20 feet above my head. I can see the glint of her eyes watching me. Footsteps thump overhead. I've made too much noise. She waves me away, but I shake my head. I mime holding my nose then wave my hand for her to drop. But she ignores me. She's hurt, and may not even be able to swim. A lot of sailors can't. I hook an elbow over the gunnel and show her both my hands, cradled to catch her, but she just stares at me. The first footsteps seem to be heading back to shore but others come out to join them. I hope they haven't spotted the canoe, but there's nothing I can do about that now. I can see Gran's arms shaking, as she tries to hold on. She's not going to last much longer. I let go of the boat, hoping the stern won't swing out into view, and I grab the pylon, intending to climb up to her.

She takes one tremulous step down toward me, her foot feeling for the next nail down, just as the humongous figure of a man leans out over the dock and peers underneath at her. I can't see details in this light, but he's too big, and his head looks wrong, big and lumpy. I gasp and he looks down toward me, which gives Gran time to step back up and jab her twig-like finger right into his eye. The man howls and disappears. Gran leans back and, looking at me with a grin of triumph, she lets go of the pylon and falls like an empty sack down into the water.

I haul her out as fast as I can, yanking at her clothes. She's not breathing well and heaving her over the gunnel is awkward. I'm rougher than I intend to be. But we're both aboard, and I'm paddling out from under the dock when more shouts ring out from the pier. I look back in time to see one man down, one kicking him, and several others kneeling beside him. They seem to be stripping the downed man of whatever it is homicidal giants carry. He tries to shove them away with one hand. The other is clapped to his face. The standing man sees us and yells. He throws something heavy that falls short of our boat. Within seconds we're far enough away that I feel more secure. I look back again and a dark figure is climbing off the pier onto the ladder with the canoe swinging from its base. As I watch, the ladder detaches from the pylon with a creak and falls outward. Man and ladder hit water with a crash. The brush along the shore wavers in response to the sound, as if there are more predators inside, just waiting for their chance …. I raise sail hastily, the boom swings out, and we're away.

"Which way?" I ask Gran. She's crumpled in the bottom of the boat, wheezing. As soon as we're far enough, I'll tend to her, but I watch her anxiously from the tiller.

"Gran?"

"East," Gran wheezes. "East … river …." I steer east, by the stars, but the river is behind us. Surely she can't want me to head back up there. Tacking upstream would make us slow enough to be a target from shore, and I don't want to go anywhere near those scary people – if they were people – again.

The wind comes up. I have my hands full for a while, but I manage to pull the unused jib over Gran, hoping it will keep her warm enough for now. We're both wet and the wind is chilly.

Something is going on with the boat. It's kicking and bucking. In the starlight, I can see long waves coming in at me. At first they hit us as chop but finally they turn to longer rollers that are easier to ride – as long as I keep my hand on the tiller.

The sun rises just as the wind dies. I tie the tiller off and kneel by Gran. We're bobbing and wallowing in those weird swells. I'm starting to feel a bit ill. I pull the jib off Gran and shake her shoulder gently.

"Gran, you awake? I'm not feeling too good. Can you give me some directions?"

Gran doesn't open her eyes, so I shake her again and put my hand to her forehead. Her skin is like ice. "Fracking hell, Gran, why didn't you tell me you were cold?" I push at her shoulder, but it's stiff and unmoving. Tears well in my eyes. I don't want to understand what I'm seeing.

"Dammit, Gran. What was so important there anyway. Nothing, that's what. NOTHING!" I yell at Gran, but she lies there with her eyes closed, ignoring me. Done with me. Done with the world.

I yell and scream at her, at the sky, at the water. But Gran would likely say it's easier where she is now. I tell her how mad I am that she's left me alone. I tell her I'm going to take her boat. But she doesn't mind anymore.

The sailboat rocks wildly as a wave hits us broadside and I finally look up. The sun is bright in the sky, and as far as I can see, as far as the horizon, there are blue waves. Spray hits me in the face and I taste salt. We've arrived at the salt sea.

• • •

The ocean is too big and rough. Waves make sailing difficult. I heave to out in the open water, under the sun. We rock so badly I think I may just pitch over the side. Who'd care? I wrap Gran in the jib and I tell her I hope she finds her mum. The ancient husk that was Gran slips over the gunnel into the water. I've tucked the bag she clutched so fiercely into her wraps. It held a book. Just a book. There is only faded, childish handwriting inside. I read a little out loud to the sea and the sky. I wonder if it's Gran's life I'm reading, from when she was a child. She loved her mum a lot. I send the book after her into the ocean.

Then I'm alone, Jack and his Jackboat; maybe named by a long-ago friend. Maybe not. If I ever meet Keycha in some other life, I'm gonna tell him his riverboat design stinks out on the open ocean. I'm so ill I can't distinguish the feeling from the sheer depression and horror of losing Gran. I almost throw my poetry book overboard after her, but then I don't.

I decide to turn back. I can't take the waves. I can't drink the water. I don't see any fish to spear. By achieving my goal, I've lost it. I turn my back on the cruel shifting horizon and head back toward that evil decayed place that took Gran from me. I hug the northern shore, intending to pass as far from the market as I can. By chance I find another river mouth, smaller than the one we just sailed down, but plenty big for the Jackboat. Since it doesn't matter where I go anymore, I sail in and find myself, once again, curving east, or just north of east.

The water turns from salt to brackish to salt again, but the waves don't pitch as badly. I unfold Aki's plasticized waterways map from where it has served as a cover for my poetry book, protecting the pages from the damp since long ago. I want to see if I can make sense of this weird place. It appears I'm on a body of water that connects to the salt sea but is protected by a long island. When I see the name of the river I turned down to get here, I start to laugh. East River. That's what Gran meant all along. Why does everyone tell me to head east?

My map shows the coast curving eventually to the north before the map ends. I wonder, if I were to follow this eastern coast to the far north, would I find the river where Aki and Harken once traded salt? I've already had enough of salt. It coats my hair, my skin, my tongue. I feel sticky all over.

I try jumping in the water to clean off and a zillion invisible squashy things caress my skin, stinging it with a zillion little stingers. I clamber back aboard, tingling painfully. The discomfort lasts a long time. I hang over the side and watch the things that did it. The current is filled with tiny creatures passing by the boat in a long ribbon about 10 feet wide, drifting away in a lazy S-curve as far into the horizon as I can see. They're little cup-shaped things, each with a brown middle made of squiggles. The cup is almost see-through. Over the next few days, the cups grow, their squiggles tangling like hair, and the ribbon widens. I suspect they're feeding on each other, because as they get bigger, there seem to be fewer of them. I scoop a few up with a bucket and leave them to dry out on the bottom of the boat. But they still sting, even dry (and worse as they get bigger) so I scrape them back overboard. I'm getting hungry, though, and thirsty. I see no large fish to hunt.

When the creatures become as big as my head, I see one with a small fish caught in its squiggles. This is a good sign, but I can't imagine fighting that thing for the fish. If it stung me so badly when it was smaller, what kind of sting would it deliver now?

I finally remember what they are, one night. The boat is gliding through what now looks like a sea of giant brown pudding creatures and I recall that I've seen things like these before, in that other ocean far and long ago to the west. And I remember something else. I had a family once. I was traveling with them. A mother, father, cousins? There were many of us. We were headed east because our ocean was dying – was it radiation? Oil? There were myriad reasons – and the western sea had emptied of all other life, filling up with poisonous creatures like these. But I'd had a family! We were fleeing the death of an entire ocean – together. I know, somehow, that they were my people, but in my mind's eye they look like the last image I have of Keycha's family out on the ice. Penguins standing in stiff rows, a long way off. I can't picture a single face. The photograph is just too faded.

When the moon comes up, I know that the pudding creatures are called *kurage* – sea moons. Jellyfish.

I laugh so hard I start to retch. I haven't eaten or drunk in days now. I let the boat wallow. I've traveled across a poisoned sea with my family and an entire continent alone, through fire and ice, using up more lifetimes than should be allowed. I've left and lost all the people I ever cared about just to keep traveling east in hopes of finding a living ocean ... and the kurage have beaten me here.

These passive little monsters are a symbol of ultimate failure, the scorpion's sting catching up with me at last, my journey pointless. I watch the gelatinous things drift for hours until I can't tell any difference between us. I become a jellyfish, a sack of pudding, aimlessly drifting wherever the currents of time take me. I drift until my lips are blackened and peeling. I don't seem to be healing well. Or at all. I don't care. I refuse to sleep. But something in me must still want to live, even now, because when my sunburnt eyes see a river mouth on shore I sail the Jackboat hard, right up onto the beach, grinding her hull into the sand.

I lay face-down in the river, sucking in brackish water. Drinking to live. I'm still lying there, weak as a beached jellyfish, when the dangerous people – the predators Gran always warned me about – find me and my too-special boat.

NEW BEGINNINGS

We have lingered in the chambers of the sea
By sea-girls wreathed with seaweed red and brown
Till human voices wake us, and we drown.
— *T. S. Eliot, "The Love Song of J. Alfred Prufrock"*

I want to die. It would be a relief. Everything hurts. I'm
sitting in my own blood, which pools in the dank water of
the culvert where I'm hiding. Other equally nasty things
drip on my head. I'm missing something terribly important. My will to survive, that thing that used to drive me so
hard, is dull and unimportant now. I'm too tired even for
the long sleep. I just can't see any reason to try again. Gran
is gone. My Aki is gone, and Harken. Keycha! My throat
swells again with unbearable loss. Would his incredible
boats have survived the melting ice? It seems unlikely the
Jackboat is really his design, though it helped to imagine
it was, for a while (*boat's gone now; book's gone too*). I was so
focused on just getting by, on traveling east, I somehow
missed so many opportunities to live and love. I grieve for
them all. My heart hurts. I wonder if I could have loved
them better. But it was the same with Gran. Just surviving made us hard and inward-turned. I feel used up. The
lens through which I view the world has narrowed, and

become clouded from loss. I'm tired. Maybe I can just end if I decide to?

Footsteps splash in the mud outside the pipe. I don't care enough to hide when a face peers in at me. There are words, lost in a haze of pain and fever. More than just my body has been beaten. Hands drag me from the culvert. I cling to my grief, which bursts forth as if for the first time. I miss them! Why should I continue on when those I love are gone? I hurt. Even my grief is selfish.

Instead of beating me, the hands smooth the hair from my face. Warm broth wets my lips and my body betrays me by sucking it down greedily. I'm wrapped in something dry and crinkly and my body warms. When I'm warm enough to shiver, another body slides in beside me and curls softly against my back. Skin to skin. My grief becomes greater just from being touched gently by another human.

Days go by in a blur. But the dark hands and their gentleness stay with me. I wake one morning to rough hair against my face. I think I can't have been in my right mind for a while. I feel certain my body would never have regenerated on its own this time; I was too beaten down. And yet, time has passed, and here I am, feeling – okay. Feeling warm and well fed. And I didn't regenerate; I just *healed*. That horrible empty gap of lost time is not there in my head. I have a hazy sense of days having passed, filled with gentle care. Somebody is lying with their back to me. I don't think I've ever clearly seen them, but I know this person somehow.

Rough dreadlocks splay across a plastic ground cover. Smooth ebony shoulders slope toward a neat waist, and one arm pins a ragged faded blue tarp around us both. I can't help touching my fingertips to that arm, patting the wild hair. Unlike the lake folks, this is someone very differ-ent from me. Why do I feel so warm toward this person? Is kindness catching? I wonder if I could melt into that unknown body and become someone other than myself. My neighbor sighs and rolls over. I touch a high cheekbone and run my finger over full lips that twitch into a sleepy smile. The eyes stay closed. So lovely. So kind. This person pulled me from the culvert, shared warmth. Let me heal so I didn't have to choose between ending and starting over. Why would they do that? I feel overwhelmed with affection for this human being who has helped me for no reason.

But all at once it's too much. Grief and love for my lost ones washes over me yet again and I collapse, sobbing, onto the slim chest. An arm curls around me in a hug while I weep for all of us.

"What's this? So sad first thing in th' morning? *Ah*, you're okay now. Feeling better and freakin' out, aye? You'll be fine." And the warm, rich voice reverberates under my ear, soothing. "Bet a feed will fix you up, right?"

My stomach grumbles, and a giggle erupts through the sobs. "Always ... hungry."

"C'mon then. You an' me against the world. No one can be sad with grub in their tum." The boy gets us both standing and I see that we are alike after all.

"You're like me?" Not a boy, not a girl, but both. (*Maybe long-lived too? Is it possible? Is this what I've been searching for? People who won't leave me behind?*) He/she stands proudly naked in a thin morning light sneaking through rusted holes in the walls of our sleeping area. There are others too, bundles of bodies sleeping everywhere. We seem to be sheltering in a huge, dilapidated metal room. I can't count how many other sleepers there are, some even now rustling awake.

"Ha! You'd be so lucky! But yeah, we all like *this* here," and he/she gestures down at his/her beautiful naked body. "Good, aye?"

"Good!" *Ohmygodsohmygods*. Thank you, imaginary friend in my head. Thank you, Keycha, Aki, Harken, Gran. Thank you for sharing your warmth with me through the long cold. "Good?" I'm crouching and *almost* crying again, but someone's arms are around me, laughing and hugging, thumping my back and assuring me that everything will be fine. Other voices are calling out, asking Joon (*his name is Joon!*) "What's the matter?" As if centuries of searching and loneliness have just been a bad dream (*except for the time I had with you*).

Joon takes me by the hand and we go in search of breakfast. The marketplace here is bustling. There is salvage like I've never seen, huge containers dredged up from the sea with pristine milled clothing and tools and glassware. There are weavers and potters making their wares right in the market. I spot windmills up on the hill above us and stare. Joon laughs and tells me they're run by the scientists up at the experimental University. They have hydroponics up there, he says, and they trade greens for what the fishermen and -women catch. "You should see their library," he says. Books! There are books here?

I barely see two faces, or hear two accents, that are alike. The market seems to be a catch-all for the tough survivors of dozens of cultures who made it east, to the coast, bringing skills to share. They are hard and alert, but don't seem predatory. They're even kind, if Joon is anything to go by. This place is rich with people. I hug myself, trying to decide if this is all real or some fever dream. Joon pulls me over to the docks to see what the fishermen are unloading.

"Breakfast!" he says.

It's horrible. The catch consists of nothing but jellyfish. Entire decks are awash with the huge misshapen bells.

"Then the salt sea is dead." I feel numb just looking at them. My joy squashed.

"Nah, it ain't dead, just a bit globby." Joon looks over the catch thoughtfully. "Not to worry; ya don't eat 'em like this. That would hurt!" He laughs.

The fishermen are donning odd-looking gloves, and I notice they don't let any skin show as they start to shift their catch.

"I got some credit at the Caf. Come on!" And Joon drags me away again. I can barely tear my eyes from the gelatinous slide of the jellies from deck to crates onshore. But I finally let him steer me to a shack right on the water. It has shuttered sides that can open whole walls and rickety tables that seem like they're made of plasticized cardboard. The whole thing looks like it could collapse any moment – and probably be raised again just as fast. Joon pushes me down onto an upended crate serving as a stool and disappears into the dim interior of the place. I look out over the water. The waves are tiny here, just lapping against the shore at the very base of the shack. There is plenty of plastic and junk swirling in the water. The salt sea is not what I expected.

Joon comes back with a pottery platter piled high with something that smells amazing. He thunks it down between us and digs in with his fingers, lifting up a pale, dripping crescent and chomping at it vigorously. He gestures at me to try.

There is a lovely sharp vinegar tang, and a satisfyingly firm texture to the food.

"What is it?" I ask, already reaching for more. "Jellyfish, shtoopid! Wha' else?" I stare at the platter. I am stupid. These things aren't responsible for the death of the oceans. Like me, they are merely opportunists. Better than some at surviving in polluted seas. Designed to continue on in the absence of competition. They have simply filled a niche. They are even useful, necessary, to the humans that feed on them. They're just another proof of the tenacity of life, not harbingers of death. It's not a crime to be adapted to one's environment. The sea moons have their place.

Unforgettable words from the poetry book the Lioness found in her poisoned city light up in my mind (*these are my words now, with my own meanings*):

The darkness drops again; but now I know
That twenty centuries of stony sleep
Were vexed to nightmare by a rocking cradle
And what rough beast, its hour come round at last
Slouches toward [the Salt Sea] to be born?

"Can I stay?" I manage to say through trembling lips. Can I have a place here too? Maybe I'm not the last of my kind. Maybe (*like Joon? Could it be?*) I'm just well adapted to a profoundly changing environment.

"Can I stay here with you?"

"I made Mother promise you could," Joon says, grinning his larger-than-life grin. "I found you and I'll look after you. We'll have each other's backs. I'll feed you up an' teach you how to fight," and he gestures widely. "You'n me!" His bright eyes shine out of the dark tangle of his dreads as if his whole soul is laughing and full of life. He's so beautiful.

Mother? Fight? More fighting? But somehow I feel I'll have the energy for it now. This is life after all, right?

And – oh my gods 'n' fishes – I think I'm in love.

ICE-LESS EPILOGUE – Jack & Joon

I heard tell, while traveling with Gran, about a strong trader-woman who became one of the first pirate queens along the northern rivers and lakes. People say she was a terror for getting the top deal – except when it came to stories. She'd give away her best salted-fish stew and seaweed beer for stories about boat-builders, lake dwellers, and folk who lived long. She was the Tale Trader, and Gran hinted she was a distant relative. I like to think it was Aki, living life to the fullest.

• • •

I sigh, staring into the lightening desert sky. The long night is over. I fleetingly wonder if my survival story can be of any use to Joon. She's the reason I'm here under this sky, chasing after knowledge in a sandy desert. Jack is alive to love Joon.

"And you?" Joon asks into the hush following the end of my tale. She strokes my cheek. "Are you living your life? Can you forget your old loves and live?

"Will you forget me one day?"

"Is that what you take from my story? When you are the endpoint and pinnacle of it all?"

"Tell me more," Joon says.

Acknowledgments

Love and thanks to my family, Tim, Lili, and Pippin, for getting us through the pandemic with creative flair, including chickens, weaving, graffiti art, and banjo playing. Yoko Inoue got me started on my trilogy project with grace, humor, and the *best* sayings and proverbs! She is so missed. Motoko Inoue, my daughter's godmother, has been a strong voice of encouragement, as is the girls' godfather, author Eddy L. Harris. Thank you Martha McCutchen, for being you, and Janet Gary Kerstetter, for always being present for the important moments. Thanks Sharon McCutchen and Brian Stewart for inspiring artwork, and the team at Can of Worms and Leapfrog Press, Tobias, Nicole, Bella, Sarah, and Mary. Thanks for the support from family and friends in OZ and NZ. And thanks so very much pirate librarian Laurie Wheeler, and authors Jane Rosenberg, Michael J. Deluca and Giselle Leeb. And most definite thanks to Kirsten Mosher and Cindy Snow, the best co-readers ever! Y'all rock!

About the Author

D.K. McCUTCHEN's speculative fiction trilogy includes *JELLYFISH DREAMING*, a Leapfrog Press Global Fiction Prize winner; *ELECTRIC ICE* (2024), winner of a Speculative Literature Foundation grant; and *PLASTIC EATERS*, in progress. *WHALE ROAD*, creative nonfiction about sailing with whale researchers through the South Pacific, was a Kiriyama Prize Notable Book and Pushcart Nominee, published in NZ and the UK with an update by JackLeg Press, US (2023). D.K. teaches writing for College of Natural Sciences, University of Massachusetts Amherst, and is an associate director of the Junior Year Writing Program.